P9-DEI-507

MURDER, TAKE TWO

Also by Carol J. Perry

MURDER, TAKE TWO

CAROL J. PERRY

KENSINGTON BOOKS
www.kensingtonbooks.com

KENSINGTON BOOKS are published by

Kensington Publishing Corp.
119 West 40th Street
New York, NY 10018

Copyright © 2020 by Carol J. Perry

To the extent that the image or images on the cover of this book depict a person or persons, such person or persons are merely models, and are not intended to portray any character or characters featured in the book.

This book is a work of fiction. Names, characters, places, and incidents either are products of the author's imagination or are used fictitiously. Any resemblance to actual persons, living or dead, events, or locales is entirely coincidental.

All rights reserved. No part of this book may be reproduced in any form or by any means without the prior written consent of the Publisher, excepting brief quotes used in reviews.

All Kensington titles, imprints, and distributed lines are available at special quantity discounts for bulk purchases for sales promotion, premiums, fundraising, and educational or institutional use.

Special book excerpts or customized printings can also be created to fit specific needs. For details, write or phone the office of the Kensington Sales Manager: Kensington Publishing Corp., 119 West 40th Street, New York, NY 10018. Attn. Sales Department. Phone: 1-800-221-2647.

Kensington and the K logo Reg. U.S. Pat. & TM Off.

First Kensington Books Mass Market Paperback Printing: September 2020

ISBN-13: 978-1-4967-3139-5
ISBN-10: 1-4967-3139-5

ISBN-13: 978-1-4967-3140-1 (ebook)
ISBN-10: 1-4967-3140-9 (ebook)

10 9 8 7 6 5 4 3 2 1

Printed in the United States of America

For Dan, my husband and best friend

Author's Note

The 1830 murder in Salem, Massachusetts, of Captain Joseph White referred to in *Murder, Take Two* really happened. Dick Crowninshield, the son of one of Salem's wealthiest and most famous families, was the alleged killer. I've long been fascinated by that story and have taken this opportunity to weave it into a mystery tale of my own. My dad, Arthur Phelps, worked for the Salem-based Parker Brothers game company, so the game of Clue, which also figures prominently in this adventure, is a familiar old friend of mine.

Look into any man's heart you please,
and you will always find, in every one,
at least one black spot which he has to
keep concealed.
—*Henrik Ibsen*

Chapter 1

"Hello. Lee? Roger Temple here. I guess you've heard about our nephew."

I hadn't heard from Roger Temple—or from his identical twin brother, Ray—for nearly a year, but I knew from Roger's "cop voice" that this wasn't a casual, just-to-say-howdy call. The Temple twins are retired Boston police officers who'd taken a course on television production I'd once taught.

I'm Lee Barrett—nee Maralee Kowalski—thirty-three, red-haired, Salem born, orphaned early, married once, and widowed young. I've worked in television, mostly in front of the cameras, since graduating from Boston's Emerson College. I'd been a show host on a Florida home shopping channel, a network weather girl, and even had a brief, ill-fated stint as a call-in psychic, but for a short time I'd worked as an instructor in television production at the Tabitha Trumbull Academy of the Arts—Salem's newest school—known locally as "the Tabby." The school was located in the sprawling old building that had once housed Trumbull's department store in downtown

Salem. Now it bustled with the activities of aspiring dancers, poets, painters, actors, and more.

"What's going on, Roger?" I asked. "And what's this about your nephew?" I sat at my kitchen table, waiting for the microwave to ding, telling me that my frozen macaroni and cheese dinner was ready. I remembered that the twins had often spoken about their sister Phyllis's boy, but I'd never met the man.

"Hey, it's been in all the newspapers. Maybe you didn't recognize his name. Cody McGinnis? He's been teaching at the Tabby like you used to."

"Cody McGinnis! Oh my goodness, Roger! No. I didn't know your nephew's name." I was shocked by this news. Astonished, actually. "I'm so sorry!"

Roger was right. It *was* in all the newspapers. Cody McGinnis, an associate professor of history at Essex County University had recently taken a nighttime job teaching Salem History at the Tabby.

Even more recently—only a few days ago—he'd become a prime suspect in a murder investigation. As a matter of fact, my police-detective boyfriend, Pete Mondello, was the lead detective in this particular case. That didn't mean I had any more information about Cody McGinnis than anyone else did. Pete doesn't discuss police business with me, especially since I've been promoted to field reporter at the Salem-based TV station, WICH-TV. The station had covered the case from the start. I'd even done a standup in front of the courthouse when Cody was first charged with the crime and so far the evidence against the twins' nephew was pretty much circumstantial—but the circumstances were downright weird.

"Well, of course the kid's not guilty." Roger spoke with conviction. "He's our favorite nephew. A great kid. A good man. That problem he had with the dead guy was no big deal. Nothing you'd want to *kill* anybody over. Ray and I are coming down to Salem in a couple of days to straighten out this mess before Chief Whaley convinces the prosecutor to file criminal charges. We've hired lawyers for Cody. We wanted to give you a heads-up—see if you want to do a little snooping for us before we get there." He'd dropped the cop voice. "We know how much you love snooping."

He was right about that. Sometimes Pete calls me and my aunt, Isobel Russell, "the snoop sisters." My sixty-something, tech-savvy Aunt Ibby and I share the big old family home on Winter Street along with our gentleman cat, O'Ryan. We also share a penchant for getting involved in things that are sometimes none of our business.

I didn't hesitate. "How can I help, Roger?"

"Thanks, Lee. Could you see what you can dig up about the victim? Samuel Bond? Not the stuff about him being a much-beloved retired professor, pillar of the community and all that crap. Nobody's as perfect as the press is making him out to be. There must be a good reason somebody offed the old SOB. And it sure wasn't Cody!"

From what I'd read in the paper, seen on TV—and from the few remarks Pete had made about the case, the old man had no known enemies. Yet he'd been mercilessly beaten to death in his own bed—and so far the evidence pointed directly to the Temple twins' nephew.

"I'll do what I can, Roger," I said, meaning it. I glanced at my kitchen clock, a vintage Kit-Cat, complete with googly eyes and a tail that swings back and forth, marking the seconds. It was six-thirty, still light outside on a pretty New England spring evening. "When will you guys be coming to Salem? Do you have a place to stay?"

"We'll be there the minute we can get away from here. I guess we'll be at Phyllis's. She's pretty upset about all this."

"I should think so. I'll call you right away, Roger, if I find anything interesting. Tell Ray I said hi. See you soon."

The microwave dinged, Roger and I said our good-byes, and O'Ryan strolled into the kitchen through his cat door and hopped up onto the windowsill directly behind my chair. The window was partly open, admitting the pleasant early June breeze. "What do you think of that, O'Ryan?" I said, not actually expecting an answer—he is, after all, a cat. But before he came to live with Aunt Ibby and me, he used to belong to a witch named Ariel Constellation, so he's not exactly an *ordinary* cat. Some say he was her "familiar." In Salem, a witch's familiar is to be respected—and sometimes feared.

I took my dinner out of the microwave, poured a glass of iced tea, picked up the pencil and notepad I use for my grocery list, and returned to my nineteen-seventies Lucite kitchen table. While the macaroni and cheese cooled, I wrote "Cody McGinnis" followed by "County U," "Samuel Bond," "Salem History," and "Tabby." O'Ryan watched from over my shoulder with apparent interest—whether in my scribbled words or my dinner, it was hard to tell.

"Roger believes his nephew is innocent," I said aloud. I often talk to the cat. So does my aunt. I guess most people talk to their pets—but it's usually along the lines of "Good dog," or "Pretty kitty." With O'Ryan, it's quite different. We talk to him as though he understands everything we say. He's definitely not your everyday housecat. I continued. "Roger wants me to do a little snooping."

"*Mmrrup,*" O'Ryan voiced his cat version of a snarky laugh. "*Mmrrup mmrrup.*"

"Well, excuse me. I'm very good at snooping."

He turned his back and faced the window, his long tail swinging back and forth in a pretty good imitation of Kit-Cat's.

"I am too," I said, and started on my mac and cheese.

"Right after dinner I'll see if anything new has turned up today."

"Mmrrup" came a muffled snicker from the windowsill. I ignored him, savoring every bite of gooey, cheesy goodness before grabbing my laptop from the kitchen counter and googling "Cody McGinnis."

There wasn't much of anything there that I hadn't already heard at the station, or read in the *Salem News* or the *Boston Globe*. Usually a murder this far north of Beantown doesn't rate much mention in the major papers, but this one was bizarre enough to get some national coverage.

Samuel Bond's bloodied body had been found by his housekeeper when she'd knocked on his bedroom door as she did every day, carrying a silver tray with his morning coffee, two slices of whole wheat toast, a small pot of marmalade, and the *Wall Street Journal*. That kind of discovery is pretty upsetting all by itself.

But it gets even worse. The Bond murder darn near duplicates one that happened in Salem well over a century ago, and that's what's creeping everybody out.

"I guess I'd better go downstairs and tell Aunt Ibby about Roger's call," I spoke aloud in case the tail-swinging cat was still listening, then opened my kitchen door and stepped out onto the maroon-carpeted third-floor landing. Looking over the mahogany railing, I could see all the way down to the first-floor foyer where, within about twenty seconds, O'Ryan skidded to an abrupt halt at the foot of the stairs, then looked up at me with a smarmy cat-smile.

He loves that trick. He races down two flights to Aunt Ibby's kitchen door, in through her cat door, and out to the front hall before I can get there.

"Smarty pants," I mumbled when I'd reached the arched entry leading to her living room.

"Aunt Ibby, it's me," I called.

Her answer came from the direction of her office.

"Come on in, dear. I knew you were on your way down here when O'Ryan streaked past me like a yellow-striped blur." My aunt's office is a neat and compact space off the living room. She sat behind her cherrywood desk surrounded by the very newest and most advanced technological gadgets, french-tipped manicured fingers flying across the keyboard of her laptop. "I'll just be a minute. Brought a bit of work home with me." Aunt Ibby is the semi-retired head research librarian at Salem's main library, and bringing work home with her is not in the least unusual.

"Take your time. I wanted to see if you're up for a bit of snooping to help out a couple of old friends," I said, knowing that would grab her attention.

It did.

"This can wait," she said, her green eyes—so much like my own—sparkling, her expression animated. "Which old friends and what's their problem?"

"You're following the news about the Samuel Bond murder, aren't you?"

"Of course. Everybody in Salem is."

"I had a phone call a little while ago from Roger Temple. Cody McGinnis is the twins' nephew."

"Good heavens. I had no idea. That *is* a problem. How can we help?"

"Ray and Roger are positive Cody's innocent. They'll be in Salem soon to help, but meanwhile, since Cody didn't kill Professor Bond, somebody else must have. They'd like us to find out what the old man did to make someone angry enough to beat him to death."

"They stabbed him too," she said, making a "tsk-tsk" sound. "A vicious killing."

"The papers say Cody had some serious issues with Samuel Bond," I said, "but nobody's been specific about what the problem was. I think Pete's pretty well convinced that the prosecutor can build a solid case against

Roger and Ray's favorite nephew, and Chief Whaley is pushing to file criminal charges."

Aunt Ibby pointed to her computer screen. "Everything here seems to show the evidence against him building. His fingerprints are all over the ladder the killer used to climb into Bond's bedroom window that night. They're also on a glass in Bond's downstairs bar."

"Well, sure. It was *his* ladder. He told the police it was stolen from his tool shed weeks before the murder."

"And what about the dagger that went missing from his desk at the Tabby?" she wondered aloud. "What about that? All of his students remembered the thing. Said he used to fiddle with it all the time while he was lecturing."

"It was a letter opener! Not a dagger!" I knew I sounded a little shrill. "And we're supposed to be *helping* the twins. Not thinking of reasons to convict their poor nephew!"

"Certainly we're going to help the twins. But it's important that we know exactly what we're up against—exactly what evidence the prosecution has—circumstantial or not."

"You're right," I said. "Remember, though, the last time Salem saw a case like this one it was eighteen thirty and the prosecutor was Daniel Webster."

Chapter 2

O'Ryan strolled into the office, hopped up onto Aunt Ibby's desk, positioned himself in front of the computer, effectively blocking my aunt's view of the screen, and proceeded to groom his magnificent whiskers.

"O'Ryan seems to think we're wasting our time searching for information online," my aunt said. "He's right. Everyone in the world has access to *that* story. We need to do what Daniel Webster did back in eighteen thirty—talk to people the press hasn't found yet."

The 1830 court case she referred to was currently prominent in newspapers, tabloids, and television in Salem and elsewhere—and no wonder. The murder of Professor Samuel Bond was remarkably similar to the nineteenth-century murder of Captain Joseph White, wealthy shipmaster and trader who'd been found dead in his Salem bedroom—beaten and stabbed to death—with a ladder leading to his bedroom window.

"Roger was quite specific about what we should look for," I told her. "To quote him more or less exactly, 'Somebody had good reason to off the old SOB.' I guess we need to help the twins figure out who that somebody is. Any bright ideas on where to begin?"

She'd coaxed the cat into her lap by then, and scratched behind his ears, prompting some sonorous purring. "I think I do," she said after a moment. "I have a couple of girlfriends who might have known the old SOB—uh—the gentleman—socially. Shall I call them?"

"Absolutely. Which girlfriends?"

"The first one who comes to mind is Betsy Leavitt," she said, mentioning one of her high school classmates, "and the second is Louisa Abney-Babcock."

Both suggestions made perfect sense. Both women moved comfortably in Salem's social circles. Betsy, probably because in her mid-sixties she was still uncommonly beautiful and still worked as a professional model—and Louisa, by virtue of tons of old money and a pedigree as long as your arm. My aunt was no stranger to the newspaper society pages either and was well-known in the area's literary and artistic worlds.

"Good idea. Do you think either of them knew the professor?"

"I'd be surprised if they didn't," she said. "I've met him a few times myself. Assisted him with some library research. He was an associate of Rupert's too, and—if you ask me—a bit of a social climber."

Rupert Pennington was the director of the Tabitha Trumbull Academy of the Arts and a special "gentleman friend" of my slim, trim, and attractive red-haired aunt—and had also been my onetime boss. "Mr. Pennington. Of course." I snapped my fingers. "They must have known one another through the university."

"That's right. Rupert occasionally gives talks on Shakespeare to the English classes at County U. Shall I invite the three of them over? Say, tomorrow evening?"

"Good idea. What are you going to tell them? That we need their help in doing some snooping?" I asked.

"In a manner of speaking, yes, but I'd phrase it differently."

"Like, how?"

She paused in her cat-scratching, prompting a pink-tongued cat-lick of her fingers, furrowed her brow for an instant, then smiled. "How's this? I'll tell them that a couple of Boston TV executives are looking for some creative people—the kind who think 'outside the box'—to help with an important project."

"You amaze me," I told her. "That's the absolute truth. Sort of."

"Word choices, my darling child," she said. "It's all about word choices."

I shook my head in admiration. O'Ryan climbed back onto the desk, watching as my aunt picked up her phone and pressed a key. "Hello, Betts?" she said. "If you're available tomorrow evening—sevenish—for an hour or so, Maralee and I have an idea for something that's right up your alley."

She made two more similar calls, then leaned back in her chair wearing a look of satisfaction. O'Ryan stretched, yawned, then—maybe bored with the conversation—vacated his desk position and trotted out of the room. "Done and done," she said. "Now we have to sketch out a presentation of sorts. Catch them up on all they need to know about the case so far, and point them in the direction of digging up any deep dark secrets Professor Samuel Bond may have had."

"I think maybe we've found the perfect snooping crew. Louisa knows everybody who is anybody just about anywhere. Betsy could charm the Supreme Court out of their robes—let alone gather dirt about an old professor. You are the research expert and word master. Mr. Pennington will be our Daniel Webster, and I'll dig around in the media world." I was excited. "Let's get started."

"Have you had dinner yet?"

"Mac and cheese."

She gave a well-bred sniff but didn't comment on my choice of cuisine. "I think O'Ryan has repaired to the kitchen for his happy hour snack. Shall we join him?" My aunt gathered up a few papers, pulled a couple of college-lined notebooks from a desk drawer, and together we walked through her living room and out into the big warm kitchen.

"Maybe we should have tomorrow's meeting here," I suggested, pulling out a captain's chair and sitting at the round oak kitchen table. "This table has always been a great place for brainstorming."

She smiled, poured some special treats into the waiting cat's red bowl, put two wineglasses on the table, and took a chilled bottle of Moscato from the refrigerator. "And for homework and school science projects and cupcake decorating and writing Christmas cards . . ."

"And for making wonderful memories," I said. Aunt Ibby had raised me in this house after my parents died together in a plane crash when I was only four. After my race car driver husband, Johnny Barrett, died in a terrible accident and I'd come home from Florida, she'd made the third floor of the house into an apartment for me.

"You're right," she said, pouring wine into our glasses. "But for right now, it's Snoop Station Central." She pushed one of the notebooks and a pen to my side of the table and kept the other in front of her.

"To Snoop Station Central," I repeated, and we raised our glasses in a toast.

At that moment we hadn't the slightest idea of what kind of mess we were getting ourselves—and our friends—into.

Chapter 3

Our meeting preparation session took over an hour. We did it in a sort of outline form—with Roman numerals and all. It felt a little high schoolish, but as my librarian aunt pointed out, it still *is* a truly efficient way to put thoughts in order. I said good night to my aunt and left via her kitchen door. I carried my outline copy upstairs with the cat darting ahead of me on the narrow, spiral-like back stairway that opens onto my living room.

O'Ryan entered through his cat door while I used the old-fashioned, knob-turning way. When I stepped inside, he was already curled up on his favorite zebra-print wing chair, pretending he'd fallen asleep waiting for me. He gets a kick out of doing that. I went along with the gag, tiptoeing past him and down a short hall into the kitchen. I tossed my copy of the outline onto the table, next to my grocery-list notepad and the laptop. Kit-Cat showed eight-forty-five. Plenty of snoop time left in the day. It was even still a little bit light outside.

I ducked into my bedroom, pulled a pair of red satin pj's from a bureau drawer, and headed down the hall to the bathroom. The pj's were loose and comfortable, and if

Pete happened to drop by after his shift was over, they were kind of glamourous looking too. About twenty minutes later, showered, shampooed, makeup-free, and satin clad, I slid into a Lucite chair and prepared to get to work.

The cat was under the table, maybe asleep and maybe still faking it. Sometimes I can't tell the difference. I'm not sure, even as smart as he is, that O'Ryan realizes I can see him through the clear tabletop. I looked at the notes I'd made on the grocery pad. Not fancy, not efficient, but as a matter of fact the words lined up nicely with Roman numerals I, II, III, IV. And V. I decided to start with I: Cody McGinnis.

I put his name into the laptop. What popped up was a serious case of TMI, most of it repetitive rehashes from newspaper articles. Not particularly useful. I decided to use Aunt Ibby's pitch to the girlfriends. "Think outside the box."

I typed in "Tabitha Trumbull Academy of the Arts— Salem History." Bingo. Up came the course description and requirements for attendance. The Tabby doesn't have a lot of requirements and doesn't give degrees. But it does give folks an opportunity to study dance, or music, or literature, or painting, or animation, or acting—or any number of other artistic pursuits. Many of the students are retirees, like the Temple twins, who've had to work at a regular job most of their adult lives, but always yearned for something else. Some are young working people who attend evening and weekend classes to broaden their personal horizons. Some of my television production students, like Roger and Ray, have gone on to work in the TV industry, and one young woman who studied acting at the Tabby is in Hollywood making movies.

Cody McGinnis had labeled his course Salem's Rich History—It's a Lot More Than Witches! *Intriguing,* I thought, *and so true.* He'd broken it up into semesters. Early Settlers; The Maritime Trade; Artists, Architects, and Adventurers. Samuel Bond's untimely passing had occurred immediately after Cody had completed teaching a course he'd called "I Love a Mystery—Salem's Most Famous Murder." McGinnis had apparently spiced up each of his courses by including field trips in the itinerary. The *Early Settlers* segment included a tour of the Pioneer Village in Forest River Park, where visitors saw what Salem might have looked like back in 1630. *Maritime Trade* students had a trip to the Salem Maritime National Historic Site with its historic wharves and buildings, along with the reconstructed tall ship *Friendship*, telling the stories of Salem's sailors, privateers, and merchants. Those interested in *Artists, Architects, and Adventurers* had museum visits and a walking tour of Chestnut Street, reputed to be the most architecturally perfect street in America. But the field trip that drew my interest most was the candlelight tour of the mansion on Essex Street where Captain Joseph White had been murdered—it's known now as the Gardner-Pingree House, and it's open for tours. Here the young associate professor had given his students a close-up look at the scene of the gory 1830 killing, including a step-by-step description of how the assassin had entered the old man's room, via a window.

Pete had dropped a hint or two that Cody McGinnis and the professor had had some differences. He'd not been specific about it, and the newspapers had barely touched the subject. During a standup outside the courthouse, I'd managed a shouted question at one of McGinnis's lawyers. "What was the argument between Cody and the professor about?" I'd yelled.

Much to my surprise, he'd answered me. "A simple disagreement between colleagues. No big deal."

I added the word "disagreement" to my grocery list notepad, giving it a Roman numeral VI, then frowned. It was a good thing the twins were paying for Cody's defense lawyers. I doubted that he could afford them, since he was working at the Tabby because he needed the money. How well were his parents set? I had no idea. Some of these questions would have to wait until the twins arrived.

I went back to the outline, put a capital letter *A* under Salem History, and printed "Captain Joseph Smith's murder," then put the same words onto the subject line in the laptop. Plenty of information there. It's a good story, after all. Some literary scholars believe that both Nathaniel Hawthorne and Edgar Allan Poe used aspects of the White murder. Hawthorne wrote about the murder of Judge Pyncheon in *The House of the Seven Gables*: "an old bachelor, and possessed of great wealth." Poe, in his 1843 "The Tell-Tale Heart" has his fictional murder boast "how wisely" and "with what caution" he killed an old man in his bedchamber.

My concentration on this historical carnage was interrupted by my buzzing phone. Text from Pete. "Feel like ice cream?"

I texted back, "Chocolate chip," then put the laptop, notebook, and notes in my room, replacing them with ice cream scoop, bowls, and spoons. About twenty minutes later O'Ryan scooted out from under the table and dashed for the living room. That meant Pete had pulled his Crown Vic into the driveway. I heard the cat door flap. That meant O'Ryan would meet him on the back steps. I headed down the hall to the living room too, pulling the door open and waiting for both of them.

I hadn't seen Pete for a couple of days, and his kiss told me he'd missed me too. We eventually made it to the kitchen without melting the ice cream. Pete put his jacket in one end of my bedroom closet where he keeps a few things for when he stays overnight. He stashed his gun in one of the secret drawers in the bureau while O'Ryan climbed onto the bed, turned around three times and lay down, his usual nighttime ritual.

I put a scoop of vanilla into Pete's bowl and a scoop of chocolate chip into mine. "Are you extra busy with the McGinnis case?" I asked.

He smiled. "Not exactly extra busy. Normally busy. Why do you ask, Nancy Drew?" He always thinks it's funny when I say "case" and compares me to that famous girl detective.

"As a matter of fact, I do have a reason," I told him. "Did you know that Cody is Roger and Ray Temple's nephew?"

He looked surprised. "I didn't know that."

It was my turn to smile. I love it when I know something that he doesn't. I told him about the phone call from Roger, without mentioning the part about my snooping, of course. "The twins are coming to Salem in a few days. They're convinced that Cody's innocent. I guess they're planning to prove it somehow."

"I wish them good luck with that," Pete said. "It doesn't look too good for the guy right now."

"Got any other suspects?"

He shook his head. "Nope."

"Most everyone seems to think the old professor had no enemies at all. Is it true?"

Pete frowned. He could tell I was snooping. "Obviously he had at least one," he said. "Are you being WICH-TV-reporter curious? Or friend-of-the-suspect's-twin-uncles curious?"

"Maybe a little of both," I admitted. "Come on. Nobody is that nice. He must have ticked off more than one person. He taught college kids, for goodness' sake. Most anybody with a bad mark blames the professor."

"Sure. But would that be enough reason to fracture somebody's skull, then stab him around the heart a few times to be sure he was dead?"

I made a face. "Yuck. Messy. But Pete, one of Cody's lawyers said the problem with Professor Bond was only a disagreement between colleagues. That it was no big deal. Was it? Do you know what the problem was?"

"Yes. McGinnis told us about that right away. The first time we questioned him. Before he even had a lawyer."

I wondered again about that legal team. I was sure they hadn't come cheap. I decided not to push my luck by asking Pete about them yet. "Can you tell me what the disagreement was about?"

He was silent for a moment, helped himself to another scoop of vanilla. "I can tell you this much. It was a big deal to Cody McGinnis. I think he's still pissed about it."

"Uh-oh. That makes him look more guilty, right?"

"Sure. Got any chocolate syrup?"

"Yeah. In the fridge. Top row inside the door. Was it something that could get a person killed?"

"Offhand, it didn't seem like it to me. But people get killed for dumb reasons every day." He poured chocolate onto his ice cream and extended the bottle to me. "Want some?"

I pushed my bowl forward. "Maybe a smidge." I waited for him to continue with casual observations, hoping for something negative about the departed beloved professor—something I could relay to the twins. Didn't happen. He savored his ice cream silently for a few clicks of Kit-Cat's tail, then changed the subject.

"The chief gave me a couple of tickets to the Sox–Rays game for next Wednesday night. Want to go?"

He knew I'd want to go! I lived in Florida long enough to become a Tampa Bay Rays fan, while he remains ever loyal to the Red Sox. "Absolutely," I said, my mind momentarily derailed from the objective. "I'll fix it up with Mr. Doan to be sure I can have Wednesday night off." Bruce Doan is the WICH-TV station manager, and also a Sox fan who believes time off for a home game is more important than a dentist's appointment any day.

"Good. You're not going to wear your Rays hat, are you?"

"Of course I am. But listen. Does Cody McGinnis have enough money to pay that team of lawyers I saw going into the courthouse?"

"Maybe. Seems some of his students started a Go-FundMe page and have raised quite a bundle of money for his defense."

I was surprised. "I didn't know that. He must have a lot of friends."

"He'll need 'em. He's not exactly Dick Crowninshield."

Richard "Dick" Crowninshield, the son of one of Salem's wealthiest, socially prominent families, was the alleged perpetrator of the 1830 murder of Captain White.

"True," I agreed. "But your prosecutor isn't exactly Daniel Webster either!"

Chapter 4

Pete was up in the morning, dressed, shaved, and ready for the day before I woke up—as usual. My alarm clock jingled at seven, and I awoke to the smell of coffee brewing and country music playing on the radio. He poked his head into the bedroom. "Want to go out to breakfast? I can't find much of anything in the refrigerator." That was usual too.

"Good idea," I said. "I'll be ready in a jiff." I padded out to the kitchen, reached up for a good morning peck on the cheek, picked up my waiting cup of coffee, and looked around for the cat. "Did O'Ryan go downstairs already?"

"Yep. Sniffed at his empty red bowl and headed for greener pastures at your aunt's place."

"That's what I usually do too," I admitted. "But a restaurant breakfast with you sounds even better." I showered, dressed, did minimal makeup in a hurry, and by eight o'clock Pete pulled the Crown Vic into the parking lot behind our favorite breakfast place. It doesn't have a name. It's in an ordinary-looking two-story house on a side street with no sign except a vertical neon OPEN sign in the window. We're regulars, like most of the customers, so the waitress, calling us by our first names, led us to our favorite booth at the back of the long room.

By the time our breakfasts—ham and eggs for Pete, veggie omelet for me—arrived, I'd already restarted the conversation about murder. "Do you think Roger and Ray will actually be able to help their nephew?" I asked. "I hope the guy is as innocent as they believe he is."

"Not going to give up, are you, Nancy?" Pete said, shaking his head with a grin. "Okay. Yes, they probably can. They're good cops. Both of them. They have the old-school methods down pat. They'll chase tips down every alley. They'll dig up every scrap of evidence. They'll ask questions lawyers never thought of. Yes. Cody McGinnis is lucky to have them on his side. Now can I enjoy my breakfast without feeling like I'm a character in 'Nancy Drew and the Case of the Murdered Professor'?"

I gave up. For the moment. "How 'bout them Rays?" I said.

Pete dropped me off in the driveway behind the house on Winter Street. We managed as good a kiss as is possible while leaning across the radio- and radar-crowded console between us and agreed to call each other. O'Ryan waited for me on the back steps and followed me into the hall. I knocked on Aunt Ibby's kitchen door. "Come on in," she called. "It's open."

"I have a few minutes before I have to leave for work." I said. "But I want to catch you up on what I've learned so far—even though it's not very much."

She looked up from her morning paper. "All ears."

"Pete says that whatever the disagreement was between Cody McGinnis and Professor Bond, Cody is still angry about it."

"Does Pete know what it is?"

"Cody told the police about it first thing," I said, "and no, he didn't tell me."

"Too bad. But the twins will have that information anyway."

"Uh-huh. Another thing. Pete says that Cody's students at the Tabby have raised quite a lot of money for his defense."

"No kidding. He must be a good teacher."

"I checked the course curriculum, which looked wonderful to me. Complete with field trips." I'm a great believer in field trips and sometimes took my own Tabby classes on several memorable ones—not always in a good way. "He even took them to the scene of the original crime."

"Captain White's bedroom?"

"Yes." I sighed. "If the Bond murder closely duplicated the White murder, well, there was hardly anybody else in Salem so familiar with the details."

"Except maybe anybody who'd paid close attention to McGinnis's class," she reasoned, "or read one of the dozen or so books that have been written about it."

"Doesn't make sense that he'd commit a crime that pointed so directly to himself, does it?"

"It doesn't to me," she said. "But then, that's probably what Dick Crowninshield thought too."

"Crowninshield had accomplices. The papers—especially the tabloids—have been speculating that there may have been others involved this time too."

"I've read that," she said. "One with a club or a lead pipe of some kind and the other with a knife."

I checked my watch. "Have to go," I said. "I'm afraid we don't have a lot of information for the twins."

"We haven't heard from Louisa and Betsy yet, remember. And Rupert knew both Bond *and* McGinnis." She wore a look of confidence as she picked up her newspaper. "You'll see. Leave it to us. We'll figure it all out."

I patted the cat, wished my aunt a good day, then backed my blue Corvette out of the garage and headed for

Derby Street. I decided to take my aunt's advice and leave murder solving to the girlfriends and Mr. P.—at least for now.

WICH-TV is housed in one of the lovely old brick Federal buildings that fortunately escaped the urban renewal madness that gripped Salem, along with too many other New England towns, back in the 1950s. I've been with the station long enough to rate my own parking space in the harborside parking lot, and when the weather is nice, I always enjoy taking a deep breath of good salt air before I go inside. It was a beautiful morning, my tummy was full of good breakfast, and I looked forward to an interesting day at work. I was scheduled to cover the opening of a new toy store first, then a tour of a historic candy store after lunch. Toys and candy. What could be more fun? I love my job. Naturally, those cushy assignments would be cancelled if there was breaking news somewhere else in town.

I crossed the black and white tiled floor of the lobby and pressed the UP button beside the polished brass doors of the elevator. We call it "Old Clunky" with good reason, and I thumped and bumped my way up to the second floor. I pushed open the glass door marked "WICH-TV" and greeted Rhonda, the receptionist. "It's a beautiful day in the neighborhood, isn't it? Am I still on for Toy Trawler?"

Rhonda is surely not your everyday average receptionist. We don't know exactly how many degrees she has, but she is one smart woman, and Bruce Doan has always left most of the scheduling up to her. She keeps track of all of the on-air reporters on a white board next to her desk. She pointed to the board where "Barrett: Toy Store: 10:00 a.m. America's Oldest Candy Company: 1:00 p.m." was written in purple dry marker. "Francine's driving and filming. I've got some prep material for both places printed out for you. I understand the owner of the toy store does a good interview." She handed me a folder.

"Thanks, Rhonda." I rifled through the pages. "I wonder why it's called Toy Trawler."

"That's easy," she said. "Remember that old restaurant on Route One that was shaped like a ship? It's in there."

"I don't think that was a trawler."

"It is now. They took the masts off and cut it in half. The owner is a retired Gloucester fisherman."

"Ship ahoy," I saluted her and tucked the folder into my hobo bag. "I'll go down to the dressing room and slap on some makeup, then find Francine and get going."

Francine is my favorite mobile photographer. We work together well, and we've produced some darned good TV. We've also been through a few pretty hairy shoots together too. I took the stairs down to the first floor, where the dressing room has a good mirror and decent lighting. Rhonda's a Mary Kay rep, so there's always a box of samples down there to work with. I cut through the long, dark room with its black painted walls and an assortment of show sets—*Sports Roundup*, *The Saturday Business Hour*, *Cooking with Wanda the Weather Girl*, *Shopping Salem*, *Tarot Time with River North*. That last one was the same set where I'd done my short-lived call-in psychic show—*Nightshades*. My best friend, River North, has had much more success in that space than I ever did.

I ducked into the dressing room and added a little more eye shadow and redder lipstick, then smoothed out and sprayed my too-curly red hair. I texted Francine. "Where are you?"

"Outside. Motor's running."

"On my way."

Francine had the WICH-TV mobile unit facing Derby Street, ready to roll. I climbed into the passenger seat. "Ever been to the Toy Trawler before?" I asked. "I haven't, but I'm dying to see what the fisherman/toy guy has done to the place."

"Captain Billy," she said, pulling onto the street. "Wait 'til you see it. I took my sister's girls there. I think adults like it even more than the kids do. He has a room full of the old collectible toys as well as the latest ones."

"Sounds like fun. Then after that we go to a candy store. Gonna be a good day," I promised, opening the facts folder Rhonda had prepared, trying once again to push all thoughts of murders, past and present, out of my mind.

Chapter 5

Captain Billy's Toy Trawler was every bit as charming and interesting as Francine had promised. She started shooting as soon as we got out of the mobile unit. I carried the stick mic, talked to the audience, and walked backward toward the gangplank entrance to the store. *Smart idea. Nautical and wheelchair accessible at the same time.* It's taken me a while to master that walking backward while smiling, talking, and facing the camera trick. Rhonda had phoned ahead, so Captain Billy, in full captain's regalia, waited for us at the entrance.

"Welcome, welcome aboard ladies," he boomed. He looked every bit the fisherman part. Think a kind of attractive cross between Spencer Tracy in *The Old Man and the Sea* and Johnny Depp in *Pirates of the Caribbean*. Francine followed the captain and me with her camera as he led me from a rubber raft full of teddy bears, to a fully outfitted yacht peopled by Barbie and all of her well-dressed friends, to a walk-in fish bowl where the Little Mermaid, the Ninja Turtles, Nemo and other toy denizens of the deep were artfully displayed.

"Come along to the game deck," Captain Billy ordered.

"This month's special is board games—all the ones you remember from when you were a kid, along with all the newest ones."

Francine and I dutifully followed him into a large room where the walls were papered with board game labels and box covers. Kids climbed on giant Monopoly game pieces and others played on a slide from Candy Land. Counters were stacked with hundreds of games. A central display featured an enormous game board from one of my favorites, Clue. "Clue is our game of the month," Captain Billy explained. "Lot of interest in it locally lately, of course."

"Why so?"

He looked at me as though I wasn't quite bright. "The murder. Lots of folks think that the game of Clue was inspired by the murder of Captain Joseph White. Happened in Salem and Parker Brothers games were made in Salem, so why not? Look, there's a game character named White, like the murdered guy, Joseph White At first they'd thought the old man had been killed with a lead pipe like the one in the game. Dick Crowninshield hanged himself with a silk scarf—so there's the noose. Perfect tie-in for me and my games with the murder of that professor."

So much for getting my thoughts away from that topic. "That's really interesting," I said. "Especially the tie-in aspect of the Captain White murder. That's something to think about, isn't it? Are you selling a lot of Clue?"

"Not only the games. People all over are throwing Clue mystery parties. Here." He handed me a colorful brochure. "All the directions for hosting a Clue party. We even sell life-size plastic weapons. The wrench, the rope, the lead pipe, the revolver, the knife, and the candlestick. Say, you ought to throw one and take the video. It would make a good TV show. I'd even sponsor it!"

Francine tapped her watch and gave me the "cut" sign.

That meant something must have come up at the station. It looked as though we'd have to leave early.

"Thanks, Captain Billy," I said. "We'll think about that. Thanks so much for showing us the Toy Trawler." I gave the store's address, hours, and website, and signed off.

Francine reached for my mic. "Come on. Let's roll. Rhonda says there's some kind of student protest going on over at the college." I hurried to keep up with her. I wore heels because, after all, I was on camera, while Francine can wear sneakers every day if she wants to.

"Is the candy store gig cancelled?"

She stashed camera and sound equipment in the back of the van, and we climbed into the front seats. "She told them we'd be a little late. They said they'd be open until nine tonight."

"Looks like we might be in for a long day," I said.

"You don't sound too happy about it." She turned on to Route 1, heading back to Salem.

"I kind of have plans," I told her.

"With Pete?"

"He's probably working late tonight himself on that murder. No, it's a get-together with my aunt and a few of her friends."

She raised an eyebrow. "No offense to Aunt Ibby, but that doesn't sound very exciting."

I had to smile, thinking of the particular friends involved. "You'd be surprised. All of them knew Professor Bond. Cody McGinnis's uncles are friends of ours, so we're all trying to put together anything we can think of that might help clear their nephew."

"That's nice," she said politely. "Listen, Lee, I don't know if this is important, but you remember my roommate's brother's muscle-bound trainer, Rocky?"

"Sure." I did remember Rocky. He'd been instrumental in helping to dig up some really important information for me not too long ago—information that may have saved Aunt Ibby's life.

"Well, according to my roommate's brother, Cody McGinnis has a membership in one of the gyms where Rocky works out. He said the cops came in the other day with a warrant and emptied Cody's locker."

Yes, that could be important. "Interesting, Francine. Thanks."

"No problem," she said. "Anyway, I doubt this student thing will take long. They're always getting riled up about some cause or other. It was that way when I was there too. I carried signs for all kinds of stuff. Save the whales. Free lunches for students. It was fun."

"Did Rhonda give us a hint about what they're protesting this time?"

"Nope. Want to give her a call?"

"Sure." I tapped in the station's main number. "And speaking of clues, that Clue mystery party idea might be something we should try. Hello? Rhonda, we're on our way to Essex County University. What's going on over there?"

We could hear the noise before we turned onto Lafayette Street. We drove onto the campus without being stopped, parked in one of the student parking lots, and unloaded the camera and mic once again. It didn't take long for us to figure out that the students weren't protesting anything at all. It was actually a rally to gather support for the Cody McGinnis Defense Fund—and it seemed to be going well. "It's almost time for the noon news," Rhonda said. "Tell Francine to send, we'll edit as you go, and maybe we'll get some of it in before twelve-thirty."

Francine motioned for me to follow her. She pointed to where much of the crowd seemed to be gathering in front of one of the school's older buildings. A man in a white shirt, his arms upraised, a megaphone in one hand, appeared to be about to speak. We pushed our way through the mass of young people—we're both getting pretty good at that—and staked out a position a few feet away from the man.

I activated my mic, and Francine began recording. "Lee Barrett here reporting to you from the campus of Essex County University, where a rally is in progress." I spoke to a young woman standing close to me. "Could you tell me who the speaker is?" I asked. "Is he a student here?"

"That's Alan Armstrong," she said, "aka Professor Dreamy because he's so handsome. He started the Go-FundMe for Professor McGinnis."

The man lowered the bullhorn and spoke into it. "Can you hear me okay?" A quick roar of approval answered. I wished we'd brought a good sound engineer with us. Filming was going to be a challenge between the bull-horn, the crowd noise, and a recording of "Where in the World but in America" playing somewhere in the back-ground.

"Thanks for coming out," he said. "This is important." The crowd noise stopped. The music stopped. Just like that. Unusual. The man had somehow commanded instant full attention. I was impressed.

"Cody McGinnis is a friend of mine," he began. "You all know that. There's no way he could have done what the papers, the TV, even some members of the administration right here in this fine university—what they're saying he did." There was a dramatic pause, and still the crowd remained silent. "Samuel Bond was a friend of mine too," he said. "Professor Bond was my teacher and my mentor when I was a student here, some twenty years ago. Now one good man is dead, and another good man is facing imprisonment. Nothing we can do will bring Samuel Bond back to us." His voice grew louder, more urgent. "But there *is* something we can do for Cody! We can help him pay for the best defense money can buy! We can facebook and tweet and instagram. We can contact all of our friends and family and neighbors. We can dig deep in our own pockets. We can save Cody!"

Cheers erupted. The man lowered the bullhorn and came down the steps directly toward me. I stuck my mic right in his handsome face.

Chapter 6

"Excuse me. Professor Armstrong? Lee Barrett, WICH-TV. A couple of questions please?"

He didn't answer right away but gave me a quite un-professor-like up-and-down look. I was pretty sure Francine's camera must have caught it. He smiled a perfect toothpaste-commercial-worthy smile. "Yes indeed, Ms. Barrett. Always happy to talk to the press. Get the word out to the community about our cause. What would you like to know?"

Who's your orthodontist? was the first question that came to mind, but I smiled back. "There's been talk around that Cody and Professor Bond had some serious differences. Do you know what the problem between them was?"

He sighed. "Ah, yes. There's always talk around, isn't there, Ms. Barrett? Usually unfounded gossip." He held up one hand. "Yes. I know what the problem was. A tiny, insignificant disagreement between colleagues."

That sounded familiar. It was almost what the lawyer had claimed—plus a couple of adjectives. "A disagreement?" I asked. "Do you know what it was about?"

"Internal university business," he said. "A minor scheduling problem in the History Department, as I understand it. Not a big deal."

Not a big deal. That's what the lawyer said.

"You said that Professor Bond was your mentor. Do you teach history also?"

"I don't. I started as a history major, then switched to political science. A better fit for me. Thank you for your interest in our funding for Cody's legal expenses. Your viewers can help." He rattled off a website and handed me a card. "Have a good day." He flashed the smile again, this time directly at the camera, and walked away.

The crowd had pretty much dispersed, but I found a few students willing to talk about the case. Two fervent male Samuel Bond fans who thought Cody McGinnis had probably done it and one girl who was just as sure Cody wasn't guilty. "I can fully understand why somebody could hate Professor Bond, though." She shook a head full of bright blue curls. "He gave me a D on my midterm. I couldn't believe it. What a jerk. I switched my major to earth science." There didn't seem to be much more of interest going on. I thanked the three, did my usual sign-off, and handed Francine my mic. "Time to go to the candy store? We seem to be back on schedule."

"Absolutely—and Rhonda says they can fit almost all of the hunky professor's speech and some of your interview onto the noon news. Good job."

"Thanks. It's lunchtime. Do you suppose we should eat some actual food before we start with the candy samples?"

"I'm afraid you're right," she said. Once again we loaded our gear into the van, then headed for the nearest drive-through. After a filling, if not particularly healthful lunch, we passed the WICH-TV building with a toot of the horn and proceeded all the way to the end of Derby Street, where the candy store is right across the street from the House of the Seven Gables. I'd glanced at Rhonda's notes about it, but I'd been there before and so had Francine. Ye Olde Pepper Candy Companie dates back to 1806 and is, after all, the oldest candy company in America—so named because one of the long-ago owners was George Pepper.

That interview went well too, and we headed back to the station with our day's scheduled stops completed and with several boxes of chocolates, fudges, truffles, and the signature lemon-flavored "Salem Gibralters" along with complete instructions on how to throw a Clue party to share with the crew. A good day's work—and I'd still be able to attend the meeting of "Snoop Station Central."

We'd put our candy haul on the curved Formica counter surrounding Rhonda's reception desk. It didn't take long for word to get around, so pretty soon several of our fellow employees, along with the boss, had joined us for an impromptu tasting party.

"So, what did you think about what the professor had to say about the murder?" Scott Palmer wanted to know. Scott's not one of my favorite co-workers, but I always try to keep things civil between us.

"He didn't say much of anything about it," I said, "except that Cody didn't do it."

"I mean about the disagreement between Cody and Bond. You buyin' it? That it was no big deal?"

It was a good question. "I think it needs a lot of investigation—a lot of explanation. I didn't see the news show myself. Did they get the interview with the three students in?"

"So," he said, stuffing a truffle into his mouth, "you're not buyin' it either."

Rhonda interrupted. "We didn't get the students in. We'll do the whole thing in the six p.m. slot."

"What did they say?" Scott wanted to know.

"Two against Cody, one for," I said.

"Men or women?"

"Two guys. One girl."

"Who was for?" he mumbled. "And why?"

"The girl," I said. "She thinks Bond was a jerk. He'd given her a D on her midterms."

"She has blue hair," Francine offered.

"Kids," Scott scoffed. "They screw around partying for a whole semester, then blame the teachers when they don't get the As and Bs Daddy is paying for."

"Not exactly worth killing over, though," Mr. Doan put in. "And that professor you interviewed didn't give much of an answer when you asked about what was going on between McGinnis and Bond."

"I know," I admitted. "He apparently agrees with the lawyers that whatever it was is 'no big deal.'"

"Get another interview with him, Ms. Barrett," Bruce Doan ordered. "You can do better. Get the answer." He pointed to the candy spread. "Rhonda, wrap up some of those dark chocolate–covered orange peels. They're Buffy's favorites."

"I'd already set some aside," Rhonda said, handing him a small candy box. "I know Mrs. Doan loves them."

"Thanks." He retreated to his office, looking back over his shoulder. "Get on that 'disagreement between colleagues' thing, Ms. Barrett. Pronto!"

I gritted my teeth and didn't answer. Scott grinned. "Need help, Moon?" Scott's called me 'Moon,' ever since I first came to WICH-TV. "Crystal Moon" was the name I chose for my phony psychic routine.

"No thanks. I can handle it." I believed I could. The twins undoubtedly knew all about whatever the problem was between the two professors. Besides that, I had a meeting in a few hours with some crack busybodies who might already have the answer to that too.

As the bounty of goodies on Rhonda's counter grew

smaller, so did the group gathered there. After a while it got down to the women—Francine, Rhonda, and me—by this time wetting our fingers and picking up little shreds of chocolate.

"So, are you going to call the hot professor?" Rhonda wanted to know.

"The kids call him 'Professor Dreamy'" was Francine's helpful observation.

"We all saw that look he gave you," Rhonda teased. "I'll bet he'll spill the whole story if you ask nicely."

I thought about calling him. Gave it a moment's serious thought. "Don't think I'll need him," I decided.

"Doan would probably like you to do it," Rhonda said. "All those college girls would watch because he's so handsome. Doan's always looking to attract a younger audience."

"That's right," Francine offered. "The only eye-candy guy we've got around here is Buck Covington."

"Don't let Scott hear you say that." I laughed. "He thinks he's all that and more." But she was right. Buck Covington is wicked handsome, and in addition to that, he reads from the teleprompter flawlessly, every time. Never needs a second take on anything. The late news ratings went up as soon as he was hired. Buck is dating my best friend, River, who is also gorgeous. They're definitely WICH-TV's "beautiful couple."

"Think about it," Rhonda advised. "Anyway, you two have another hour or so before you clock out. Got any time fillers in mind?"

"I have to get an oil change on the van," Francine said. "I'd better get going."

"I've got some more research to do on Dick Crowninshield," I said. "I think I'll use the computer in one of the data ports if that's okay."

"Sure." Rhonda handed me a key to one of the secure

little cubicles where reporters can work without interruption or background noise. The data ports were one of Mr. Doan's better ideas, and I use them often.

I closed the dataport glass door behind me, tossed my handbag onto the desk, and typed in "The murder of Captain Joseph White Salem." Even though the crime happened almost two hundred years ago, there's still a surprising amount of information about it on the internet. What I hoped to find was some more ties between the murder of Samuel Bond and the killing of Joseph White. It would all be coincidental, of course, but Bruce Doan would like it, and it could make a great story. Maybe I'd even get an investigative reporter shot on the late news with it.

It was pretty much agreed by all concerned that Dick Crowninshield had killed the old man for money. He was simply a hired killer who, rather than face the consequences of his crime, had hanged himself in his jail cell with a fine silk scarf. Nothing was stolen or even disturbed in the captain's bedroom. The same was true of the Bond killing. Nothing missing that we know of. There were accessories to the White murder. A man named Frank Knapp and his brother Joseph were later hanged for their part in the crime. Did Bond's killer work alone?

I noted both things on one of the index cards I always carry in my purse. Did they mean anything? Maybe not, but I guessed they were worth a Roman numeral apiece. I jotted down VII—Bedrooms; VIII—Accomplices. I'd figure out the ABCs and 123s later. I added a PS to the bottom of the card. I didn't know what else to do with it. "Cops emptied Cody's gym locker." I closed and locked the dataport door, returned the key to Rhonda, and left for home—anxiously awaiting the evening's meeting with my own willing accomplices.

Chapter 7

Rupert Pennington had arrived early, impeccably dressed as always. Tonight he sported a tweed jacket with leather elbow patches and a melon-colored ascot. By seven o'clock he'd arranged five chairs around the kitchen table and placed a copy of our outline, along with a brand-new notebook and pen, in front of each place. Aunt Ibby stood at her kitchen counter, putting the finishing touches on a plate of dainty sandwiches. A nice Merlot chilled in a hammered aluminum bucket, coffee would be ready with a touch of a button, and assorted exotic tea bags awaited boiling water.

I stood in the front hall, facing the big mirrored hall tree, listening for the doorbell. I peered at my reflection. Usually after work I'm makeup-free, wearing comfortable sweats or even pajamas. Tonight I dressed up a little, knowing that Betsy would be a model-perfect fashion plate and Louisa would be understatedly elegant. I didn't want to embarrass my aunt by looking tacky, so I'd chosen a nice, middle-of-the-road blue denim jumper with a white blouse. Good enough, I decided, and hurried to pull the door open as the first chime of "The Impossible Dream" sounded.

Betsy whirled through the door in a cloud of Flowerbomb, looking fabulous in pink shantung, long platinum hair in a perfect upsweep. She gave me a side hug and an air kiss. "This is so exciting, Lee," she said. "Thinking outside the box is so *me*! I can hardly wait to see what Ibby has in mind." Louisa Abney-Babcock, immaculate in a gray linen pantsuit, arrived shortly after Betsy, and the two hurried to the kitchen with me right behind them.

After Mr. Pennington had bowed graciously, kissed hands, and pulled out chairs for all of us, Aunt Ibby got down to business. With her usual appropriate "word choices," she laid out the problem.

"You've all read or heard about the recent heinous murder of Professor Samuel Bond," she began, "and are surely aware of the name of the prime suspect in the matter—Cody McGinnis."

There was a murmur of "dreadful thing," and "terrible, terrible," along with a subdued "tsk-tsk." Aunt Ibby proceeded. "We—Maralee and I—learned yesterday that the suspect is the nephew of two dear friends of ours. They believe wholeheartedly in Cody's innocence. I've asked you, Betsy, and you, Louisa, to join me in doing some unbiased digging to see what we can learn about Samuel Bond. Our friends, retired police officers, by the way, don't believe Professor Bond is as perfect as the media make him out to be. Rupert, I know you've been friends with both the victim and the accused, so this doesn't have to involve you. Maralee is of course a journalist and must try to maintain neutrality. But we three girls"—those green eyes sparkled—"we three can do all the digging we like!"

"Like *The Golden Girls*!" Louisa clapped her hands. "Wonderful!"

"No. We'll be like *Charlie's Angels*!" Betsy exclaimed. "And Rupert, you can be Charlie!"

Mr. Pennington colored slightly and made eye contact with my aunt. "There are some things," he said, "a man just can't run away from."

Betsy and Louisa looked puzzled. My aunt winked. "John Wayne. *Stagecoach*. 1939." Those two have been quoting old movie lines, trying to stump each other for years.

And so, as Julius Caesar said, the die was cast. I wasn't sure whether the *Charlie's Angels* thing was exactly what my aunt had in mind, and it undoubtedly wasn't what the twins had asked for, but there it was. Three women and one gentleman "of a certain age" were about to take on a real time life-and-death challenge.

Aunt Ibby stood, picking up her pen. "Let's each write down what we know—personally—about Samuel Bond. Good, bad, and in between. Lee, you and Rupert are excused from this part if you don't want to do it." She glanced around the table. "Then we'll share what we've written and see what we come up with."

"I don't know anything about him," I admitted. "Does anyone want coffee, tea, or wine? I can handle that."

Everyone agreed on wine. Mr. Pennington uncorked the bottle and poured. I put the plate of sandwiches on the table, sipped my wine, and watched the others write in their notebooks. The room grew quiet, except for an occasional muffled giggle from Betsy as she bent over neat backhand script. Louisa alternated between minutes of frantic scribbling and moments of elbows on the table, hands covering both eyes, deep thought. Aunt Ibby worked steadily for five minutes or so, then closed her notebook with a firm "that's that" slap, poured a cup of coffee, and nibbled on a cream-cheese-and-olive-on-rye-bread mini-sandwich. Mr. Pennington followed my aunt's lead—coffee and sandwich—then stood, apparently studying the Hood's Milk calendar on the back of the kitchen door.

When all of the erstwhile Golden Girls/Charlie's Angels had closed their notebooks, the digging up dirt on poor, dead, unable-to-defend-himself Professor Samuel Bond began in earnest. From the start it was a gossip fest.

Betsy went first. "The first time I met Sam Bond was around ten years ago at a benefit auction for the Animal Rescue League. Mr. Leavitt and I had donated a lovely Emile Gruppe painting. I wish I had it back now. Well, anyway, Sam was working that crowd as though he was running for congress. Practically begging for invitations to the various A-list events represented in that room. Such a climber! It worked for him to a certain extent." She laughed. "Got himself invited to a couple of hundred-dollar-a-plate dinners."

Louisa nodded. "I sponsored one of those dinners. It was at Hamilton Hall. We were raising money for a new pediatric outpatient facility for the hospital. We had to redeposit his check twice. Bounced the first couple of times." She shook her head. "Why people spend money they can't afford to impress others, I don't know. But it seems to me Samuel has been living beyond his means for a very long time."

I've rarely ever heard my aunt speak disparagingly of others—excepting certain politicians—and this occasion was no exception. "His late wife was a library volunteer years ago," she said. "A sweet woman, but she always seemed so sad. I had the impression that the marriage was not a happy one."

"For years I didn't even know he was ever married," Betsy said. "He sure didn't act it. Almost every time I saw him he was hanging around with his students or trying to crash an A-list party."

"Ever see him with Cody McGinnis?" Aunt Ibby wanted to know.

"I'm not positive," Betsy put in, "but when I saw the newspaper photos of Cody, he looked familiar. It *may* be because I've seen him with Sam. Have you ever seen Cody, Lee?"

"Not really. I only saw the back of his head when he was going into the courthouse with his lawyers. All I've heard about him lately is that apparently the police have cleaned out his locker at a gym he belongs to."

"That might be important," my aunt said, "since the police are involved. Did Pete tell you that?"

"No," I admitted. "It's thirdhand information. I haven't seen anything about it in the papers or on the news. Might be just gossip."

"Let's make a note of it anyway," Aunt Ibby said, and scribbled in her notebook. "But back to Betsy's point. Have any of you seen Cody and Sam together?"

Mr. Pennington stopped his perusal of the cow-of-the-month portrait. "I've seen them together," he said. "Many times."

All heads turned in his direction. "Where?" Aunt Ibby wanted to know. "When?"

"It was usually at school functions, of course," Rupert Pennington said. "That was most often where I saw Samuel. He and Cody McGinnis were, as you know, associates in the university's history department."

"Nothing unusual there," Betsy said. "What we need is dirt. Or at least suspicion of dirt."

"I don't know if this qualifies at that level," he said, "but Samuel, Professor McGinnis, and that poli-sci professor you interviewed, Lee, often dined together, went to the theater together, and occasionally traveled together."

"I knew they traveled together," Louisa said. "I ran into them a year or so ago on an Alaskan cruise."

"I'm generally pretty tight-lipped about library business," Aunt Ibby said. "What happens in the library stays in the library. Some folks in Salem wouldn't like the type of books they read to be common knowledge, if you get my drift. But since Samuel is dead, I guess I can tell you that those three men were collaborating on a book. They asked for my help with the research."

"That's interesting," Louisa said. "When I met them on that cruise, they were with another man. Occasionally I sat with the four of them at dinner. And now that you mention it, their conversations were always about writing."

"Aunt Ibby," I asked, "do you know what their book was about?"

"As far as I could tell by the questions they asked, I don't think it was exactly a textbook. I believe it was a how-to book showing students how to study for exams, how to take notes effectively, how to research and write a term paper—that sort of thing. They called it *You Can Do This.*"

"Cute title. It sounds like a worthwhile project."

"I agree," she said. "They apparently had a contract with a well-known publisher. Now, I don't know if this is important or not, but someone else was working with them. They had an editor. I overheard them talking about 'the editor.' Somebody who was putting the thoughts and ideas of the three into publishable shape. Maybe that was the man Louisa saw them with. They were pretty secretive about it, as if they didn't want people to know that they needed help to write this book. And between us, they needed a great deal of help!"

"It sounds almost as though they'd hired a ghostwriter, doesn't it?" I asked.

"Could be quite important, I should think," my aunt said. "Whoever that is might hold some extra insight into all three of those men."

"Brrr." Louisa pretended to shiver. "Ghostwriter sounds strange—under the circumstances, doesn't it? So it looks as though we three women need to find him. Or her."

"We can do it, I'm sure," Betsy said. "And if we're going to be *Charlie's Angels*, can I be Farrah? I have the best hair."

Chapter 8

After the three guests had left, Aunt Ibby and I worked on our outlines. Top on our new information list was Aunt Ibby's announcement that there was someone—an editor—who had contact with Professors Bond, Armstrong, and McGinnis.

"Why didn't you mention the book collaboration earlier?" I asked. "When I first told you about Roger's call?"

"Remember, Maralee, we didn't even know that Cody was Roger and Ray's nephew until you got that call. Then Professor Armstrong showed up on your newscast, and things started to fit together. Academic types ask me for help all the time. Nothing unusual about it at all. Publish or perish, as the saying goes, and many of them need a great deal of help to produce anything even remotely publishable."

"Did any of them mention a name for this mysterious 'editor'?"

"No. They referred to 'the editor.' I don't know if it was a man or a woman. Maybe it isn't even important. I'm kind of curious."

"Does 'editor' get a Roman numeral?" I asked.

"Hmm. No. I think it's more of a subheading. We need a numeral for Bond-McGinnis-Armstrong collaboration, though. 'Editor' goes somewhere under that."

"Did the book they were writing have a chapter on how to make an outline?" I gave the three names Roman numeral IX in my notebook, then held the page at arm's length. "It all looks quite orderly, doesn't it?"

"It does," she said. "But murder is never orderly."

I helped her clean up the kitchen. We finished the coffee, nibbled on a few leftover dainty madeleines, then O'Ryan and I climbed the front stairs to my apartment.

It was still fairly early. I changed to pj's—white cotton printed with fiftieth-anniversary Sesame Street characters. Kit-Cat showed eleven o'clock. I turned on the bedroom TV and tucked my notebook away in the bureau, wondering if either the Toy Trawler story or the candy store tour would be on the WICH-TV late news. O'Ryan had followed me into the bedroom. I plumped up my pillows and slipped under the covers while he made his usual three turns, then lay down at the foot of the bed.

Buck Covington began the newscast with an interview Scott Palmer had done earlier with Salem Police Chief Tom Whaley. It appeared to have been shot in the chief's office. Chief Whaley does not like live interviews, and I wondered how Scott had managed this one.

"Chief Whaley," Scott began. "The medical examiner has released some new information today about the stab wounds on Professor Bond's body. He says that the wounds were made by a 'long dagger.' This would seem to preclude the idea that a small letter opener which has gone missing from the suspect Cody McGinnis's desk was the murder weapon. Is that correct?"

"Yes," the chief said. "The idea that a letter opener was involved came from the media. It was never the position of this department."

"Does the department now have a knife like that in evidence?"

"We do."

"Is it the murder weapon?"

"We don't know that. At this point it's simply an item of interest."

I was surprised by the answer. From the look on Scott's face, he was surprised too.

"Whose knife is it?"

"It apparently came from Professor Bond's own kitchen."

"Is that where it was found?"

"No."

Scott leaned forward, looking expectantly toward the chief. "No? Where then?"

The chief looked even more uncomfortable than usual. "As I said, we aren't representing that this knife is the murder weapon."

Scott pressed on. "Where was it found?"

"It was at the university."

"County U?"

"Yes."

"Where?"

"In Professor Bond's office."

It was a "holy cow!" moment. I could tell that Scott was momentarily speechless. That doesn't happen very often. It gave the chief a chance to escape, and he took advantage of it.

"Thank you, Scott," he said. He stood so quickly his chair tottered slightly, and he made a quick exit from the room.

"Uh—thank *you*, Chief Whaley," Scott said, recovering enough to do a quick wrap-up of what he'd learned, along with a standard sign-off. "Stay tuned to WICH-TV, everybody, for continuing coverage of this rapidly unfolding story."

Not unfolding so rapidly, I thought, then stopped thinking about murder completely when my own image appeared on-screen. (Can't help it. Was my hair okay? Do I look fat in those jeans?) I decided that the interview with Captain Billy went well, and the shots of the kids on the giant game pieces were adorable. Buck moved on to coverage of Salem's newest public park, named for Abolitionist Charlotte Forten; a story about a kid's big catch of an enormous halibut; and a detailed report on a city council meeting.

My friend River North's show follows the late news, and I often manage to stay awake long enough to watch *Tarot Time.* River features scary old movies and TV shows, like *The Twilight Zone*, and takes calls from viewers, reading the beautiful cards for them. The show is wildly popular and, to Bruce Doan's delight, sometimes outpulls the big network late-night programs.

I was happy to see that the night's movie was a true classic—Stephen King's *Misery.* River, as usual, looked amazing in a black velvet off-shoulder gown with a sparkling jeweled spider above her left breast. Silver moons and stars were woven into her long black braid. She sat in a giant fan-backed wicker chair, facing a matching table. There was another chair opposite hers, which usually meant that Buck Covington had stayed after the news and was on hand to shuffle the cards—the viewers loved that part—and since Buck and River had started dating, he'd become quite adept at some fancy card handling. Because sometimes a card being read is upside down, which usually yields an opposite meaning from the right-side-up position, Buck riffled the cards, holding them so that the tops in each hand faced each other. That way they get mixed well.

O'Ryan, on hearing River's voice, abandoned his foot-of-the-bed position and snuggled in beside me. He loves

River. After she gave a few words about the movie, and
as Buck shuffled the cards, she took her first call.

"Hello, caller. Your first name and birthday, please?"

A woman's reply was hesitant, soft voiced. "My name
is—um—do I have to?"

"No. You don't have to give your name and birthday if
you're not comfortable with that. Could you speak up a
little louder, though?"

"All right. River, I'm very worried about one of my
children. Can you read his future?"

"I'm sorry." River shook her head, and the moons and
stars in her hair quivered and sparkled. "I can't read for
your child without his permission. I believe that would be
an invasion of his privacy. Would it help if I read for
you?"

"Yes. Yes. I think it could help."

River placed her hand onto the deck of cards in the
center of the table. She bowed her head. "I dedicate this
deck to serve others with their spiritual growth, for wisdom, knowledge, and to bring healing and peace to all
who seek its guidance."

"That's nice. Thank you, River."

I recognized the same ten-card arrangement she uses
most often, beginning with a single card in the middle of
the table to represent the caller. I recognized that card as
"The High Priestess," and I understood why she used it.
In readings River has done for me, she's used it to represent Aunt Ibby. She told me the card often signifies a
mother or a mother figure. Made sense, since the caller
had mentioned a son.

After she'd reshuffled the cards, River completed the
layout and the overhead camera revealed the first six
cards in the form of a cross and four more in a vertical
row beside it. All the cards faced up. River touched the
second card, which she'd placed across the priestess card.

"The Three of Swords," she said. "You see rain and clouds in the background, and a heart pierced by three swords. In the Kabbalah, this card sometimes represents a sorrowful mother." She looked toward the camera. "You've already told me you are concerned about your son. Are you fearing a separation?"

A softly spoken "Yes."

"Next we see the Ten of Wands. A man is shown carrying ten wands, each of them flowering. It is a heavy burden, but the man plods on toward the beautiful city in the background." River smiled. "It seems as though the load is more than he can manage, but your son is brave. His plans have been disrupted, but he still struggles onward."

A stronger voice. "Yes."

The overhead camera activated as she touched the next card. "The Knight of Pentacles, reversed," she said. I squinted, leaned closer to the screen. The card showed a man on a horse. A knight in armor, he wore a red tunic and red gloves. The camera once again focused on River. "Perhaps there's a man with dark hair, dark eyes in your son's life. That man is careless with money. Not always trustworthy." She moved on. "Here's the Eight of Pentacles. This man—perhaps your son—is working at a trade, a profession. He's in the apprenticeship stage of what is to come. He earns less money than he hopes for."

"He deserves more. He's earned it." The caller's voice was louder.

"The Wheel of Fortune is your next card. It's reversed too. For the time being, there'll be setbacks in your plans. You will need courage, but eventually, things will be so much better."

"You think?"

River smiled. "I think."

The Six of Wands was next, showing a man on horseback. "This is good news, caller," River pronounced. "A victory is ahead. Perhaps in the field of arts and sciences. Does that make sense?"

"It certainly does. But when does the victory come?"

The next card was not a pretty one. The Four of Swords showed a knight lying on a tomb. River spoke quickly. "It's not a card about death. It's sometimes about a temporary exile, though, a separation from the familiar. There will be a change back to normal activity in the future."

"But you don't know when?"

River moved through the rest of the reading fairly quickly. I understood why. She was on a schedule involving commercial breaks, station IDs, and the start of the movie. The remaining cards covered some information about putting one's house in order, more changes of plans, the appearance of an interesting-sounding blonde woman, but nothing indicating a set time for victory or normal activity, which the caller seemed to want. Not surprising. River wished the woman and her son courage and love and golden white light and moved on to a message about Lorelei's love magic candles at Crow Haven Corner.

O'Ryan and I watched the start of the movie and another card reading. This one involved safety of possible travel abroad and the advisability of hiring a dog sitter while the family was away as opposed to a boarding kennel. The cards indicated that it would be safe to travel and that the dog might prefer staying at home. I felt drowsy, and O'Ryan was already asleep, showing a total lack of interest in the comfort of dogs.

I turned off the TV and lay awake for a while thinking about the nameless, birthdate-less, worried mother, fearing separation from a son, who thought he should earn more money, who was involved with the arts and sciences, and whose plans had been disrupted. And who does the Knight of Pentacles represent? Is he the mysterious editor? The ghostwriter?

I decided that first chance I got I'd ask River about that knight. And maybe I'd ask River's call screener, Therese Della Monica, if she'd recorded that sad mother's number. Just in case.

Chapter 9

I sat down for breakfast in Aunt Ibby's kitchen—still nothing much in my refrigerator—when my phone dinged. A text from Roger Temple announced that he and Ray would be in Salem on Wednesday night. "The twins will be here tomorrow," I told my aunt. "It looks like Cody's about to be formally charged with the crime."

"Oh dear. That doesn't sound good," she said. "I'll talk with Rupert and the Angels and see what they've learned so far that might be helpful."

I smothered a snicker at the casual way she mentioned "the Angels," and spread homemade strawberry jam onto a thick slice of sourdough toast. "Did you see Scott Palmer's interview with Chief Whaley on the late news? About the knife?"

"I didn't, but it's in this morning's paper. Strange."

"Sure is. At least we know the murder weapon wasn't Cody's letter opener," I said. "But why would one of the professor's kitchen knives turn up in his office?"

Aunt Ibby sipped her coffee thoughtfully. "I know my kitchen knives have turned up occasionally in the break room at the library," she said, "when I've baked a birth-day cake for someone and brought a knife along to cut it."

"I hadn't thought of anything like that," I said. "It probably isn't the murder weapon anyway."

"If it is," she pointed out, "it could have Samuel Bond's blood on it somewhere. Bloodstains are pretty hard to get out."

"They should be through testing it by now. We'll probably know today whether it had prints or blood or birth-day cake or anything interesting on it."

"There wasn't anything about it on the morning news," she said, "but I saw your report on the candy store. Made me hungry for chocolate."

"I need to go shopping," I said. "I'll pick some choco-lates up for you. Need anything else?"

"I'll give you a list. I want to get some of those sardine-flavored treats for O'Ryan, and I'll need a few things if Roger and Ray want to get together with all of us on Wednesday evening."

"Oops. Hope not. Pete and I have tickets to the Sox game. The twins will probably want to spend time with their sister anyway."

"Of course. Maybe I'll have the Angels over and we can work on the case."

I smiled, thinking of Pete's book title—*Nancy Drew and the Case of the Murdered Professor*. "Good idea," I said. "See if they have any ideas about who the editor is. Jot down your grocery list, and I'll see you after work."

It was such a pleasant day that I thought about putting the top down on the Corvette, but decided against it. Maybe on the way home I would, though. Salem can be lovely in late spring/almost summer. Pleasant weather, and the traffic isn't too bad before the annual influx of tourists begins in earnest.

I pulled into my parking space, locked the car, and took a couple of deep, refreshing breaths of salt air. For me, that works as well as one of those energy drinks. I skipped the elevator and climbed the metal staircase, wondering what Rhonda's white board would offer for my day.

"Glad you're here a little early," Rhonda said. "Scott's out with a sore throat. So you and Francine are kind of doubled up with his assignments as well as your own." I didn't question that. Wasn't even surprised. Mr. Doan would be happy if everyone did double jobs every day. As it is, almost everyone at the station wears more than one hat. My job is sometimes like that of a substitute teacher. I've subbed for Scott many times, and he's done the same for me. I've answered phones for Rhonda, done investigative reports on short notice, and once even filled in for Wanda the Weather Girl.

I looked at the white board and read aloud the items neatly printed in purple marker. "City council meeting at city hall: 10:00 a.m. Mayor meeting with mayor of Salem's Japanese 'sister city' at noon: Hawthorne dining room. A new mural to be unveiled at the El Punto neighborhood: 2:00 p.m. Police chief will hold presser about McGinnis arrest: TBA. As time permits, visit the no-kill animal shelter, the new display of figureheads at the Peabody Essex Museum, and schedule another interview with Professor Armstrong." That last one was underlined in red, probably by the station manager.

"Is Francine here yet?" I asked. "Maybe we have time to visit the animal shelter on the way to city hall."

As though on cue, Francine arrived, joining me at the white board. "Holy cow! We'd better get rolling right now." I agreed, told her about my animal shelter idea, and we hurried down the metal staircase and out to the parking lot. We climbed into the mobile van and began our workday.

"Shall we promise each other that neither of us will fall in love with a puppy or kitty this time?" Remembering the difficulty I'd had passing up an adorable black kitten the last time we'd visited, I raised my right hand and promised. Anyway, I wasn't sure how O'Ryan would feel about welcoming a new pet.

The volunteers at the shelter gave us an excellent tour of the facility. We met the veterinarian on duty, petted a sweet St. Bernard and a pair of brother and sister cockapoos. I didn't cuddle any kittens, and we came away with a good twenty minutes of material, which would get edited down to a couple of short spots that could run almost anytime a filler was needed. Mr. Doan calls those "evergreens."

City hall was already in full swing, dealing with a citizen's committee demanding that the city council arrange for more neighborhood security. There were several FREE CODY signs being waved with enthusiasm, mostly by young student types. The committee spokesman gave an impassioned request for more patrol cars. "There may still be a vicious, house-breaking killer wandering our streets, looking for another victim—like poor old Sam Bond." I managed a short interview with the spokesman, a few words with a young sign-carrying girl who'd taken Cody's Salem history course, and a longer Q and A with Councilor Lois Mercer, who's helped me out several times when city business rated prime time, front-page coverage—which this murder clearly did.

"We've already passed on the request to the police department," Mercer told my audience. "We've been assured that the chief will address the situation later today. Although the police have arrested a person of interest, it seems entirely possible that there is still a killer loose in Salem." She waved a hand toward the crowd, which had begun to leave the chambers. "We listen to our citizens. They are frightened."

The Hawthorne Hotel, where the mayor's meeting with the Japanese mayor was due to start at noon, was only about a mile away, but parking could be a problem because the hotel is close to the Witch Museum, where lots of tour buses line up every day. Francine lucked out with a space, and we had five minutes to spare before the dignitary was supposed to show up.

Meanwhile, the "Free Cody" group had learned about the mayor's meeting, grown in number, and had lined up across the street from the hotel. I did a quick standup commentary while Francine zoomed in on the chanting protesters. There was a significant presence of security on both sides of the street. When a black limo bearing a Japanese flag pulled up at the front entrance, I was in a perfect position to see the expected dignitary step from the limo. He looked quite young against a background of sign-waving, noisy students calling on him to tell the mayor to free Roger and Ray's imprisoned nephew. I recognized the blue-haired girl.

Rhonda hadn't had time to fill me in on the visiting mayor's name. I was only a couple of feet away from him, so I had to wing it. "Good morning, your honor," I said. "I'm Lee Barrett. WICH-TV. Is this your first visit to Salem?" I held the stick mic toward him, belatedly hoping he spoke some English. He did. Turned out he'd been an exchange student in California for a year and spoke it well enough for us to have a conversation.

"It is, indeed," he said. "An interesting city. But tell me, Ms. Barrett, what is a 'cody'?" he gestured to the loud crowd across the street. "And why must it be freed?"

OMG! Hasn't his staff briefed him on what's going on in his sister city? Or is he having fun with the lady reporter?

"Local story, sir," I said. "A sad one. A prominent citizen has been murdered, and a popular history professor is a suspect. His name is Cody McGinnis, and some of his students believe—quite strongly—in his innocence."

His expression was appropriately grave. "Yes. A sad business." He moved toward the open doorway of the hotel. "Thank you, Ms. Barrett."

Francine and I flashed our press credentials and, along with reporters and cameras from a couple of Boston stations, followed the procession of dignitaries, both Japanese and American, to the dining room where our mayor waited to greet the guests. A polite guy wearing a Red Sox cap and carrying the latest Tascam DR-44WL audio recorder held the door for us. I pointed to the neat portable unit and whispered to Francine. "Way better than mine, and we're supposed to be professional."

We made ourselves as unobtrusive as possible, and Francine began filming. I'd do a voice-over later at the studio. For the moment I was an observer. The welcoming speech was the usual kind, with translator and signer helping. Our mayor is excellent at this, and her Japanese counterpart responded with similar goodwill. He reached what appeared to be the conclusion of his remarks, then added, "I noticed the gathering of students outside. It reminded me of my student days in California. It is a very good thing for citizens to make known their feelings to those of us in office, isn't it?" He paused, then smiled. "So often the young people are right."

What had started as an ordinary piece of fluff filler TV had suddenly become news.

Once back in the van, I put my phone on speaker and called Rhonda. "Do we have any idea when the chief's presser is going to happen? The student protest about Cody McGinnis being held is growing, and our sister city mayor dropped a good pro-student quote we can use along with whatever the chief has to say. Besides that, the city council is dealing with citizens' groups who want more protection from a killer who might be loose in Salem."

"Sounds good," she said. "Listen, why don't you two get over to the police station now? I'll send Old Jim over for the mural unveiling. That way you'll be on hand as soon as Chief Whaley is ready."

"We're on our way."

"Okay if we stop for a hamburger?" I asked. "The mayors didn't invite us for the dinner."

"Sure, but don't forget to get that interview with the hot professor. Doan is expecting it."

"I know. I'll get it done," I promised. "See you later."

I fumbled in my purse for the card Professor Armstrong had given me. Francine had already turned the van in the direction of McDonald's. "While we wait for the chief to show up, I'll try to get in touch with Professor Dreamy."

"He gave you his number?" Francine gave one of her raised-eyebrow smirks.

"It's a business card, silly. He probably gives them to everybody."

"I saw that look he gave you." We joined the fast-food line. "Want the usual?"

"Sure." She ordered two number fives with Diet Cokes. "All our viewers saw the look too," I said. "He probably gives that look to every woman he meets."

"Go ahead and call him. I'll bet he answers right away." My call went to voice mail. It was my turn to smirk. I left a brief message, as instructed, and we headed for the police station. When we arrived, the lectern the chief uses was already in place, and it looked as though his mic was being installed. We were the only media vehicle there so far, but I knew that wouldn't last long. I'd taken my first mouthful of hot fries, when there was a tap at my window. I rolled it down quickly. Pete's office is on the street side of the building, and he must have seen us drive up.

"Hi, babe," he said. "Saw you rolling by. You're early. I think Chief's still busy putting on his dress uniform for the occasion. Hi, Francine."

"Hi, Pete," she said. "Doan's got us doing double duty today."

"I see that. Lunch and presser at the same time?"

"Triple duty," I said. "Lunch, presser, and trying to set up an interview all at once." I pointed to my phone in its holder on the dash. "Have you talked to Professor Armstrong at the university yet?"

"Not personally. I know we took a statement from him. Said he was friends with McGinnis and Bond both. Kind of conflicted there, I suppose."

"I guess so. Mr. Doan seems to think he's important. He's being quite insistent that I talk to the man. I hope he'll return my call. I don't want to have to chase him around the campus."

The phone, still on speaker, buzzed. "Hello?" I said.

The male voice was smooth and a little husky. "Hello, Lee. This is Alan. I've been hoping you'd call."

Raised-eyebrow smirk again from Rhonda. "Told ya."

Pete raised his eyebrows too.

Chapter 10

I raised one finger in a "wait a minute while I take this call" signal.

"Uh, yes, Professor Armstrong. I know you're very busy, but I wonder if you could spare the time for a short interview." Pete leaned in a little closer, his arms folded on top of the open window, obviously listening to every word.

"On TV?"

"Of course. WICH-TV. Francine and I can arrange to meet you at the university if that's the most convenient for you. Or if you prefer, we can shoot it at our studio."

"Who's Francine?"

"My photographer. She was with me yesterday."

"Oh, yes."

Long pause. Was he thinking it over? I remembered the underlined-in-red "Schedule another interview with Professor Armstrong." Mr. Doan was serious about this. I had to convince this guy to agree to it. "We'll keep it as brief as possible," I promised, "but I'm sure our viewing audience wants to hear more from you, Professor."

"All right, but you can drop the 'Professor.' Call me

Alan, Lee." It sounded like a smooth, slightly husky, command.

Francine's smirk was back.

"Certainly, Alan," I said, making a face in Francine's direction. "When and where would be convenient for you?"

Another pause. "I suppose the lighting and sound at the TV studio is superior to the outdoor version?"

"We have more control there, yes."

"I can arrange to meet you at the station tomorrow evening then, Lee. Sixish? And Lee, I'm looking forward to it."

Pete shook his head, moved away from the window, and made a swinging-a-bat move. "Ball game," he whispered.

"Professor—I mean, Alan—can we make it earlier in the day? I have a previous engagement tomorrow evening."

Long, heartfelt sigh on the other end of the phone. "Lee, dear, as you've already noticed, I am a very busy man. There are so many demands on my time—some from larger media venues, to tell the truth. And I *do* have a unique slant on this murder. I'd love for *your* station to be the first to hear about what I know. But, if you can't make time for me . . ."

I looked at Pete, shrugging my shoulders. *What shall I do?*

He put down his imaginary bat, smiled, and whispered, "It's okay."

I knew he understood. There've been times when his work interfered with our plans and other times when mine had. "All right, then, Alan," I said. "I'll plan to see you at the station at six tomorrow evening."

"Perfect," he said. "And Lee, you won't be sorry."

I'm sorry already. "Looking forward to it," I lied. "Goodbye."

"Oh, Pete," said. "I wish I didn't have to do this. But, Mr. Doan . . ."

"Don't worry about it, babe," he said. "I'll give the tickets to Marie. She and Donny love the Sox. We'll go to another game soon. I promise." Yes, Pete's sister and brother-in-law are named Donny and Marie.

"Thanks for understanding," I said. "I'd better call Rhonda and see if she can schedule Marty for a six o'clock in-studio shoot tomorrow." I've worked with Marty Mc-Carthy since my first day at WICH-TV. She's a friend as well as a crack videographer. My mind raced, trying to plan ahead. "The news desk will still be working on the five o'clock. Maybe we can use the *Saturday Business Hour* set. Then we can run the interview on the late news." I looked back at Pete. "The interview shouldn't take too long. Maybe we can do something afterward."

"I've already got Wednesday night off," he said, then did that silly Groucho Marx thing wiggling his eyebrows. "I'm sure we'll think of something. Gotta get back to work. I'll call you later. So long, Francine."

"See ya, Pete," she said, waving as he left. "Here come some more mobile units. Chief must be about ready to get started."

I called Rhonda, quickly explained what was going on, checked hair and makeup in the visor mirror, and climbed out of the van. Together Francine and I organized camera and mic setups and took our positions as close as we could get to the chief's lectern.

Media interest in the Samuel Bond murder had clearly grown. I recognized reporters from two of the local Boston stations, along with a FOX network crew, a representative from the History channel, and even a member of a well-known ghost-hunting team. The long-ago murder of Captain White had surely captured the attention of the public far beyond Salem. The chief, tall, distinguished, and handsome in a dress uniform and a chest full of medals, approached the bank of microphones, cleared his throat, and began to speak.

"Thank you for coming. I'll attempt to update you briefly on the matter of the recent death of Professor Samuel Bond. As you may know, we have made one arrest. My staff, as well as our state of Massachusetts advisers, are continuing a thorough investigation into the circumstances of Professor Bond's death. There has been some significant progress in the case, the details of which will be forthcoming later. Certain materials have been turned over to the forensics unit for further analysis. I wish I had more to share with you today, but please be assured that we are moving as swiftly as possible in a forward direction. Thank you for your understanding."

The shouted questions began. A guy I recognized from WBZ-TV yelled, "Is it true you've got the killer's shoes?" *So someone else has heard about the cops raiding Cody's locker.* I poked Francine's arm. Her gym-rat contact was right.

"There have been several items collected and sent to the forensic labs," the chief said. "I'll have no further comment on that." I tried asking a question. "Chief Whaley, since you've found the knife, are you looking for two killers now?"

He frowned in my direction. Then shook his head. "As I just said, a state forensics team is working on evidence we've gathered, including some new items of interest." He stepped back from the podium. "That's all we have for now. I'll notify the press as soon as there is any further relevant information. Good afternoon."

He answered a few more questions as he moved toward the door of the station—mostly about any connection to the White killing. As usual, he looked relieved when the door closed behind him.

"That's kind of a letdown." Francine stowed our equipment neatly in the side of the van. "Nothing much new there."

"I know. The only new thing was the fact that they've gathered some more evidence they're not going to tell us about. How'm I supposed to make a news alert spot out of that?"

"Beats me," she said. "What's a 'new item of interest'?"

"Could be darned near anything," I said. "And 'items of interest' mean 'things,' not 'people,' I suppose."

Chapter II

Francine may have exceeded the speed limit on the way back to the station. There was a good chance we'd be able to get this footage ready in time for the five o'clock news. Also, I was anxious to let Mr. Doan know that I'd secured an interview with Professor Armstrong. I was sure he'd be a lot more happy about that than I was.

Super-efficient Rhonda had already contacted Marty and arranged for the in-studio interview with Professor Dreamy. Mr. Doan seemed pleased about it, although he wondered aloud why I couldn't do it immediately, in time for the early news.

"What does he think we are? Magicians?" Francine grumbled. "How many places can we be in one day? Dogs and cats. City hall. A couple of mayors. The chief of police. Whew!"

"When you line it up like that, I'm impressed with us," I told her.

"Yeah. We're worth more money," she said, and we both laughed at that idea.

So did Rhonda. "Fat chance of that for any of us. Hey, Old Jim should be back pretty soon from the mural unveiling at El Punto. So you can do the voice-over and add that to the list. If you hurry, you might even have time to check out the figureheads at the Peabody Essex Museum."

"Let's save that one for another day," I said. "It'll be too interesting to rush through. I'll wait for Old Jim and talk about the murals." I like talking about El Punto. It's a fairly new attraction in Salem—a three-block outdoor art museum that has revitalized a previously rundown neighborhood. Now over seventy-five large-scale murals, many by world-famous artists, decorate existing buildings. It's an artistic extravaganza, changing the formerly bypassed streets into a welcoming riot of color and excitement.

Old Jim is a darned good photographer. He keeps trying to retire, but winds up filling in every time the station needs him. He's usually relegated to the aged Volkswagen van instead of the much newer mobile unit Francine drives, but he doesn't mind.

We fixed up a screen that looked as though I was actually standing in front of a giant mural of a rainbow-colored cat with a bird on his shoulder. Then as Jim's camera panned the three blocks, I encouraged viewers to visit the place. We wrapped it up and exchanged high fives. By then it was time for me to leave, satisfied with my day's work well done. I could hardly wait to get home to see what Aunt Ibby thought about the chief's information—such as it was.

I made a quick trip to Shaw's with Aunt Ibby's grocery list, then hurried home. As soon as I hit the remote and opened the garage door, I recognized Betsy Leavitt's Mercedes in the driveway. Had my aunt called an emergency meeting of the Angels already? I parked and walked quickly toward the house, where O'Ryan waited on the back steps. He met me halfway, and together we went in. I knocked on my aunt's kitchen door, while the cat scooted inside.

I heard my aunt's voice. "Come in, Maralee, it's open. We're in my office." I hung my purse on the back of a kitchen chair and followed the cat. All three of the Angels were there, gathered around the cherrywood desk. There wasn't a chair for me, so I stood behind Louisa.

"Hello, Angels," I said, trying not to giggle. "I didn't see your car, Mrs. Abney-Babcock."

"Betsy picked me up, dear—and please call me Louisa. I feel that we're going to see a lot of each other for a while."

Aunt Ibby and Betsy agreed. "We're giving every spare minute to this case," my aunt pronounced. "I've already contacted the twins and told them not to worry. We're on the job."

Oh boy. You've told two professional police officers, who are related to the chief suspect, not to worry because three senior citizens are "on the job"?

"What did they say?"

"They're delighted, of course," Betsy pronounced. "Who wouldn't be with a professional researcher and two close personal friends of the deceased helping their cause."

Word choice, of course. It's all about word choices.

"You're right," I said. "Who wouldn't be?" I pointed to the computer. "Anything new to report so far?"

"We're trying to make sense out of what the chief said—or didn't say—about the shoes. I'll bet your third-person source from the gym was right, Lee," Betsy said. "I'll bet the cops have Cody's shoes and they'll try to match them up with footprint casts from Bond's backyard."

"Did he say anything else after the cameras were turned off?" Louisa wanted to know. "And why didn't he answer your question about two people?"

"He was in a big hurry to get away, that's for sure," I said. "I'm pretty sure his comment would have been 'no comment.'"

"We'd like to know if the police *actually* have Professor McGinnis's shoes—and they're a match—or are they saying that he *has* a pair that *could* have made the prints?"

"Yes. That's a very good question. Maralee? Why didn't you ask the chief that?" My aunt cocked her head to one side. "You were right there."

I had to admit it. The question hadn't occurred to me. "The chief left in such a hurry," I rationalized, "that there were lots more questions we all could have asked. But I think Pete will tell me the answer to that one. I'll let you know."

"Good," Aunt Ibby said. "You do that. Meanwhile, we're putting together a plan of action right now. We—the three of us—know many people in this city. I mean, we know people who know other people, if you know what I mean." A conspiratorial head nodding and eye winking went on between the Angels.

I didn't know exactly what that meant and was almost afraid to ask. I changed the subject. "Where's Mr. Pennington? Isn't he supposed to be helping?"

That met with frowns. "No. He's just Charlie. He doesn't have to *do* anything. We'll report what we find to him, and he can organize it."

"I see." And I did—sort of. "I'm sure the twins will contact me as soon as they get to town," I said.

"Those fancy lawyers haven't been much help so far, have they?" Aunt Ibby mused.

Louisa gave a well-bred "Humph," then continued, "a fancy suit and a nice haircut doesn't always mean brains and competence."

"True enough," we all agreed.

"Have you made a contact list of those people who know people? I may know some people who know people too," I suggested. "As a matter of fact, I have an appointment tomorrow evening with someone who not only had a close working relationship with Professor Bond, but with Cody McGinnis as well."

Three pairs of eyes turned toward me. "Who is that?" Betsy asked. "Another professor? Or even a student?"

"Oh, dear," Aunt Ibby put one finger to her mouth. "I hope we're not going to hear one of those dreadful stories about a college professor having an inappropriate relationship with a student!"

"Surely not Samuel Bond!" Louisa was emphatic. "Perhaps Cody McGinnis, though. He's younger—in his thirties, I believe—and according to the newspaper pictures, quite attractive."

"Yes. That must be it." Betsy's nod was affirmative. "Is that it, Lee? Have you found a whistle-blower on the campus?"

"Whoa, ladies!" I held up both hands. "The idea of any kind of inappropriate relationship had never even occurred to me. No. Mr. Doan wants me to interview Professor Armstrong. Alan Armstrong. I have no idea what he's going to tell me, but he says he has a 'unique slant' on the murder."

"A unique slant sounds promising," Louisa said.

"Professor Dreamy." Betsy patted her perfect hairdo. "That's what the college girls call him. What a doll."

"You know him?" Aunt Ibby leaned forward, eyes wide.

"Well," Betsy batted her eyelashes. "Not in the biblical sense, but yes, I know him fairly well. Watch out for him, Lee. He's a terrible flirt."

I'd already figured that out but didn't say so. "We're meeting at the station," I said, "and Marty will be filming the whole thing. No problem."

"Please be careful," Betsy advised again. "Now, where were we?"

"I think we got a little bit sidetracked there," I suggested. "Remember, we're supposed to be concentrating on figuring out who—besides Cody—might have had a reason to kill Samuel Bond."

"Can you arrange somehow to talk to Cody himself?" my aunt wondered. "Now *that* would make a great interview."

"It would," I agreed, "but even before he was officially arrested, according to all the published reports I've seen, he'd been instructed not to leave Salem and not to speak to the press."

"The judge told him that?" she asked.

"Sure. Even if the judge hadn't, his lawyers would have told him the same thing." I was sure about that. "But maybe after the twins get here, we'll have some more to go on."

"Looking over our notes so far"—Aunt Ibby held up a few sheets of paper—"we've come up with some *possible* reasons someone might want Samuel Bond to die."

"Let me grab a chair from the living room," I said. "I want to hear every word of this." I pulled a small Victorian rosewood lady's chair into the small room. "Okay. Shoot."

"Well, first of all," my aunt said, "it seems that Samuel was in financial trouble." Louisa nodded, so I assumed this was one of the items she'd contributed. She sits on the boards of several banks. Aunt Ibby continued. "He recently applied for a large loan that was denied by a local bank, and his checks written to several merchants have all been retuned for insufficient funds. At least one credit card has been cancelled."

"That's bad news for anybody," Betsy said. "But do people get killed for a few bounced checks?"

"Kind of depends on who you owe money to—and how much," Aunt Ibby said. "Here's another one. According to Gladys Miller over at Triple-A, Sam came in for new passport pictures a couple of days before he died.

She thinks he could have been planning a trip out of the country."

"Had he bought tickets yet?" I asked. "This might be important."

"Nope. No tickets. No reservations. Maybe he was merely thinking about traveling. No crime there." She turned a page.

"This next one is admittedly gossip. It comes from one of my own neighbors. About a month ago she was pet sitting for a lovely standard poodle in the house right next door to Bond's place. It's usually a quiet neighborhood, so one night, quite late, when she took the poodle out to do his duty, she was surprised to hear loud voices coming from next door. Men's voices. She thought she heard two distinct voices, and she *thinks* one of them could have been Professor Bond, but can't swear to it." My aunt paused, looked around the room, and continued.

"She says that although the sound was muffled, because of the high fence between the properties, and she couldn't hear every single word, she's quite sure that one of the men—she couldn't tell which one—said something like, 'You've stolen from me for the last time. This time you're not going to get away with it.' Then, the voice she thought could have been Samuel Bond let loose with such a dreadful stream of cuss words that she covered the poodle's ears and ran straight back into the house."

"Do the police know about this?" It was my first thought. My first question.

"Of course not. I told you. It's plain old gossip. She can't prove a bit of it."

"Even so," I said. "It could be important."

"Yes," said Louisa. "Stealing puts a whole new perspective on it, doesn't it?"

"Stealing was involved in Captain Joseph White's murder." Aunt Ibby looked thoughtful. "Although the actual theft took place *before* the killing. A man named

Joseph Knapp opened Captain White's iron chest four days before the murder and stole what he thought was the old man's will."

"Maybe that's what happened this time too!" Betsy put her notebook down on the desk. "Wouldn't that be a delicious coincidence?"

"Pete doesn't believe in coincidences," I said to no one in particular. "Anyway, nothing was stolen this time. Nothing is missing."

"Nothing that we know of," Betsy insisted. "I *love* coincidences. I say we should investigate it."

"If Samuel was in debt to the extent Louisa's contacts say he was, some sort of stealing could be involved." My aunt spoke cautiously. "Perhaps we should at least consider the possibility."

All three raised their hands as though some sort of parliamentary procedure was in place—which it wasn't.

"Motion carried," said my aunt.

"But there was no . . ." I gave up. No one was listening to me anyway. I shook my head and looked down at the desk, noticing a large envelope marked "The Ultimate Alaska Cruise" and bearing the logo of a well-known cruise line. "What's this? Someone planning a cruise?"

"Oh, no, that's an assortment of photos from a recent trip I took," Louisa offered. "Remember? I told you that was where I saw the three professors and the other man. Together. They're in some of the pictures. I thought everybody might be interested."

"Could I look at them?" I picked up the envelope.

"Of course," she said. "Betsy and Ibby have already seen them. You may borrow them if you like."

"Thank you." I tucked the envelope under my arm. I excused myself from the Angels' meeting and, with O'Ryan following me, headed up the front stairs to my own apartment. I had to admit, Robert's Rules of Order aside, they had dug up some pretty good information. Some more Roman numerals were lining up in my head. Gladys Miller's tip about the passport picture was worth following. So was Louisa's bank information. Was Samuel Bond broke? Was he planning to leave the country? Questions about the shoe prints and the possibility of professor-student hanky-panky were further down on the list, along with backyard cussing. I thought that, overall, the twins would be pretty darned impressed with what we'd dug up on the departed professor in such a short time.

Pete phones me most evenings, but I knew that he had practice with his PAL peewee hockey team that night, and he usually takes the team out for ice cream after practice. If he did happen to call, I planned to ask the question about the killer's shoes. Were they actually Cody's or were they only the same type of shoes the police had found in Cody's locker?

These were the questions I hoped I'd dare to ask Pete— if he called. Meanwhile, as a large cat circling around my ankles making pitiful little starving-kitten sounds reminded me, it was past our dinnertime. I treated the cat to a can of White Meat Chicken Primavera with Garden Veggies and Greens in a Classic Sauce while I microwaved a bag of penne and vegetables in Alfredo sauce for myself. For dessert we shared some leftover vanilla ice cream. See? All the healthy food groups and very few dishes to wash.

When my phone rang a few minutes before ten o'clock, I reached for it, assuming it was Pete. I glanced at the caller ID as I was about to hit the little green phone icon. Oops. Alan Armstrong.

I let it ring.

Hey, if it's important, he can leave a message.

I added the Angels' findings to my outline—which was beginning to resemble preparatory notes for a master's thesis—and closed my notebook with a self-satisfied thump. I added Louisa's envelope of photos to the pile. I'd put in a darned good day's work.

"Ready for bed, O'Ryan?" The cat sat on the windowsill, looking out into the darkness. "Okay," I said. "I'm going to take a shower. If Alan Armstrong calls, don't answer it." Laughing at my own little joke, I padded down the hall to the bathroom.

When I returned, showered, shampooed, and paja-maed, O'Ryan was already asleep at the foot of my bed—and there were two identical messages from Alan Armstrong on my phone. "Good cat. You didn't answer it," I whispered as I read Alan's texts.

"Can we meet at five in the Hawthorne Hotel lounge for a little one-on-one time before the filmed interview? I have some information that isn't for public consump-tion."

Great! What was I supposed to do? Meet the man Betsy had so recently warned me about and perhaps pick up information that could not only help the twins defend their nephew, but could get me an exclusive for WICH-TV? Or should I turn down the invitation, miss out on something that the twins should know about, risk letting another reporter get the scoop, and at the same time to-tally tick off Bruce Doan?

I knew I didn't have to answer right away. It was late enough so that I could say I was asleep when he sent the messages. That would give me some time to think it over. I also knew that my curiosity would probably overrule in-stincts and good sense. I'd undoubtedly be at the Hawthorne lounge at five o'clock the following day. The cat at the foot of my bed stood up, looked at me, shook his head, then turned around three times and lay down again.

"Yeah. I know. Curiosity killed the cat. Don't rub it in. Let's hope it doesn't kill me."

Chapter 12

Wednesday started out a lot better than the previous day had. Scott was apparently cured of whatever ailed him, and he'd already left in the Volkswagen with Old Jim when I arrived. The white board, with my assignments in purple marker, looked fairly easy. I told Rhonda that she could post my five o'clock meeting as soon as I confirmed it.

"Great. Doan will be pleased. He's been getting pretty antsy about you talking with the hot professor. He must think the guy has some important information about the killer."

"I hope he has *something* worth reporting. Pete and I had tickets to the Sox game."

"Oh boy. Those are hard to get these days."

"I know. The chief gave them to him." I peered at my purple-inked assignments. "Speaking of the chief, no presser scheduled today?"

"Not yet. Don't worry. You'll be the first to know if he does." She glanced down at the row of security screens under the Formica counter. "Francine has pulled onto the lot. I've prepared a little cheat sheet for you about the museum figureheads. Dates, famous carvers, not much else."

"That's okay. The museum has those info cards on everything. Those busty beauties are so fascinating, the camera will tell the story better than I can."

I was right about that. The museum shoot went so smoothly Francine and I were back at the station within one hour. We weren't scheduled for anything else until noon, so while Francine worked on editing the tape for the noon news, I used one of the dataports and reluctantly returned Alan Armstrong's call.

"Hello, Professor . . . Alan. Lee Barrett here. Sorry I missed your call last night."

"Good morning, Lee." I could almost hear that perfect-teeth smile in his voice. "Did you get my text?"

"Sure did. You'd like to meet at five, right?"

"Yes. In the lounge at the hotel. Is that convenient for you?"

"No problem," I said, stretching my own lips into a smile. "Five o'clock. See you there."

"I'll look forward to it. And Lee, I think it'll be worth your while."

I certainly hope so.

"Thanks, Alan," I said. "I'll see you at five."

"It's a date, then. Would you like me to pick you up?" He sounded hopeful. "I'd be happy to."

I'll bet you would. And no, it is not a date.

"No thanks." I said, still fake-smiling. "It's right on my way to the station. Bye now."

I sat back in my chair, glad that call was over with. If Professor Dreamy was going to spill some useful information, Bruce Doan would be pleased. I planned to ask him straight out who was the editor of the book the three professors were writing. The twins would be proud of me. The Angels might even be impressed. And no matter what, Donny and Marie would be happy with those tickets. I closed the dataport and went back upstairs to the reception area.

"Okay, Rhonda," I said. "Meeting with Alan Armstrong at five confirmed. Any chance I can get paid overtime for it?"

"Not too likely," she said, picking up her purple marker. "But I'll ask the boss. Miracles do happen."

Francine pushed open the metal door leading from the newsroom. She was breathless. "You won't believe what Scott did while we were taking pictures of wooden boobs! I saw the transmission. Oh crap! We should have been there."

"Calm down," Rhonda commanded. "What happened? I didn't know Scott was back yet. He didn't check in with me."

"He's not back." Francine sank into one of the turquoise-and-chrome chairs. "Old Jim sent the footage ahead. They'll be here in a few minutes."

"So what did they get?" I pleaded. "What's got you so excited?"

"Cody McGinnis's mother," she said. "Old Jim spotted her. He went to school with her. Phyllis McGinnis. Recognized her right away. She was walking down Bridge Street big as life—all by herself."

I sat in the chair beside her. "Don't tell me they got an interview."

"Kind of," she said. "Poor woman was walking to the dry cleaners. She said she was going to pick up his good suit because he needs it for court. She was crying. Tears running down her face. 'He wants to look nice,' she said. 'He's afraid they'll make him wear one of those awful orange things.' She was absolutely sobbing."

"They got that on tape?" I was jealous already.

"Yep. Sure did."

"Nice human interest angle," Rhonda said. "What else?"

"She didn't say anything about the case," Francine said, "even though Scott pushed. You know how pushy Scott can be!"

"That's for sure," I said. "Did she tell them anything else at all?"

"Only that Cody is a good boy. Scott tried to get her to say that she was confident he'd be found innocent. Then he tried to get her to say she was worried about his chances, but she kept right on crying. Then she wished Scott a nice day and kept on walking. She went into a dry cleaners. It looked like Scott was going to follow her, but in a few seconds someone inside locked the door and put up the closed sign."

"So it wasn't an actual interview," I said.

"You've got to admit, it's better than anything anyone else has come up with lately," Rhonda said. "The part about needing his good suit for court is kind of sweet. And the sobbing mom is pitiful."

"Yeah, I guess it is." I had to agree.

"We don't have to be anywhere for a couple of hours yet." Francine glanced up at the starburst clock. "What do you say we take a ride around and see what we can find? Maybe we'll get lucky too. Maybe we'll see a bank robbery in progress or a famous movie star having a beer or even a fireman getting a cat out of a tree."

"Worth a try," I said. "Let's roll."

"It would be better if the fireman got a dog out of a tree," Rhonda suggested as she wrote "local investigation" in purple marker.

Francine and I discussed which direction we should take as we rode down in the elevator. "We haven't done the witch shops lately," I said, thinking of the commercial about the love magic candles I'd seen on River's show. "We could see what our local psychics and mystics and card readers have to say about the murder."

"I like it." We hurried across the parking lot and

climbed back into the mobile unit. Francine headed toward Washington Street. "How about Christopher's Castle? Chris Rich follows all that stuff, and he loves the publicity."

"Good idea." She was right. Christopher Rich stocks all kinds of magic paraphernalia in his shop—crystal balls, tarot cards, Ouija boards, magician's supplies. And he is the consummate publicity hound. "We might get the feel of what the whole supernatural community is thinking with that one stop."

Not unexpectedly, Chris seemed overjoyed to see us. Especially since we were carrying camera and mic. "Come in, come in! Two of my favorite women in the whole world. Welcome to my castle!" He did one of those deep bows with the hand-sweeping gesture that you see in movies about old-time royalty. Corny, but he does it well. "You're here in time to see my new line of tuxedos and top hats for magicians and adorably skimpy outfits for their lovely assistants."

"Sure. Interesting. We can cover that," I promised, "but at the same time, we're interested in hearing your take on what Salem's paranormal community thinks about the Samuel Bond murder."

Chris approached a male mannequin in magician's garb and motioned for me to join him next to it. Francine aimed her camera in his direction. "The whole city is buzzing about it," Chris said. "Can we show the merchandise while we dish the dirt? Have a look at the satin lapels, the black pearl cuff links."

"We'll weave it in." I picked up the stick mic with the WICH-TV logo on it and joined him beside the mannequin, which bore a remarkable resemblance to David Copperfield. "Ready, Francine? Is this light okay?"

"Good enough," Francine said, then "On one," and began the slow backward count. "Ten, nine, eight . . ."

"Lee Barrett here at Christopher's Castle, one of Salem's

best-known shops for all things magic and metaphysical.
We'll be talking to shop owner Chris Rich about not only
what's new in the world of paranormal paraphernalia, but
we'll get his take on exactly what his psychically tuned-
in patrons have to say about the recent Samuel Bond murder, along with its strangely similar counterpart, the
Captain Joseph White murder of eighteen thirty."

"Thank you for visiting us here at Christopher's Castle,
Lee!" He grinned at the camera and put his arm across the
mannequin's shoulders. "As you said, we have all of the
very newest, trendiest merchandise in the world of magical
arts. Christopher's Castle is where the stars of the psychic
world shop every day."

"I'm sure they do," I said. "Chris, everyone in Salem is
talking about the recent tragic death of Professor Samuel
Bond. In fact, because of the similarity in circumstances to
the Captain White murder in eighteen thirty, the story has
attracted national interest. Your patrons, with their varied
special talents, must have some interesting thoughts on the
case. Could you share some of what you've heard from
them on the subject?" Chris edged away from the mannequin and put his hand on a nearby counter where an assortment of colorful small boxes was displayed.

"Happy to help, Lee," he said. "You're absolutely right.
Some days it seems as if the murder is the *only* thing people
are talking about. Yesterday there were several of our tarot
card readers here—they were checking out my exciting assortment of tarot card bags and boxes. Anyway, some of
them had already done readings for friends of the deceased Professor Bond, and the findings seem to be about
fifty-fifty—between Cody McGinnis being guilty or someone else."

"Any clues about who the someone else might be?"

"Not exactly, but the Knight of Pentacles showed up
for almost all of them. That might mean something."

Yes, it might!

"Anything forthcoming from the witch community?" I asked.

"Many of them say that they're stocking up on crystals. The protective ones—you know, like black obsidian, smoky quartz, labradorite." Big smile at the camera. "I carry them all here at Christopher's Castle." He dropped his voice. "Most of my witches believe there's a killer loose in Salem and at least half of them are talking about bloodstains." He frowned. "Have you heard anything new about bloodstains?"

That caught me by surprise. "Uh, no, I haven't." *Are the witches seeing bloody handprints?* "That's interesting, Chris," I said. "I've always admired your beautiful display of crystals. Are some of the other magical items attracting special attention because of the murder?"

"Ouija boards!" he exclaimed. "They are simply flying out of here. And pendulums! These are tools that answer questions—and people in Salem want answers about this murder." He frowned. Scowled, actually. "We are not getting answers from the police. Perhaps the police should pay a visit to Christopher's Castle. They might learn a lot about *both* of the murders."

"Both murders?"

"Of course. The murder of Samuel Bond and the murder of Captain White. The similarities between them cannot be simple coincidence, can they?"

How was I supposed to answer that question? I dodged it. "Thanks for your insight into this mystery, Chris," I said. "It's always fascinating for us to visit with you."

Francine panned the camera around the large room for a few seconds, then came back to me. "Lee Barrett reporting from Christopher's Castle in downtown Salem."

As Francine and I gathered our gear, she whispered, "Do you think maybe you and I should pick up a couple of those protective crystals? Just in case? I mean, we're going to be poking around, talking to people who knew the dead guy. You even have a date with one of them."

"It is *not* a date."

"Okay, a meeting then. But it's only a crystal. A piece of jewelry. What could it hurt, right?"

My first instinct was to laugh, to brush the suggestion off, to say it was all nonsense. But hey, as she said, what could it hurt? Besides, the crystals are quite beautiful. Francine bought a black obsidian ring. It was pretty, but definitely not for me. Sometimes I see things—pictures, scenes that other people don't see—in reflective surfaces, like mirrors or windows or polished metals—and especially in shiny black obsidian. I've learned that I'm what is known as a scryer. Nostradamus was one. Jeane Dixon too. River says it's a special gift and calls me a "gazer." I don't think of it as a gift at all, even though I have to admit it's come in handy a few times.

I chose a smoky quartz pendant. I was pleased with my choice and even more pleased when Christopher Rich gave us a 20 percent discount *and* put our purchases into his fanciest blue velvet gift boxes. I slipped the box into my purse, thanked him sincerely for his time. The information about what the Christopher's Castle crowd thought about the murder was going to play well to the WICH-TV viewers. I was sure of it.

Chapter 13

Between the figureheads and Christopher's Castle, we'd managed to use up most of the morning. Our next appointment was at noon, so we headed back to Derby Street to pick up our information on the destination.

"What are you going to wear for your date . . . um, your meeting?" Francine asked, with a glance at my jeans and plain blue chambray shirt. "Not that, I hope."

"I hadn't thought about it," I admitted. "Probably a different shirt—pink maybe. It'll be a sit-down interview, so I don't have to change my jeans." I stuck out one foot. "Brown booties, I like 'em. Comfortable."

"Yeah, but I'm talking about the Hawthorne lounge cocktail hour. You'll be with Professor Dreamy! Everyone will be looking at you." She pointed at my bootie-clad foot. "I think it calls for heels. And a skirt. Yeah. Short skirt and heels."

"No," I said firmly. "No way. I told you this is not a date, and I most certainly am not trying to impress the professor, let alone the early cocktail crowd at the Hawthorne."

"Okay. I'm just sayin'."

"Remember, if Doan hadn't insisted that I talk to this guy, I'd be deciding what to wear to a baseball game with my man."

She sighed. "All right, but will you at least wear some decent boots? Like with heels?"

It wasn't an unreasonable request, and anyway, she was right about the boots. "I'll do it," I said. "Only for you."

Our noontime assignment was another easy one—a tree dedication. A Boy Scout troop was planting an oak tree at the senior citizens' home on the site of the old Salem High School to replace one that had been toppled in the most recent hurricane. I did a brief interview with the troop leader, then the Scouts, a couple of seniors, and then the man from the tree nursery took over the rest of the shoot. Easy-peasy. We were back at the station by one-thirty. A glance at the white board showed no more outside jobs for us until my five o'clock.

"I'll get with Marty and be sure the *Saturday Business Hour* set is ready for us," I said. "She was going to get some appropriate props for the desk and some visuals. Photos of Bond and maybe even one of Dick Crownin-shield."

Francine left to take the mobile unit through a car wash, and I told Rhonda I'd have to leave early. "Francine insists that I have to change this outfit for the Armstrong interviews."

Rhonda agreed with Francine. "Yep. You should. If you're going to be seen in public with Professor Dreamy, everyone in the place will be looking at you."

I sighed. "So I've been told." We agreed that I'd leave for home at three—and that I'd remain on the clock until after the six o'clock shoot. Good deal.

At exactly three o'clock I backed the Corvette out of my parking spot and headed home. Aunt Ibby's Buick was missing from the garage. Even though she's supposed to be semi-retired, she still spends several days a week at the library.

O'Ryan waited on the back steps, and then hurried along the flagstone path to meet me. I bent to pat his fuzzy head as he maneuvered in, out, and around my ankles so deftly that I maintained my pace without tripping over him. I let myself in, and the two of us climbed the twisty staircase to my apartment and headed straight for the bedroom.

"You can help me pick out something to wear that's appropriate for three places." I tossed my purse onto the bed, opened my closet door, and counted the venues off on my fingers. "A meeting at the Hawthorne, an on-camera interview at the station, and probably something with Pete later."

O'Ryan hopped up onto the bed, sitting up very straight, ears pointy and alert, golden eyes focused on me. He appeared to be interested in the project. I pulled out the pink silk shirt I'd already planned to wear. "I thought I'd wear this and the same jeans I have on," I told him. "Okay?" He cocked his head to one side, maybe considering that option, then bobbed his head up and down. I put two pairs of my best high-heeled boots on the bed. "What do you think? The Jimmy Choo silver ankle boots or the Yeezy midcalf python print wedge?" He stuck out a paw and tapped the Jimmy Choo.

"I agree," I said, although it's possible he passed on the python print because he's very wary of snakes. "There then. That's settled. The pink shirt, the same jeans, and the silver boots."

The cat sat on my purse. "You want me to change purses? I don't think so. I have all my stuff in that one and it goes with everything." He backed up, trying to stick his head inside the open top of my favorite Jacki Easlick hobo. It was comical. I laughed. "You can't fit inside, big boy," I told him. "I can't take you with me." He was not deterred. Not only did he fit his head inside, but one paw as well. *What is he trying to do?* The purse wiggled and wobbled for a bit, then the cat backed away with a blue velvet box clutched in his paw.

"I get it," I said, rescuing the box from his claws. "You want me to wear this tonight."

Did O'Ryan know somehow what was in the box? I've long since given up on trying to figure out how he does the things he does. Did this mean there was something important about the pendant—or was he simply being nosy because I had something new in the purse? Either way, the pendant on its slim silver chain would look fine with the other things I'd chosen.

I showered, tried hard to tame my too-curly hair, put a quick press on the jeans, and did a more-careful-than-usual job on my makeup. Kit-Cat showed four-fifteen. I planned to get to the hotel at exactly five if I could manage it. If I got there early, would it look as though I was anxious to see the handsome professor? If I was late, would I appear to be rude and possibly mess up the interview?

Parking is always iffy around the Hawthorne. Even though I live only a couple of blocks away from the place, sometimes I've had to drive around for a while to find a convenient space. I pulled on the jeans, buttoned the pink blouse, and slipped on the silver boots. Last of all, I fastened the new necklace. O'Ryan watched every move. "Okay. Satisfied? I'm wearing the smoky quartz for protection. Protection from what, I'm not at all sure."

He stared at me for a moment, gave a nod, jumped down from the bed, and strolled out of my room without a backward glance. I felt as though I'd been approved and dismissed. "Okay," I said to the retreating cat. "I'll be back as soon as I can." I meant that sincerely. I knew that this was important to Mr. Doan, and I hoped that whatever it was that Alan Armstrong had to tell me would turn out to actually be "worth my while" as he'd promised.

Considering the almost–five o'clock traffic, and the questionable parking situation in the vicinity of the Hawthorne, I lucked out. I parked in the hotel's overflow lot with five minutes to spare. Plenty of time. Even a couple of minutes to check my hair and makeup in the visor mirror.

Big mistake.

The flashing lights and swirling colors that always precede a vision filled the oblong space where curly red hair and mascaraed lashes should have been. The colors faded. I squinted, trying to make out exactly what I was seeing. River had told me that the pictures I saw this way might be from the past, the present, or the future. This one, like most of them, didn't make much sense no matter where it had come from. It was a book—no, a magazine or a big booklet. I wasn't sure. It had a blue paper cover and wasn't very thick. I couldn't read the title because there was a large red stain covering most of the words. Boom. It disappeared. It had lasted only a few seconds.

I sat there for a moment, then slowly pushed the visor up. I got out, locked the Vette, and walked across Essex Street to the front door of the hotel. It was five o'clock on the dot. Alan Armstrong reached the door exactly in time to hold it open for me.

"Nice timing," he said.

Chapter 14

With a gentlemanly hand at my elbow, he steered me across the lobby and into the lounge. Francine and Rhonda had been right. It seemed as though everybody in the room turned and looked at us. At least every woman in the place did. Professor Dreamy wore jeans too—well-fitted ones, with a lightweight knit white cotton polo, also well fitted. (I knew the attention wasn't directed at me, but I was glad anyway that I'd changed shirt and boots.)

We were seated at a small table at the rear of the room. "Do you like wine, Lee?" he asked, motioning for the waitress.

"It's a little early for wine for me," I said. "I'd like a Diet Coke."

"Perhaps next time we'll meet a little later. They have an excellent wine list here." He ordered two Diet Cokes and favored me with that toothpaste smile.

There's never going to be a next time.

"Mr. Doan is very interested in what you might have to share with us about your friend's death," I said, pulling pen and steno book from my purse. "Do you mind if I record?" I reached into the hobo for my recorder. "Sometimes I have trouble reading my own hen scratching."

The smile faded the tiniest bit, but he agreed. "Of course."

I turned the recorder on, spoke my name, the date, and the location, adding "Interview with Professor Alan Armstrong," and picked up my pen.

"Professor Armstrong," I began.

"Alan," he said, smile turned on full blast.

"Alan," I corrected. "I understand that you and Professor Samuel Bond were friends as well as colleagues. Had you known one another for a long time?"

"Over twenty years. He was my teacher, my mentor when I was a student, and my friend above all."

I already knew that from his rally at the university, but I've learned that people don't always give the same answer to the same question every time it's asked. I tried another one. "Some people say that Cody McGinnis and Professor Bond had a recent disagreement. I understand that Professor McGinnis is your friend also. Can you tell me what the disagreement was about?"

He sighed, lowering his lashes (incredibly long ones for a man). "I'm sorry to say so, but it may have been serious enough to completely end a friendship of long standing."

That was a surprise. Last time he'd agreed with the lawyers that it was a minor disagreement among colleagues. "Oh, what a shame," I said, being careful not to sound too pushy. "What happened?"

"Of course, you realize, I wasn't present at the altercation."

Another surprise. I didn't know there'd been an actual altercation. I pushed a tiny bit. "I do understand," I said. "So, did Professor Bond tell you about it?" I scribbled "AA not present at fight" on the pad.

"Oh, no. Sam wasn't one to discuss such things. It was Cody who told me. He was terribly upset about it."

For God's sake, man, get to the point!

I didn't say anything. I've learned that sometimes it's better to wait for the subject to continue without prompting. I sipped my soda and waited.

He sipped his own soda and continued. "It was quite a row, according to Cody. Of course, I can't swear to it. I wasn't there."

You already said that. I smiled with what I hoped passed for sympathetic understanding and waited.

"Cody believed that Sam was going to approve his application for a full professorship. He was counting on it. As head of the university's history department, a chaired professor, it was up to Sam to make the final decision. It meant tenure, an increase in pay, and frankly, more respect. Cody wanted those things. There was only one opening. Sam turned him down in favor of a woman in the Sociology Department."

"Uh-oh. So Cody confronted him about it?" I wrote "Cody denied full professorship."

"Sure did. Cody said the friendship was over and that he was through doing half of Sam's work while Sam focused on research."

"The confrontation didn't lead to actual violence, did it?" Two college professors duking it out seemed unlikely to me.

Alan lifted toned shoulders. "Not that I know of. But Cody was the most upset I've ever seen him, and we've been friends for many years."

"You even started the GoFundMe for his legal defense," I prompted. "Couldn't Cody simply apply for the position again?"

"Sure. But it will take another year or more, and he's got a big student loan to repay. That's why he took that extra job at the Tabby."

"Have you ever seen Cody do anything—um—anything violent?"

"Nothing like hitting someone over the head and stabbing them, if that's what you mean." He scowled.

"I didn't mean anything," I apologized. "You said he was very upset."

"You're asking if I think Cody is capable of murder." He stated it flatly.

"Yes. I guess I am." I glanced at my watch. "Do you?"

"I don't know," he said. "And that's the truth. We'd better get going if we're going to keep our six o'clock appointment at your station." He signaled for the check. I turned off the recorder and put the pen and notebook away.

"May I ask one more question? It can be off the record if you like."

"What is it?"

"I understand that you, Cody, and Professor Bond have been working on a book."

"We've co-authored one. Yes."

"Could you share with me who your editor is?"

He sat very straight in his chair, frowning again. "Editor? What gave you that idea?"

Can't tell him without throwing my aunt under the bus, can I? "I heard it around somewhere," I lied, remembering *"What happens in the library stays in the library."*

He seemed to relax. "Can't believe everything you hear. You should know that, Lee." He managed a snicker. "As if we three couldn't put together a simple how-to book without help."

"Of course. Thank you for your time, Alan," I said. "When we do the on-air segment, will you include this same information?"

"Not exactly," he said, smile back in place. "Will you ask the same questions?" Not waiting for an answer, he took my elbow once again, glancing around the room and acknowledging with a nod of his head the adoring looks aimed his way, and guided me toward the lobby. "I thought you might appreciate a heads-up on what the possible outcome of this mess might be when the facts finally come out." He paused when we reached the hotel's front door, tightening his grip on my elbow, still smiling.

"Are you appreciative, Lee?"

I didn't answer. "See you at the station," I said, and walked quickly toward my Vette.

Chapter 15

On the way to the station, I thought about Alan Armstrong's answer to my question about the editor. What was the big deal? Lots of writers hire editors to polish their work before they submit to the publisher. In fact, probably most of them do. What's so different about this one, even if he or she is actually a ghostwriter? Who cares anyway? Can the three of them be so vain that they can't admit that they need help sometimes? It's not as though a little how-to book for college students is headed for the best seller list.

Marty, as usual, was prepared and ready to shoot well ahead of time. She'd neatly rearranged the *Saturday Business Hour* layout so that it looked almost like a brandnew set. The big world globe had been replaced with a fake ficus tree borrowed from River's area, a modern glass-and-brass clock stood in place of the vintage desk lamp, and the four-drawer file cabinet had disappeared entirely. A famed print of Grant Wood's *The Midnight Ride of Paul Revere* hung on the wall, the photos of Joseph White and Dick Crowninshield lay on the desk, and a pair of red upholstered club chairs replaced the straight-back versions favored by the Saturday morning host.

"Nice job, Marty," I said. "Shall I sit behind the desk and put the guest in one of the red chairs?"

"I think so. Gives you the position of authority, you know?"

"Sounds good."

"Besides, it'll cover up those jeans. You've been wearing them all day. Viewers notice that stuff."

There was no answer to that. Anyway, Marty's usually right about details like that one. I hid my briefcase under the desk, along with my lower body.

Details. That's what I need from Alan Armstrong.

"Is the guest here yet?" she asked.

"He should be along any minute," I told her. "His car was right behind me."

I'd no sooner spoken the words when Alan, led by a smiling Rhonda, entered the long, darkened studio. "Right this way, Alan," Rhonda said. "It's the lighted set dead ahead. I see that Lee is all ready for you."

Alan's voice carried clearly in the high-ceilinged room. "Oh, Rhonda! It's dark in here. Want to take my hand so I don't get lost?"

I could tell that Rhonda was stifling a laugh. "Don't worry, Professor. I'm sure you know your way around. There you go. Straight ahead."

Alan joined us without further comment about darkness. I introduced Marty, and the two shook hands. Somewhere along the line, between the hotel and the station, he'd managed to change his shirt, exchanging the white polo for a colorful, camera-friendly print. I took my designated spot behind the desk. Alan sat in a red chair, pulling it a little closer to the desk.

"So, are you ready for me, Lee?" Somehow he made even that innocuous question sound suggestive. In my mind Professor Dreamy grew less dreamy by the minute. *Does he think every woman is a starstruck teenager?*

"Thank you, sir," I said. "I believe I am. We'll record for about fifteen minutes, do some editing, and the finished interview will air in the seven o'clock hour and also on the late news."

Marty took her position behind the big studio camera, wheeling it into the three-sided cubicle, focusing on Alan and me. "Counting down, Lee. Ten, nine, eight . . ." At "one," she pointed to me, and the tally light clicked on, indicating that the camera was recording us.

"Hello, ladies and gentlemen," I began. "Lee Barrett here with my very special guest, Professor Alan Armstrong." Marty had posted Alan's bio notes on the teleprompter. I read them carefully, throwing in a few adjectives I knew he'd appreciate, like "popular teacher," and "well-known educator." I aimed a big smile in Alan's direction. "Professor Armstrong, you've been in the news lately, not only here in Salem but nationally as well. Tell us a bit about your support for your fellow university professor, your close friend and associate Cody McGinnis, who has been named as a suspect in the murder of another of your friends, Professor Samuel Bond."

I leaned back in my chair, still smiling, and awaited his answer. Marty pointed the big lens in his direction. "Thank you for your interest in my efforts to help Cody, Ms. Barrett," he said, his expression on that movie-star face totally earnest and utterly adorable. The station had run promos all day for this interview, so I was sure a good number of Armstrong's fans would be waiting anxiously to see him on TV. "Cody, as many of your viewers may know, is an associate professor at Essex County University and at the same time an instructor at the Tabitha Trumbull Academy. We teachers don't earn a great deal of money, you know. We teach out of our love of learning, our great love for our students." Self-deprecating shrug. "I am not a wealthy man either. So I started a GoFundMe page for Cody. I'm proud to say the student community has stepped up to the challenge and we have already raised more than twenty thousand dollars for Cody's defense!" He gave the contact information for the fundraiser. "Lawyers are expensive. Perhaps the viewers of WICH-TV will help."

I was surprised by the sum collected. "That's a significant amount, Professor Armstrong. I'm sure Cody McGinnis is grateful."

"I guess he is. I haven't been in touch with him since all this started."

"Is that by his choice or yours?"

"It may be mutual," he said. "As you might imagine, I'm a bit conflicted over all this. Both men have been important in my life."

"I understand that the three of you have been working together on a publishing project," I said. "Of course the death of Professor Bond and the Cody McGinnis situation must have brought that project to a halt. How do you feel about that?"

He appeared to bristle at the suggestion. "Fortunately, we'd finished the actual manuscript before all of this unpleasantness occurred. It's more or less fallen to me to deal with the marketing aspects of the project. I've been working on that."

I thought about Louisa's mention of the editor she saw with the men in Alaska, and Aunt Ibby's recollection of the conversation in the library. I decided to press for an answer again. "I suppose you'll be working hard with your editor, tying up all the loose ends."

The perfect brow wrinkled into a frown. Alan Armstrong stood so fast he nearly knocked the chair over. Then, favoring me with a big smile, he tapped his watch. *That looks like a Rolex—or a very good fake.* "Good heavens, look at the time. It's been a joy talking with you, Ms. Barrett. I must get back to campus. Thanks again, ever so much, for your interest in helping Cody during this difficult time."

He faced the camera and gave the hand-to-the-throat universal "cut" signal. Marty's head popped up from behind the camera hood. She stood in front of the desk, hands on her hips. "What's the matter?" she said. "You leaving already? I've got you booked for ten more minutes."

I stood and faced him. "Alan, I have more questions. You were going to talk about Cody being denied the full professorship. Besides, didn't you want to say something about where people can contribute to your fund? What's wrong?"

"I don't like the direction your questions were heading, Lee. Some things need to be kept confidential. I don't like your attitude at all. Don't call me again." He moved toward Marty, both hands in front of him as though he intended to push her. She stepped aside as he quick-walked toward the exit door.

He apparently hadn't noticed that the yellow tally light was still on, that the camera was still recording.

Chapter 16

"What the hell was that all about?" Hands still on her hips, Marty watched the retreating figure, then turned off the camera.

"Not exactly sure," I told her, "but the good professor seems to be very touchy about the idea that there's an editor involved with the book project he and the other two have been working on."

"Guess we'll have to go with what we've got." She shrugged. "It's shorter than I expected, but we've been promoting this guy all day. Gotta use it. You want I should delete that extra footage? The part where he blew up?"

"We certainly can't run it, but for sure hang on to it. He's worried about something, and the cops may be interested in whatever it is." I looked at my own watch—not a Rolex. "Well, at least I'll get home early." I sighed. "Maybe Pete and I can go somewhere and watch the game on TV." I looked around at the red chairs and the Grant Wood print. "Can I help you put the *Business Hour* back together?"

"Nah. I'll drag the fake tree back over to River's set

for tonight's show. The rest of it can wait until Saturday. I'll get the night security guard to help me with it."

"Speaking of River's show. Do you know if Therese Della Monica is the call screener for her tonight?"

"Yep. I think Therese's already in the building." Marty pointed toward the news department. "Doan's got her working part-time doing some phone soliciting for new advertisers. The kid's got a good phone voice."

Therese had been one of my Television Production 101 students at the Tabby. She has a good voice, and she's a pretty blonde with a future on camera, I'm sure. She's also busy learning to be a witch. "Thanks, Marty," I said. "I need to ask her a question."

Sliding the photos of White and Crowninshield into my briefcase, I headed for the row of glass cubicles adjacent to the news department. Therese has one. Scott Palmer has one too. So do Buck Covington and Phil Archer. I don't rate an office yet, but an occasional trip to a dataport serves the purpose for me.

I knocked on the glass door. Therese took off her headphone and waved me in. "Hello, Lee. What's going on?"

"Hi, Therese. Quick question. Do you keep track of phone numbers from River's callers?"

"Sure do. You asking about the lady who's worried about her son too?"

"Too? Why? Who else is asking?"

"Scott Palmer. I gave it to him this afternoon. Wait a sec. I have the phone log right here." She reached for a black-covered book. "Here you go." She scribbled a number on the back of a business card. "I have my own business cards now," she said. "See?" I turned the card over and read THERESE DELLA MONICA, SALES CONSULTANT. She smiled. "Cool, huh?"

I thanked her for the number, agreed that her card was cool indeed, and headed for the parking lot. *Damn Scott.*

He beat me to it! I hoped he hadn't used the number to call the poor distraught woman, and I was positive River wouldn't appreciate his contacting her tarot callers. I decided to call Roger Temple. If this was his sister's number—and I was convinced that it was—I wanted to tell him about the tarot reading. I used the metal staircase down the two flights to the parking lot exit, unlocked my car, sat in the front seat, and called Roger's number.

"Hello, Lee," he said. "I was about to call you."

"Are you and Ray in Salem yet?"

"Arrived about twenty minutes ago. We're at Phyllis's place."

"How's she doing?"

"About as well as could be expected, I guess. We're going to take her and our brother-in-law, Joe, out to dinner, try to cheer them up a little."

"Good idea," I said. "I wanted to give you a little heads-up on something." I gave him a quick rundown on the call to River's show and gave him the phone number Therese had given me.

"Yes. That's Phyllis's number all right. But Lee, what harm could it do? I know River wouldn't say anything harmful, even if that hocus-pocus stuff of hers is all baloney."

"It seems Scott Palmer has the number too, and I wouldn't want him harassing your sister. Can you guys kind of monitor her calls for a while? Scott is a good newsman, but he can be—well, persistent."

"Sure. That's the house phone number. We'll have her leave it on voice mail for now. How's the snooping going? Can we get together tomorrow some time and catch up?"

I had no doubt that Doan would approve a meeting with Cody's uncles no matter what else was on the white board. "Tomorrow for sure," I promised.

"Ray and I are going to have a sit-down with Cody first thing in the morning. Then we'll see what the lawyers have to say. We'll be checking in with Tom Whaley around one o'clock to see what new evidence Salem PD has come up with. How does your afternoon look?"

"This has turned into kind of a team effort," I said, searching my mind for a way to explain the *Charlie's Angels* thing. *Word choices,* I reminded myself. "My aunt and I have located some acquaintances of the deceased professor who have the kind of information you're looking for," I said. "I'll round them up and get back to you about the exact time we can all get together tomorrow. Will that work?"

"Sounds like a plan," he said. "Talk to you tomorrow. Thanks, Lee, and thank your aunt for us too. Oh, by the way, Ray wants to know if she's still single."

"Aunt Ibby? Ray? Well, yeah. Sure. She's still single." *I could have made better word choices with that response!* "See you guys tomorrow."

I aimed the Vette for home, glad this day was over. I passed the Hawthorne Hotel, recalling the day's strange interactions with Alan Armstrong. I mentally echoed Marty's observation. *What the hell was that all about?*

The usually charming Professor Armstrong had clearly lost his cool when the subject of the editor had come up. I wondered what Roger and Ray would think about it. Besides that, I was anxious to open Louisa's Ultimate Alaska Cruise photo envelope. Getting a look at the mysterious "editor" hadn't seemed like such a big deal last night, but it had certainly become one during the past twelve hours. I hoped they were nice sharp pictures.

Aunt Ibby's Buick was in the garage, and Betsy's Mercedes and Louisa's Lincoln were in the driveway. The Angels were obviously in session. I'd locked the garage, when O'Ryan popped out of the cat door onto the back steps, then ran all the way down the flagstone path to meet me. I picked him up. "Why the special welcome?"

I carried the purring armful of stripy yellow cat into the house. "Okay, cat," I said, putting him down. "Upstairs or downstairs? Your choice." He didn't hesitate, but started up the twisty staircase. I followed, a little surprised, knowing that it was close to happy hour at Aunt Ibby's—an occasion he rarely misses.

O'Ryan is much faster than I am at stair climbing—and between the house on Winter Street and WICH-TV—I climb a lot of them. I attribute his speed to the fact that he's lighter and has twice as many legs. As usual, he was inside when I got there—not in the zebra chair, though, and not faking sleep. He waited, pacing impatiently, then led me through the hall to the kitchen, where he jumped onto the neat pile of materials I'd left on the table, sending outline, notepad, and assorted printouts flying. He pounced on the Ultimate Alaska Cruise envelope.

I nudged him aside, straightened out the papers, and picked up the envelope. "You didn't need to remind me. I was going to look at this first thing."

"Meh," he said.

"What do you mean, 'Meh?' I was too!" I declared, opening the pronged clasp and sliding a thick stack of glossy color photos onto the table. At first glance they seemed to be mostly pictures of Louisa in a variety of shipboard and shore excursion settings. Does the woman never wear the same outfit more than once? I decided to separate the Louisa-alone shots from the ones showing groups.

I pulled my biggest magnifying glass from the kitchen junk drawer and began close examination of faces. Particularly men's faces. The first one I recognized was, not surprisingly, Alan Armstrong. Of course, he was the only one of the three I'd seen in person. I'd seen TV and newspaper photos of Cody McGinnis and Samuel Bond, but that's different. A group seated at a dining table offered the first picture showing Louisa, Armstrong, Bond, and McGinnis, along with two women I didn't recognize and a youngish-looking man with an unruly mop of black hair and sunglasses. Could he be the mysterious editor?

Chapter 17

I didn't even bother to change clothes—just kicked off the boots, slipped into flip-flops, picked up the stack of photos with that dining room group shot on top, stuck my phone in my jeans back pocket, and opened the kitchen door onto the front hall. "Come on, O'Ryan," I said. "Let's show this to the Angels. Maybe Louisa has this guy's name." Cat and I descended the two flights of polished oak stairs—much prettier, broader, and straighter than the back-door version, with a sweet wide bannister—perfect for a little girl to slide on—and arrived in the foyer outside Aunt Ibby's living room. There's an antique hall tree just inside the front door, with a full-length mirror and a lift-up seat. I paused for a brief moment to check my appearance.

Mistake. Flashing lights, swirling colors, and—surprise! The red-gloved Knight of Pentacles, plumed helmet and all, looked back at me. Instead of sitting astride a red-bridled horse, he rode a giant dog-shaped Monopoly game piece like the ones I'd seen at the Toy Trawler. The knight raised his right hand. The red glove didn't look quite right. I realized that it was a rubber kitchen glove—like the ones my aunt uses for cleaning the oven. The palm of the glove was red, though. Bloodred.

Blink! He disappeared. *Damned visions never make the least bit of sense.* More annoyed than enlightened, I followed the cat.

"Aunt Ibby, it's me."

"We're in the kitchen, dear," she called. "The Angels are here. We're having a brainstorming session. And some wine. Come join us."

The three were gathered at the round oak table. In front of each woman was an open spiral-bound notebook, a couple of pens, and a full wineglass. An untidy pile of books and newspapers dominated the center of the table, along with an aluminum ice bucket where a bottle of Cabernet Sauvignon chilled. Aunt Ibby manned a laptop.

"Wow!" I was seriously impressed. "You three look like you mean business!"

"Naturally. What did you expect?" She pointed to the ice bucket. "Pour yourself a wine and join us. We're working on contacting friends who might be helpful in solving the case. Did you bring your phone?"

"Sure." I patted my back pocket, then added Louisa's photos to the stack on the table. I pulled up a chair and sat down. "Here's a picture of the man I think might be the editor." I held the group shot up so everyone could see it. "He may be in some of the other pictures too, but I was in a hurry to show you all this one." I pointed to the man with sunglasses. "Do you know his name, Louisa?" I handed her the photo.

"Eddie," she said. "His name is Eddie. Offhand, I don't remember his last name." She passed the picture to Betsy. "Have you ever met him, Betts?"

Betsy shook her head. "I don't think so. You, Ibby?"

Aunt Ibby put on her reading glasses and peered at it. "Hmmm. He does look familiar. I think maybe I've seen him at the library. He may have had something to do with the bookmobile project. I don't remember his name, though."

"Did you talk to him, Louisa?" I asked. "Where was he from? Did he seem to be with the professors besides at dinner? Did he always wear the sunglasses?"

Louisa laughed at my multiple questions. "First, yes, we talked. Second, he was originally from Iowa but now he lives in Marblehead. And yes, he was almost *always* with one or more of the professors whenever I saw him." She frowned. "Sometimes he wore regular glasses. Dark rims. Sometimes no glasses at all."

"What did you talk about?" Betsy wanted to know. "He's kind of good-looking, in a scruffy sort of way. I like that shaggy hair."

"We talked mostly about Alaska," she said. "He said he was writing a magazine article about the indigenous people and their homes and buildings."

"A writer? Maybe he's also an editor," I said. "Did you talk about anything else?"

Louisa looked down and blushed. "Dancing," she said. "He offered to teach me the merengue."

"Awesome," Betsy raised her wineglass. "Did you dance with him?"

"Of course not," Louisa scoffed. "I'm a very rich old woman. What possible interest would a young man have in me besides my money? I politely declined." She raised her own glass. "Besides, I already know the merengue."

"Good for you, Louisa," Aunt Ibby said. "Too bad you can't remember his last name though. He *does* look familiar. Chances are he's been in the library. Maybe he has a card."

"I would have danced with him," Betsy insisted. "And I'm a rich, um, *middle-aged* woman. I'd remember his last name too."

"No problem." Louisa picked up her tablet. "Why

don't I call him up? We can ask him about the professors and everything else?"

"You have his number?"

"Yes. He gave it to me. It's under 'Eddie.'"

"Do you think he'll talk to you?" I worried, "I mean, about everything else?"

"Yes," she said, refilling her glass. "I told you. I'm a very rich old woman. He'll be happy to talk to me." She reached into a to-die-for nineteen-eighties Judith Leiber snakeskin clutch and pulled out her phone. O'Ryan, noting the snakeskin, darted under my chair. "What questions would you like me to ask?"

"Before you make the call, Louisa," my aunt said, "this may take some more thought. If your Eddie *is* indeed the mysterious editor, he's also a suspect. Perhaps we should save this information for Ray and Roger to handle."

Louisa hurriedly put her phone down on the table. "He's not *my* Eddie, but I see your point. What if he is a killer? I don't want to be hobnobbing with such a person. What would people think?"

"Why don't we make a note of 'Eddie the Editor' along with that phone number and pass it on to the twins?" I suggested. "After all, we're only supposed to be snoopers, not actual interrogators."

"Snoopers?" Betsy raised a perfectly arched eyebrow.

Oops. Bad word choice.

"Investigators," my aunt corrected. "We investigate and pass our information on to the proper authorities."

"Yes," Betsy agreed. "Investigators. That's what I'll tell the girls when I get my hair done tomorrow."

"You plan to talk about the case at a beauty parlor?" I asked. "Is that a good idea?"

"It's a perfect idea," Betsy insisted. "Where is there a better place to get the dirt about people?"

Aunt Ibby agreed. "True."

"It's a fine idea, Betts," Louisa said. "You'll find out things the police wouldn't dig out in a million years. But about your hair. Going to do Farrah?"

"Of course."

A brief discussion about Betsy's hair was interrupted by the chime of the front doorbell.

"Expecting company?" I asked. O'Ryan had already bolted from the room.

"Oh, would you get it, dear? Rupert said he might stop by."

"Should we call Rupert 'Charlie?'" Louisa asked.

"I certainly wouldn't recommend it," my aunt warned.

I followed the cat and, avoiding looking at the hall tree mirror, opened the door. "Hello, Mr. Pennington. They're meeting in the kitchen tonight. Come on back."

"Good evening, Lee. I'd hoped you'd be here. I need to ask a great favor of you." This wasn't the first time I'd heard those words from my former boss. I managed a smile and led the way to the kitchen. He was greeted with a flurry of greetings, happy faces, and an already-poured glass of wine.

Not just a favor this time. A great favor. I can hardly wait.

Mr. Pennington selected one of the captain's chairs and joined the group. "I can't stay long this evening. Chamber of commerce event in half an hour, but Ibby tells me you three have made some progress with our little investigation," he said. "I hope we can be helpful in clearing Professor McGinnis's name. Soon. Very soon." He glanced around the table, making eye contact with each of us. "Meanwhile, this whole dreadful mess has caused some difficulty at the Tabby." His expression was doleful, heartrending, thoroughly pitiful. He is, after all, a Shakespearean actor.

"How so, Rupert?" my aunt asked.

"There are several more days in the semester," he moaned. "Several more days of Salem history to be taught to waiting, willing students, thirsty for knowledge. Several days of full-tuition paid classes, and alas, there is no instructor."

"I understand that it's possible Professor McGinnis might be released on bail," Betsy said.

He shook his head. "Even so, inviting the dear, good, innocent man into that classroom would simply invite hordes of press people with cameras into the Tabby. Disruptive, disagreeable people." He looked at me. "Present company excepted, of course. Anyway, his attorneys wouldn't want him to do it."

Now the eye contact was with me alone. He tilted his head and put one finger under his chin. "So I thought to myself, who do I know who is familiar with that historic building, has a teaching degree, and is fully capable of teaching a few evening classes?"

"Lee," responded two voices.

"Maralee," responded the other one.

"Who, me?" said I.

"Sure. What an opportunity!" Betsy bubbled happily. "You'll be in there with Cody's students. Get their perspective on all that happened—both now and back in eighteen thirty. Great idea, Rupert."

"And maybe find out who pinched his letter opener," my aunt put in.

"I guess I'm voted in," I said. "I'll have to run it by Mr. Doan. It would mean I wouldn't be available for any evening gigs for a while. I'd like to do it. Did Cody McGinnis leave a lesson plan?"

"Not exactly," he said. "I found some notes in his desk that might be helpful. But Lee, you may feel free to handle this class as you see fit. I have every confidence in your teaching ability."

"How many students are we talking about?" I asked. My own classes at the Tabby had been small, five or six students at a time.

"Five, at last count," he said. "All adults. Two dropped out right after the—um—unpleasantness."

"Five's a good number," I said. "But I may want to contact the two dropouts too. Would that be all right?"

"Of course." He smiled. "Now that that's settled, I must be off to my next appointment. I'll let myself out." He paused, and with a meaningful look at my aunt, he recited, "I think we made some excellent progress."

She put one finger to her mouth, narrowed her eyes, then snapped her fingers. "Louise Fletcher. *One Flew over the Cuckoo's Nest.* 1975. Good one, Rupert. You almost had me."

With a bow to each of us, he made a rather grand exit. A moment later we heard the front door close.

"Well then, that's settled. I think he only came to the meeting because he wanted to recruit you, Maralee. Let's get back to work on our investigation." Aunt Ibby picked up her notebook. "I did a little snooping—investigating—at the library today. Cody McGinnis was a frequent borrower—worked his way through virtually all of our Salem history books, and we ordered a few we didn't have through the county system. He visited the stacks a few times to access some of our outdated academic history publications."

"His selections were always in the field of Salem history, I suppose," Louisa said.

"Pretty much," my aunt agreed. "He chose the occasional best seller. He's fond of mysteries. The academic history magazines were more general in content—not simply Salem material—more like world history."

"I have something in my notebook too," Betsy said.

"But I'm not sure whether it's important or not. It's something that happened a long time ago. I remembered it because we've been talking about Sam Bond."

"Let's hear it," my aunt said. "That's what brainstorming is about. Toss all the ideas on the table, no matter what they are."

"Okay. Here goes. After Mr. Leavitt and I parted company, I dated a man—very briefly—who worked for Sam. He was a gardener or pool man or something. I don't remember his name. Awfully cute. Great body. Anyway, he told me that Sam had a terrible temper. Used to blow up at the slightest thing, screaming and swearing and kicking things. He quit the lawn job or pool job or whatever it was. Said he got tired of being berated constantly."

"Interesting," Aunt Ibby said. "I've known the man casually for years and never saw the slightest hint of that kind of behavior. From what I've heard, his students seem to be fond of him."

"That's true," Louisa said. "There was a group of earth science students from County U on the Alaska cruise, and Professor Bond interacted with them very pleasantly."

"I didn't know there were students on the cruise!" I handed her the stack of photos. "Are any of them pictured here?"

"Probably. They pretty much kept to themselves, taking ice and rock samples and such." She pointed to another dining room picture, showing a group of young people gathered at a buffet table. One of the girls stood out particularly. Blue hair. "How about this one?" I asked, touching the picture. "Did you ever meet her?"

"I didn't," Louisa said. "But I remember her. Now that you mention it, she *did* interact with the professors occasionally. Mostly having drinks in the lounge. Not that there was anything wrong with that, mind you. The students were all of age, I'm sure. Even so, I remember a little gossip about it."

"Gossip?"

"Uh-huh. A few of the women were trying to figure out whether Professor Bond was that girl's mentor—or whether Professor McGinnis was her boyfriend."

Chapter 18

I was about to ask a few more questions about the girl with the blue hair, when Pete called. Recalling the earlier eyebrow wiggling conversation, I realized the call might well be of a personal nature. "Excuse me," I said. "It's Pete. I'll take it in the hall."

Trying to ignore the muffled giggling that followed me, I returned to the foyer. With my back to the mirror, I sat on the low seat. "Hi," I said. "What's going on?"

"Not much," he said. "I was watching the news. Saw you and Armstrong. Seemed like a pretty short interview to miss a game for. What happened?"

I looked at my watch. "I didn't see it. I'm at Aunt Ibby's. Was it awful?"

"No. Not awful, but it was short, and he didn't drop any bombshells after all."

"I know. It was supposed to be longer. He was going to tell about an argument between Cody and Bond, but when I asked about his editor, he ended the shoot and walked out."

"His editor? Who's that?"

"I don't know yet. And apparently, he didn't enjoy being asked about it."

"An editor, huh? Listen. Want to go to Greene's Tavern and watch the game?" he asked. "I can come right over now and pick you up."

"Love to. Give me half an hour to get changed. Toot the horn out front when you get here, and I'll be right out."

I excused myself from the ongoing brainstorming session, and with the envelope of photos under my arm and O'Ryan leading the way, I headed up the front stairs. I took a quick shower, dumped the pink shirt and my much-maligned jeans into the laundry chute, brushed my hair, and did a minimal makeup job—mascara, blush, and lip gloss.

I stood in front of my open closet, studying the contents—kind of the way I sometimes stand in front of the refrigerator—just staring. Not focused on wardrobe at all, I thought about the Knight of Pentacles guy posing beside a giant game piece. I shook the disturbing picture away, pulled out pale blue denim Bermudas and my away-game Tampa Bay Rays T-shirt, and dressed for my date with Pete.

Greene's Tavern is one of our favorite places. We'd become regulars, along with a friendly crowd of mostly local folks who enjoyed the long, old-fashioned dark wood bar, wide comfortable booths, plenty of big-screen TVs, even a huge stone fireplace for cool evenings. The "pub grub" menu is limited but always good. The owner is Joe Greene, whose daughter Kelly had been one of my first TV Production 101 students at the Tabby.

With my NASCAR jacket over my shoulders and Rays cap on my head, I waited for Pete outdoors on the front steps rather than trust to luck in the foyer facing that hall tree mirror. I started down the steps to the sidewalk as soon as I saw Pete's Crown Vic rounding the corner onto

Winter Street. "We might even make it in time for the first pitch," he said as I slid into the front seat.

We didn't quite make the first pitch, but we didn't miss any major action. Friendly greetings were exchanged when we walked in, along with the expected remarks about my Rays gear. Kelly showed us to our favorite booth—far enough back so that Pete could watch the room—and just close enough to one of the big screens. We ordered pizza with double cheese, half peperoni and half sausage, and two light beers. It's great to be in a relationship where we can carry on a conversation, drink beer, eat pizza, watch a ball game, interrupt each other to jump up and cheer occasionally for opposite teams, and still keep track of what the other person is talking about.

"Sorry the TV interview got cut short," he said, "but how did the one at the hotel work out?"

"Better, I'd say. According to Alan, Professor Bond turned a thumbs-down on Cody's bid for a full professorship. Cody took it badly. He believed he deserved it, and he'd been counting on finally getting tenure and the raise in pay that goes with it."

"Yep. That goes along with what Cody told us. Anything else?"

"He balked at the editor thing when I asked him about it at the hotel. Pretended that he didn't know what I was talking about."

"We'll need to find him, whoever he is." Pete raised his glass toward the screen. "Man on first," he exclaimed, then finished the thought: "Any ideas about where this editor might be? If he exists?"

"We think we may have pictures of him. Louisa was on an Alaskan cruise last year and all three professors were there. So was another man. Youngish. Dark hair, dark eyes. Might be named Eddie."

"Who's 'we'?"

"Aunt Ibby and a couple of her friends—you've met

Louisa and Betsy—they're doing a little investigating for the twins," I admitted.

He pretended to hit himself on the forehead. "Wonderful. But seriously, can I have a look at those pictures without getting a warrant?"

"Sure. Aunt Ibby thinks she may have seen him in the library, and he looks a little bit familiar to me too. And besides that, Louisa has Eddie's phone number." It was my turn to jump up and cheer. "Struck him out!! You go, Baz!" I yelled, then sat amid glares from the Sox faithful. "And what makes you think *they're* not serious? Aunt Ibby and the—um—the others." I'd darn near said "the Angels."

"Sorry. I'm sure they are. They won't get in over their heads, will they? Your aunt has a bit of a reckless streak sometimes, you know." He frowned. "You say one of them has this guy's phone number?"

He was right about my aunt. But I felt confident that she'd keep a lid on her inner Wonder Woman out of deference to her best friends, and with Mr. Pennington more or less riding herd on the whole bunch. "Mrs. Abney-Babcock has it. She's going to give it to the twins. I'm sure they'll be working with the Salem PD."

"Yes. I talked to Roger this afternoon. We've got a meeting with the chief lined up for tomorrow." Cheers and high fives erupted all over the room as Jackie Bradley hit a double, driving in the first run for the Sox.

Kelly arrived with our hot, melty, cheesy, crispy thin-crust pizza. "Saw you on TV tonight with Professor Dreamy," she said. "Is he as nice as he looks?"

How am I supposed to answer that?

I decided to tap dance around it. "I don't actually know him at all," I said, "but his students seem to be very fond of him. And did you know he's already raised almost twenty thousand dollars toward Cody McGinnis's defense fund?"

"I wondered what you thought," she said. "Some of the people I know at County U think he's pretty stuck on himself."

"Do any of your friends at State have anything to say about Professor Bond?"

"The dead guy? Oh yeah. That he was a wicked hard marker. Sometimes, even if you knocked yourself out on a paper, even if you were sure it was an A, he'd give you a D and suggest you switch majors. It happened to at least three of my friends. They said he wasn't fair at all."

I remembered what the Japanese mayor had said. *"Often the young people are right."*

After that first Red Sox run things got progressively worse for my Rays. Pete was kind enough not to rub it in, and steered the conversation away from baseball. "It'll be fun for you to see the twins again, won't it? That class you taught at the Tabby helped to get them into TV."

I told him about Mr. Pennington's invitation for me to fill in at the Tabby for the last few sessions of Cody's Salem history class. "Only five students," I said. "Not long enough to teach them much. Anyway, Roger and Ray are perfect Boston investigative reporters. Their *Street Beat* show is quite a hit. What could be better than a couple of ex-cops covering their old beats? One of them in the North End and the other one in Southie. Besides—identical twins? What could be more appealing to an audience than that?"

"I'm afraid the evidence against the nephew is pretty compelling, but I know Roger and Ray are hell-bent on proving his innocence. I'm looking forward to working with those two."

"Roger told me Ray was asking about Aunt Ibby. He wanted to know if she's still single."

Big smile. "What did she have to say about that?"

"I haven't told her. Mr. Pennington was there."

"Is he working on solving the mystery too?"

"Kind of. Speaking of that, did you happen to see my spot at Christopher's Castle?"

"Sorry, babe. Missed that one." He didn't sound regretful, but I understood it. Pete's not much interested in magic tricks or costumes.

"Well, it has to do with blood. Chris says about half the witches in town are talking about the blood at the crime scene. And I've—um—seen something in a mirror that has to do with blood. A handprint. Is there something new about blood going on that would help me understand the damned vision?"

"Nothing really relevant. I guess I can tell you about it. A bloody print turned up in the old fellow's bedroom. Turned out it belonged to a student. We've already talked to her. Seems she cut herself on a broken shot glass a few days earlier. The housekeeper vouches for her."

"A female student in Professor Bond's bedroom?"

"Looking for a Band-Aid, according to the housekeeper. She says the good professor sometimes entertained a select group of students on Saturday afternoons."

A certain female student immediately came to mind. So I asked the question. "What color hair does this female student have?" I almost knew in advance what the answer would be, so when Pete said blue, I wasn't the least bit surprised.

After the game ended (Sox 6–Rays 2) and the crowd thinned out, Pete and I stayed at Greene's for a while, enjoying coffee and sharing an order of Joe Greene's special pizza-dough cinnamon rolls. "So how did you know about the blue hair?" he asked.

"She keeps showing up in my notes," I told him. "When I first talked to Alan Armstrong at the college, she was there. She said that Samuel Bond had given her a D. Seemed pretty annoyed about it. Then I saw her again, waving a FREE CODY sign, across from the Hawthorne when Francine and I covered the Japanese mayor's visit."

"I guess that hair makes her pretty hard to miss," Pete said.

"Right. She's also in Louisa's pictures from the Alaskan cruise."

Pete leaned forward, cop face in place. "No kidding. Was she with any of the professors in the pictures? Or with the guy who might be the editor?"

"Not in any that I saw. She's at a buffet with some earth science students."

"Oh." He sounded disappointed.

"Louisa said she'd seen her in the lounge, though, drinking with both Bond and McGinnis. Shipboard gossip was whether Bond was her mentor or Cody was her boyfriend."

"Oh? That's interesting. Any other blue-hair sightings?"

"Not offhand. But I have Louisa's pictures at my place."

"Are you inviting me to come up and see your etchings?" Groucho eyebrows, broad wink, and quick imaginary mustache twirl.

"Absolutely."

Pete signaled for our check, we said so long to Kelly and Joe, and we left our coffee unfinished, but planning ahead, put the rest of the cinnamon rolls in a doggie bag for breakfast.

The Angels' and Mr. Pennington's cars were gone when we arrived, and the lights were out in Aunt Ibby's kitchen. Pete parked in the driveway, and we followed the solar-lighted path to the back door, where O'Ryan waited. We climbed the back staircase, trying to be quiet when passing Aunt Ibby's second-floor bedroom. O'Ryan was already inside. He'd bypassed the zebra-print wing chair and headed straight for the kitchen, where he'd climbed onto the table and seated himself on the Ultimate Alaska Cruise envelope.

"Looks like O'Ryan is anxious for us to look at pictures," I said. "Shall I put some decaf on?"

"He's simply a cat looking for a soft place to sit." Pete scoffed at the idea that O'Ryan's selection of seating material meant anything. "But yeah, we might as well take a look." He took a quick glance toward the bedroom. "And it's still early."

I loaded up the Mr. Coffee, then put my jacket and hat into the closet while Pete shooed the cat onto the floor, slid the photos from the envelope, and arranged them on the tabletop. "Got a magnifying glass?" he asked. I pulled one from the junk drawer and stood beside him.

He put the photos of people with easily discernible features and those of Alaska scenery aside and concentrated on group shots. "Louisa must have pictures of her trip on her phone," he said. "Did she show you any of those?"

"No," I said. "I never thought to ask her."

"Too late to call her now," he said, looking at Kit-Cat. "Maybe tomorrow you could find out if we can take a look."

"I'm sure she'll be glad to share any she has." I took a smaller magnifying glass from the drawer and began to study the pictures in Pete's discard pile. "Look," I said, pointing to a tiny blue spot on a shore excursion picture of Louisa standing in front of a Heritage Coffee Shoppe. "Isn't that her? Inside the window?"

"I think you're right." He peered through his magnifying glass. "It's the back of her head, but what are the chances it's some other blue-haired girl? Good job, babe." He reached over and ruffled my hair. "Did I ever tell you you'd make a good cop?"

"Couple of times. But look, can you make out the face of the man beside her? Your glass is more powerful than mine."

"He's in profile, and he has a cap pulled over his hair."
He handed me his magnifying glass. "See what you think."

"I don't know," I said honestly. "Maybe you can get
this one blown up."

"I'd like to take the whole stack and get our guys to go
over them. I'll check with Mrs. Abney-Babcock in the
morning about these and any personal ones she has."

"That's a very good idea," I said.

He put his arm around my waist and steered me toward the bedroom. "Right now I've got an even better
one."

Chapter 19

In the morning, over coffee and reheated cinnamon rolls, we talked about our plans for the day. Pete's appointment with the chief and the twins wasn't until one o'clock, which left him plenty of time to get in touch with Louisa about the pictures, and to ask her for Eddie's phone number. He'd also see what he could find out about the so-far-nameless blue-haired girl. I needed to sit down with Bruce Doan and get his thoughts on my teaching Cody's class at the Tabby for a few nights. I intended to pitch the idea that I might even be able to interview one or two of the students. Their thoughts about the murders, both historical and present day, could make good TV.

"I'm going to need to get Cody's lesson-plan notes," I said, "and I'll need some time to do my own class prep. I'll ask Aunt Ibby to bring home some books so I can do some serious cramming." I also meant to call River and tell her about my knight-on-a-game-piece vision, but I didn't mention that. "Besides," I added, "I'll show Mr. Pennington the pictures. He might recognize somebody we've missed."

"Leave some time for me," Pete said, "or maybe I'll

have to sign up for your history class." He gave me a quick kiss. "I'll call you later. Love you."

"Love you too," I said, and watched as he and O'Ryan left together. A few minutes later, after doing hair and makeup, rinsing our mugs and sweeping up the cinnamon roll crumbs, I stuffed the envelope of pictures into my hobo and followed.

I stopped at Aunt Ibby's kitchen, where O'Ryan was already happily hunched over his red bowl while my aunt worked the *Boston Globe* crossword. In ink.

"Can you get in touch with Betsy and Louisa?" I asked. "We need to figure out a time to get the twins and the Angels together today."

She looked up from the paper, big smile in place. "The Twins and the Angels. Sounds like we're talking about a baseball game, not a murder investigation. Will it be in the evening?"

"Not sure. I'll be talking to Roger later, and by the way, Ray wanted to know if you're still single."

"He did? For goodness' sake." She put down the newspaper and leaned forward. "I'm not sure I'll be able to tell which one is Ray. They have name signs in front of them on *Street Beat*. If they still dress alike, I'm afraid I can't tell them apart."

"I'm sure you'll figure it out," I told her. "Meanwhile, in case Mr. Doan okays my doing the history class, can you bring some basic Salem history books home for me?"

"Happy to."

"I didn't know you watched *Street Beat*."

She picked up her paper. "I find it informative."

"And the show hosts are kind of cute?"

"That too. I'll call the Angels and select some books for you. Anything else?"

I kissed the top of her head on my way out. "You're cute too," I told her. "I'll call you."

Bruce Doan was not only willing to give me the necessary time away from the station to teach the history class, but actually gave the idea his blessing. "It would be even better if we could get a camera in there," he said. "But interviewing the students would be good too. I'm thinking we set up Francine right outside the school. That's almost as good. That way you can ask them anything you want to about Cody. Maybe we can get something the cops don't have." Big smile. "Maybe even something those big-shot Boston TV twin cops don't have."

"I need to make a few phone calls right away to get things in motion," I told him. "Is it okay if I ask Rhonda to adjust my schedule this morning so I can get started?"

"Sure. I'll tell her to clear the decks for you today. Top priority on this one, Ms. Barrett. Anyway, Scotty can handle both your job and his at the same time. The guy's a whiz."

Thanks a lot. I gritted my teeth, plastered on my fake smile, and reluctantly agreed about Scott Palmer's whizziness. It's kind of true. He is a good reporter, but handling both jobs at the same time? I think not.

By the time I returned to Rhonda's desk, she was already erasing the white board. She's a whiz too. "Fancy new assignment for you, Lee," she said. "Doan says you get carte blanche for the day! Secret-agent stuff?"

I laughed. "I hadn't thought of it that way, but yeah. Why not? Guess I'll start by locking myself in a dataport. I don't think it's going to take all day, though. Should be done by noon, so there's no need to put poor old Scott on overload."

Rhonda handed me the key, and I hurried down the metal stairs. My first call was to Rupert Pennington. "I have Mr. Doan's approval to teach the history class," I told him. "Can you and I get together soon to go over the schedule?"

"I am delighted, Ms. Barrett," he said, and his tone of voice indicated that he was. "Will you be able to begin teaching next Monday evening?"

That was a surprise. "So soon?" I said. "Perhaps I should come over and take a look at Professor McGinnis's notes this morning. Like maybe right now?" He agreed, and I clattered up the stairs again, wishing I'd worn sneakers instead of heels.

"Finished already?" Rhonda looked up when I burst into the reception area. "I've already sent Francine off with Scott to interview a woman who saw a flying saucer over the Charter Street Cemetery this morning."

"Not finished," I started out the glass doors heading for the elevator. "Just getting started."

I rode Old Clunky down to the street level, sparing my high-heeled feet, happy to remember that there was always a pair of gym sneakers in my car. This was apparently going to be a day for moving fast. I arrived at the Tabby and looked around the school parking area to see if my old space was taken. It was occupied by a good-looking Subaru, so I wound up with a spot near the store's original loading dock, now used mostly by the Theater Arts Department for moving stage sets and furniture in and out of the building.

With white Skechers replacing navy Gianni Bini's, I walked around to the front door of the Tabitha Trumbull Academy of the Arts. It was a little nostalgic. I'd enjoyed my time as an instructor there as well as a short but eventful volunteer stint as a property manager for one of the school's summer stage productions. The big glass doors parted automatically as I approached. That was something new. We used to have to push them open. The reception desk was situated as I remembered it at the base of the enormous staircase leading to the old department store's shoe department, where I'd taught my Television

Production 101 classes. I could hardly wait to climb those stairs and get a peek at whatever class might be meeting there now.

The young woman at the reception desk wearing a student badge identifying her as Susan asked for my ID and issued me a visitor pass. "I'm here to see Mr. Pennington," I told her.

"I know. I recognized you as soon as you walked in. He's expecting you, Ms. Barrett," she said. "I guess you know your way to his office. You used to be a teacher here before you got to be a TV star."

"Hardly a star," I said. "But thanks, Susan, for recognizing me."

I hurried up the stairs, pausing at the mezzanine landing and peeking in at my old classroom area. I wasn't surprised to see that the Trumbull's shoe department signage was still there. Mr. Pennington likes to preserve the ambiance of the original locale. Even the elevators are marked with the old floor designations, like "Second floor: Millinery, foundations, notions, fabrics." The Thonet chairs were still here, lined up classroom-style, but I couldn't tell from a quick glance what subject matter might be being taught there. I continued up the stairs to the second floor. Mr. Pennington's office door stood open. "My door is always open," he often insisted. It was true. I knocked anyway.

"Come in, my dear Ms. Barrett." He stood, extending both hands toward me. "I was so pleased to get your message. I've already called Bruce to let him know how grateful I am for his understanding and how very pleased I am to have you back here at the Tabby even for a short period of time."

"Glad to help out," I said, and—at that moment— meaning it.

"Please sit down, Ms. Barrett." He waved toward a chair beside his desk. "I have Professor McGinnis's notes here, and you may be happy to know that you'll have your same classroom back again. It seemed to be a perfect location for the Salem history classes. A nice big screen for PowerPoint presentations and plenty of storage room for books and such."

"That's nice." I had mixed emotions about that location. I'd noticed that among the vintage shoe department signs on the wall, the giant shiny black patent-leather pump was still there. It had more than once shown me unwelcome visions.

He handed me a slim folder of typed and handwritten notes along with some photocopied book pages and a brochure about the Gardner-Pingree house where the Joseph White murder had occurred. I gave the papers a quick once-over.

"These will probably be useful, and Aunt Ibby is going to check out a few Salem history books for me. I think I'll be able to cobble something together. Do you have a list of names and contact information for my students? I'd like to call each of them to get a feel for what they might expect from me."

He handed me another sheet. "Here you are. Names, addresses, e-mails, and phones for all, including the two dropouts. You'll have three men and two women in class. The dropouts are also both women." I tucked it into the folder, then pulled Louisa's envelope from my purse.

"I have some photos I'd like you to examine. These are from an Alaska trip Louisa Abney-Babcock took last year. All three of our professors were present, and I wonder if you can identify any of the others in the pictures." I pushed the envelope across his desk and watched as he studied each photo.

"I know this young woman," he said, pointing to the blue-haired girl. "She was one of Professor McGinnis's students. She's one of the dropouts. Lucy Mahoney."

I pulled a pen from my purse and scribbled "Lucy Mahoney blue hair" on the sheet he'd handed me. "Good. Anyone else?"

"Not yet." He placed the photo on the table and inspected the next one. "For goodness' sake," he said, lifting the picture closer to his eyes. "Yes, it's him. For goodness' sake. I didn't know he'd gone on a cruise." He turned it toward me, tapping his forefinger on a clear likeness of Louisa's Eddie. "That's our Mr. Symonds."

"*Our* Mr. Symonds?" I asked.

"Yes. Edwin Symonds. He teaches dance here. Adult classes in tap, ballet, and ballroom."

Chapter 20

Shocker! Naturally about a million questions leaped to mind. Mr. Pennington was able to answer some of them. "Edwin Symonds," he related, "has a degree in journalism and writes for a number of publications on a wide variety of subjects. He also has an extensive background in the field of dance."

Mr. Pennington warmed to the subject, telling me that Edwin's mother had been a popular and successful dance teacher back in Iowa, and young Eddie, from early childhood, had been both dance student and assistant instructor. He'd danced professionally onstage and even been an extra in dance scenes in several Hollywood movies. "We're lucky to have him on staff," he said. "His classes are very popular. Would you like to meet him?"

"I certainly would," I said. "Sounds like he'd make a good subject for an interview."

He glanced at the clock on his desk. "He has a tap class right now. Why don't you call me later in the day, and we'll set something up." He dropped his voice and looked around as though he thought someone might be listening. "This isn't for publication yet, but the Theater

Department is about to start rehearsals for our first musical—*Oklahoma!*—and Edwin is doing the choreography. We are truly blessed to have him."

"A musical. That *is* exciting."

"Don't tell yet," he warned. He opened a file cabinet and handed me a printed sheet. "Here's a brief bio on him." I said thanks, promised not to tell about the musical, and said I'd call him later about interviewing Edwin Symonds. I'd have quite a few questions for the dance teacher—none of them about dancing.

I decided that since my new position as history teacher was to begin the following week, I'd better e-mail my prospective students right away. I aimed the Vette back toward Derby Street. As soon as I'd parked beside the seawall, I texted Pete. "Did you know the blue-haired girl is Lucy Mahoney, one of McGinnis's students?" By the time I'd reached Rhonda's reception desk and picked up the dataport key once again, Pete had answered. "Lunch? Pick U up noon? Have photo blowup."

"Meet you at Ariel's bench. 12," I replied. Ariel's coven had erected a comfortable bench in her honor beside the station, overlooking the harbor. It made a pleasant meeting place, memorializing a rather unpleasant witch. I returned to my quiet dataport, pulled the papers Mr. Pennington had given me from my purse, and began electronically introducing myself to Cody's students. I decided to use first names. I sent the same brief message to each of them—Harrison, Conrad, Carl, Kate, and Penny, along with the dropouts, Lucy and Shirley. I still had time to read Cody's lesson-plan notes before my lunch date with Pete.

While the typed, handwritten, and photocopied notes didn't actually amount to a complete lesson plan, they did at least give me a general idea of how these last few classes should be conducted. Cody had concentrated on the actual scene of the murder of Captain Joseph White—

and his notes were pretty darned graphic. According to Cody, the old ship captain's still-warm body was found lying diagonally across the bed. On his left temple was every indication of a crushing blow—even though the skin wasn't broken. Blood had oozed onto the bedclothes from a number of wounds. The doctor who'd performed the autopsy testified that there were thirteen stab wounds on the body—all in the area of the heart, some in the chest and some in the back—and all delivered with such force that several ribs were broken—but that Joseph White was likely already dead from the blow on the head when the vicious stabbing occurred.

Both the blow to the head and the stab wounds near the heart sounded eerily similar to the way Samuel Bond's body had been found. It was no wonder, I thought, that the Salem history teacher with so much knowledge of the long-ago crime would be suspected of one that nearly duplicated it. *But why? Why would Cody murder his fellow professor?*

According to the 1830 newspapers, Dick Crownin-shield had apparently killed Joseph White because he'd been paid to do it. The court records said he hadn't acted alone. I couldn't believe that Cody McGinnis was a hired killer. But were there others involved in Samuel Bond's death? I was anxious to meet and compare notes with Ray and Roger. And doubly anxious to have the twins meet the Angels.

I called Aunt Ibby. "How're the plans for the meetup with the Angels going?"

"They've both cleared their calendars for the next twenty-four hours. Do you want to call Roger and see when the twins can arrange to get together with us?"

"Sure you don't want to call Ray yourself?" I teased.

"All right, I will," was the surprising answer. "I'll let you know what he says."

"That'll be fine," I agreed. I told her what I'd learned

from Mr. Pennington about Edwin Symonds and Lucy Mahoney. "I'm going to have lunch with Pete. He has an enlargement of one of Louisa's pictures he wants to show me. Talk to you later."

At noon I was comfortably seated on Ariel's bench, eyes closed, enjoying the warmth of the noonday sun on my face. Pete pulled into a space behind me and gave a tiny toot of the horn. I joined him in the front seat of the Crown Vic. "Do you have a whole lunch hour or do we grab fast food someplace nearby?" he asked.

"I have plenty of time," I said. "I'm sort of on special assignment now that I'm taking over Cody McGinnis's Tabby class. Doan thinks it'll give me access to information from the students that maybe nobody else will have. Worth a try, I'm thinking."

"Good. I have a meeting with the twins at one, so we'll have almost a whole hour. Maybe we'll go somewhere with chairs and tables. So, is blue-haired Lucy one of Cody's Salem history students?"

"She was. Dropped out after he stopped teaching the class. And I learned even more. Eddie is Edwin Symonds. He works at the Tabby."

"Dance teacher. We've got that."

"He's also a journalism major. Got that too?"

"Yep. Feel like a roast-beef sandwich? Bill and Bob's?"

"That sounds good." The best roast-beef sandwich in Salem with a view of the harbor is a good choice in any season. "I can hardly wait to see that blowup. Who's in it?"

"Besides Lucy Mahoney? I still don't know."

We took a right off Beverly Bridge and parked in front of the iconic Salem foodie landmark. Even though it was lunchtime, we lucked out and got our favorite table. Pete put a very large brown envelope on the table and ordered our food—we rarely change the selection—roast-beef sandwiches, fries, coleslaw, and Diet Cokes.

"Can I look at it yet?" I asked, fairly itching to reach for the envelope.

"Yep. But even enlarged, it's pretty blurry. That window it was shot through was frosty or steamy or dirty. Anyway. It's still not great."

Carefully, I opened the envelope. "Boy, you weren't kidding about blowing it up. This must be sixteen by twenty. Right?" I put the photo on the tabletop, then stood so I could look straight down at it. The blue-haired girl had her back to the window, but the distinctive hair pretty clearly identified her as Lucy Mahoney. The man's face was partly obscured by the lettering on the restaurant window, and his hair was completely tucked under a knitted black Boston Bruins watch cap. Even his ears were covered.

"I'm not sure about him," I said, "but I certainly recognize that!" I pointed to an object on the table between the couple's coffee mugs.

"The fancy cell phone?" Pete looked puzzled.

"Not a cell phone. That's a Tascam DR-4HWL audio recorder."

Chapter 21

I sat down and turned the photo back toward Pete. "I'm thinking the man with Lucy blue-hair is Louisa's Eddie—the Tabby's Edwin Symonds. The reason the other pictures of him looked sort of familiar was because I'd seen him at the mayor's dinner at the Hawthorne. Polite guy. Wearing a Red Sox cap. Only I was paying more attention to his recording equipment than to his face."

"Do you think he'll show up in any of the footage Francine shot that day?"

"Maybe. There were several media people there. Someone must have caught him on camera." I thought about it. "Is it important? Why wouldn't he be there? He's a writer."

"The baseball cap. A witness says a man wearing a Sox cap was seen hanging around near Samuel Bond's house the night of the murder."

"Half the men in Salem have Red Sox caps," I scoffed. "You have one." I paused. "But it's kind of weird, though. Wait a sec." I fished into my bag and pulled out Cody McGinnis's lesson-plan notes on the Joseph White murder. "Listen to this. 'Several witnesses told authorities that they had seen a man wearing a 'glazed cap' like the one Frank Knapp often wore, late at night behind the White property.'"

Our order number was called. Pete picked up our meals and set them on the table. "Smells great," he said, and took a bite of his sandwich.

"Well," I prompted, "is that a weird coincidence or what?"

"You mean about the hats? The Sox cap and a glazed cap—whatever that is?"

"I think it means shiny. Like waxed, maybe. Anyway, there are sure a lot of coincidences between the White and Bond murders."

"I don't believe in coincidences. Are you going to eat all your fries?"

"Yep." I stuck a few fries in my mouth for emphasis. After a few minutes of thoughtful chewing, I tried another topic. "I'm anxious to see Ray and Roger. I can hardly wait to hear what they've got to say."

"Me too. So's the chief, even though he seems to be sure we've already got the right man."

"Roger is just as sure that you don't. Aunt Ibby is calling Ray today to invite them both over to our place this evening." I took a sip of soda. "She and Louisa and Betsy have been busy digging up all they can about Samuel Bond. They're trying hard to help."

Pete smiled. "Sounds like an episode of *The Golden Girls*."

"Uh—close but not exactly. Try *Charlie's Angels*."

He frowned. "That's even worse. I hope they're not getting in over their heads. Say, can you get me invited to this meeting? I think the Angels might need a few ground rules."

"Sure. I'll let you know as soon as she tells me what time everyone is going to be there."

Pete had been keeping careful track of the time, so we left the restaurant at twelve-forty-five carrying the wrapped remains of our sandwiches. On the way back to WICH-TV, I called my aunt on speaker. "Pete would like to join the group tonight," I told her. "He thinks you Angels could use a few ground rules. For your own safety."

"Glad to have him," she said. "I talked to Ray, and the twins will plan to be here at around six. Rupert can't make it, but the girls will be here for sure. This is exciting, isn't it?"

Pete shook his head. I rolled my eyes. "Sure is," I said. "Were you able to find some books for me? Mr. Pennington wants me to start on Monday."

"So soon? Yes. I think I've found some material that will be helpful. See you when you get home."

"Your aunt is too excited about this. Could be a problem." He pulled into the station parking lot and stopped beside the door to the downstairs studio.

"I'm sure she'll behave," I promised, climbing out of the car. "The others will too. All three are very smart women. See you at six?"

"Wouldn't miss it for the world. Gotta go. Can't keep the chief and the twins waiting."

I tapped my code into the pad beside the door and entered the long, dimly lighted studio. I stopped at the *Saturday Business Hour* set, noting that it had been restored to its original condition, then opened the green metal door, and with still comfortably sneakered feet, hurried up the stairs. There was not much more I could do on my "special assignment" until the meeting at Aunt Ibby's. I intended to resume my regular schedule. No point in letting whizbang reporter Scott Palmer show off any more than necessary.

I greeted Rhonda with a salute. "Reporting for duty," I said. "Got anything for me that doesn't require heels?"

"Francine is still on the road with Scottie," she said. "But Old Jim can shoot from the waist up if you ask. Want to take a ride in the VW over to the Ropes Mansion? The garden is in full bloom. You can tiptoe through the tulips—with your sneakers on."

"Good deal," I said, and that's how I came to be sitting under a wisteria arbor, babbling about flowers—from asters to zinnias—while Scott Palmer was across town, scoring a live interview with the poodle sitter my aunt had told me about. Only by this time the woman's account of the yelling match she'd overheard coming from Samuel Bond's backyard had undergone significant revision. Wide-eyed, she described how *someone* had screamed obscenities at Professor Bond, and how *someone* had accused him of stealing something of *great* value, and had *maybe* actually threatened his life. "'You won't get away with it this time.' That's what the guy said," she reported. "'I won't let you get away with it!'"

When Old Jim and I returned to the station, Marty was already at work editing Scott's transmission while Mr. Doan watched (admiringly) over her shoulder. It wasn't hard to figure out whose report was going to show up on the early news—and I knew I should have been the one who'd had it.

I wasn't about to let Scott beat me to another one. "Come on, Jim," I whispered. "We're going over to the Tabby to talk to a dancing book editor." I stopped at my car, traded Skechers for heels, and called Rupert Pennington. "I'd like to come over and interview Mr. Symonds," I said. "Is he still in the building?"

"He is indeed. I saw him heading for the coffee shop a moment ago. He's on a half-hour break between classes. Shall I ask him to wait for you there?" The Tabby has an on-site Starbucks—new since I was teaching there.

"Yes, thanks. We're on our way." I did a quick read-through of the bio Mr. Pennington had given me. I was about to confront the mysterious editor without a list of preplanned questions to ask. This was going to be a seat-of-the-pants project for sure. "We'll use the handheld camera and a couple of clip-on mics, Jim," I said. "We'll try to keep this low-key. I hope we don't attract a bunch of Save Cody sign wavers."

This time I recognized Edwin Symonds without the distraction of that much-better-than-mine recorder. Actually, Edwin Symonds in black spandex dance tights was a bit of a distraction in itself. He was almost a head shorter than high-heeled me, with a well-muscled, compact body. Mr. Pennington had apparently told him to expect us. He was sitting alone in one of the booths reading when we approached. Putting his book aside, he stood to greet us, moving with a dancer's grace. I walked ahead of Jim, hand extended. "How do you do, Mr. Symonds. I'm Lee Barrett. WICH-TV."

"Yes. I recognize you, Ms. Barrett. Please call me Eddie." He gestured toward the dark brown upholstered high-backed bench. "Won't you join me?"

"Thank you." I motioned for Jim to move forward. "Mr. Pennington suggested that we meet. Can you spare a few minutes to share your thoughts with our audience on some current Salem happenings?"

"All right."

I took the seat opposite him. I clipped one mic to my collar and handed him the other one while Jim moved to the open end of the booth, positioning the camera. Eddie smiled, clipped the mic on with professional ease, and brushed a lock of thick black hair away from his eyes. "May I assume that your questions will concern my association with certain university professors currently in the news?"

I liked his frankness. No *verbal* tap dancing. "Yes," I said. "This won't be live. We'll edit later at the studio. May we begin?"

"Go for it."

Jim began a slow count. The tally light clicked on.

"This is Lee Barrett, speaking to you from the new Starbucks inside the Tabitha Trumbull Academy of the Arts in downtown Salem. My guest today is Edwin Symonds, a dance instructor here at the Tabby. Mr. Symonds . . ."

He wagged a finger back and forth in a playful gesture. "Eddie," he said.

"Eddie," I corrected, "has an impressive background as a professional performer in several disciplines of dance. Here at the Tabby, he teaches tap, ballet, and ballroom. The school is fortunate to have an instructor of your caliber. Are your students here mainly adults?"

"Yes. I have a few youngsters, high school and college-age folks, but most of my students are of the baby boomer generation." Big smile. "Still movin' and groovin'!"

"That's great. Dancing is wonderful exercise and fun at the same time."

"Sure is. I have a few senior citizens in my classes too. A few come for the ballet barre work. Most of them enjoy ballroom, and some want to learn some good old country line dancing." He dropped his voice and winked. "Quite a few local ladies are interested in pole dancing. We've even installed a stripper pole under one of the old overhead stock shelves. It's wonderful exercise." I had a quick mental image of the Angels so exercising. It was a disturbing thought.

Enough chitchat. Let's get down to murder.

"Eddie," I began, "two of your friends have been in the news lately—and not in a good way. This must be a difficult time for you, and I appreciate your being willing to talk with us about it."

His friendly smile faded. "Thanks, Lee—may I call you Lee?" He didn't wait for an answer. "You're right. My good friend Sam Bond is dead—apparently murdered." Big sigh. "That was hard enough to accept, but then, within days, my friend—and fellow teacher here at the Tabby—Cody McGinnis was being questioned by the police. They think he killed Sam! It's outrageous. I know for a fact he couldn't have done it."

"You seem quite certain about his innocence," I said.

A disarming smile. "I'm very sure. You'll see soon enough."

I pursued that line of questioning briefly, but got only smiling assurances that his friend was innocent. Moving on, I tried another tack. "I understand that you, Professor McGinnis, Professor Bond, and"—I paused, pretending to look at my notes—"Professor Armstrong were very close. That you all even traveled together sometimes. If you don't mind my asking, if you remember, when was the last time you four were all in the same place—at the same time?"

Eddie didn't even pause to take a breath. "It was the weekend before Sam died. He threw a little celebratory dinner party."

"A celebration?" *A party? First I'd heard about that.*

"Yes. Those three had recently finished writing a book."

"You must have been helpful to them," I said. "I understand you're an accomplished writer as well as a fine dancer."

He gave a modest little lifting of one shoulder. "I helped move a few commas around, straightened out some grammar, tried to blend their different styles. Things like that. It wasn't a book in my field. It's totally their baby. I just helped out a little here and there. Sam didn't want it to be known around that I was involved at all. Called me a 'ghostwriter' and swore the other guys to secrecy. Guess it doesn't matter now that he's gone."

"Can you tell us about the book?"

"A how-to book, more or less. A book for college kids. How to study for exams. How to prepare a term paper. Things like that. We call it *You Can Do This*."

"Was anyone else there? Besides you four?"

"Sure. Cody and I brought dates."

"Did Professor Bond have a date?'

"No. Neither did Alan."

Professor Dreamy without a date? Hard to believe.

"Did you see any indication that night that there was any—um—any animosity between Professor Bond and Cody McGinnis?"

"You sound like a cop, Lee," he said, smiling again. "But no, no animosity. It was a little tense. Cody had found out that he wasn't going to get the full professorship after all. But he understood how university politics works. He'd have to wait another year or so. That's all."

"Cody—Professor McGinnis—seems to have a lot of friends on his side. They've already raised a great deal of money for his defense."

"Yes. Twenty thou I heard." He whistled. "Lot of friends."

"So there were no arguments, no unpleasantness the last time you four were all together? Celebrating the new book?"

He laughed. "Well, Cody's date got a little drunk and smashed a shot glass in the fireplace. But she cleaned it up."

Chapter 22

I wasn't about to violate station protocol by asking who the dates were—at least while Jim was filming. Unless glass smashing was a popular new fad Lucy with the blue hair had been Cody's date—which also provided an answer to the Alaska cruise gossip-fest question about which professor she favored.

I let Eddie's comment about the glass-smashing incident pass with a "Oh, well, those things happen," and searched my mind for another question. His hand still rested on the book he'd been reading, his fingers covering part of the title. "I see that we interrupted your reading, Eddie," I said, pointing to the blue paper cover. "Research for another of your many magazine articles?" He didn't move his hand.

"Uh, no. Not exactly. It's nothing that interesting. A bit of academic fact-checking."

A portion of the title was visible. Without being signaled, Old Jim moved in for a closer shot, then smoothly backed away. Smart guy. Real pro. He knew I wanted to get a closer look at the few exposed letters.

"I interviewed Professor Armstrong earlier, Eddie," I

said, reestablishing eye contact and smiling. "He told me that he hasn't seen Professor McGinnis since this whole— unpleasantness—started. What about you? Have you visited or talked with him at all?"

"Well, sure. We've been friends a long time." Eddie moved the book down onto his lap and then eased it into a black backpack that lay on the seat beside him. "He's staying at his mom's. I went right over as soon as the buzz started about Cody being the one who killed Sam. I couldn't stay long, but I talked with him long enough to know he's telling the truth. He didn't do it."

"Have you seen him since then?" I prodded. "He must be feeling pretty isolated."

"I haven't," he admitted. "I've kicked a few bucks into the fund, but no, I haven't seen or talked to Cody."

I decided to get back to questions about the dead professor. "There have been some allegations that Samuel Bond had a bad temper. That he sometimes berated people, treated them badly."

"If that's so, I never saw it." Eddie leaned toward the camera. "Oh, Sam could be outspoken. He told it like he saw it. If a student did badly in his class, Sam took it personally. Like you were somehow disrespecting the subject if you didn't do your best work on one of his history assignments. He might even suggest that you switch majors."

Lightbulb moment. "Were you ever a history major?" I asked.

He looked surprised. "Freshman year," he said. "Turned out journalism was a better fit for me."

"Yes," I agreed. "Your success in writing would certainly bear that out." *Pop!* Another lightbulb. "By the way, do you happen to know whether or not Cody McGinnis switched majors when he was a student at County U.?"

"Darn near." Headshake and a wry smile. "Cody almost flunked Sam's world history class. He thought about switching to English literature, but he switched schools instead. Transferred to Boston University in his sophomore year. That's where he got his history degrees."

"Interesting," I said. And it was. Alan Armstrong changed majors after receiving a low mark from Samuel Bond. Cody McGinnis had almost done so and Lucy blue-hair had done the same.

Is this a pattern? Of what? I made a quick mental note to pursue this line of thought—but certainly not at that moment—not with Old Jim recording every word. I tried another tack.

"Eddie, you and Cody McGinnis and Alan Armstrong spent a lot of time with Professor Bond. Were those 'working sessions'?"

"Pretty much. When a group of writers gets together on one project, it can be difficult to accommodate everyone's writing style." He gave a helpless, palms-up gesture. "Then there's the 'he gets more space than I do' complaint." He smiled. "I got that a lot."

"You must be a good coordinator."

"I try to be. The meetings were sometimes a little contentious. Mostly we got together at Sam's. He had the biggest house—a mansion, really—and a pretty good bar. I listened and took notes while the three of them hashed things out. Of course, Sam didn't like it to be known that I was involved. He didn't want anyone to think they were using a 'ghostwriter,' especially one he considered an untenured, Iowa cow-college-educated hack like me." He shrugged and smiled. "It was okay. He paid me for my time."

Bet he took notes with that cool Tascam recorder. "But you all went on an Alaska cruise together, didn't you?"

He raised a surprised eyebrow. "Yes. We did. You've done your research, Lee."

"A friend was on the same cruise."

"I see. It was billed as a spring break cruise. Students

and teachers got a hefty discount—even dance teachers! It was too good a deal to pass up." He looked at his watch in that deliberate way people do when they want to get away from you. I took the hint.

"Well, thank you very much for talking with us, Eddie. Do you have a website you'd like to share with prospective dance students?" He gave the Tabby's site and mentioned a new YouTube video of a class in Haitian-Creole ballroom dancing.

We shook hands all around, and Old Jim and I packed up our gear. We exited the Tabby via the front door, said goodbye to Susan, and zipped down Washington Street to Derby a good deal faster than Francine would have dared. "You'll want to get with Marty about the editing right away, I figure," Old Jim said. "With any luck this'll make the five o'clock. The ten o'clock for sure. Might even get a smile out of Doan."

"It went better than I'd thought it might," I admitted, "since we walked in on him with no prep time."

"Good-natured guy," Jim said. "He seemed willing to answer all your questions."

"He did. Thanks for grabbing a shot of that book cover. Maybe we can take a close look at that frame and figure out the title."

"I saw you zooming those big green eyes in on it. You think it's important for some reason?"

I laughed. "Actually, I haven't the slightest idea what it might be. I'm kind of nosy, I guess."

He gave me a stern look. "Not nosy one bit. Instinct. That's what you've got. Reporter's instinct." We made a fast turn into the station parking lot. "Mark my words. It's important. You'll see."

I liked his assessment. "Reporter's instinct." I liked it a lot.

"Thanks, Jim," I said.

Chapter 23

Marty was ready and waiting for us. She'd already done a quick run-through, taking out pauses, a couple of coughs, and some ambient sounds of clinking coffee cups and chatter from nearby customers. "Good job, Moon," she said. "Take a look and see what else needs fixing. How come you get all the good-looking guys to interview lately?"

"Lucky, I guess." I sat beside her and peered closely at the screen. Looked good to me. I paused the video at the shot of the blue book. "We can leave this out of the broadcast," I said, "but I'd like a blowup of it for myself. I want to try to figure out what the lettering says."

"Done," she said. "Maybe I can help. Okay if I fool around with it too?"

"Are you kidding? You're the expert at this stuff. Fool around all you want." I squinted at the screen. "Looks like so much alphabet soup to me. His fingers covered most of it. Can you send this frame to my e-mail?"

"Done," she said again, and I knew it would be. By then I felt pretty good about my day. I was glad to learn that the poodle sitter hadn't had much of anything new to share with Scott and that my interview with the dance teacher had gone so well.

"Guess I'll see if Rhonda has anything else for me, then I'll head for the barn."

"Have a good evening." She gave a little salute. "Too bad you missed covering the announcement about the history teacher getting bail though. You would have milked it a little more than Scotty did."

"Bail? What? Cody made bail? When did this happen?"

"Late this afternoon. They haven't made a big deal out of it. A police spokesman read an announcement. Didn't take any questions or give any details. Just said that the man had been released on bail." She shrugged. "Scotty was the only one here so he took it. He just read the same announcement word for word. You'll see it on the evening news I suppose."

Scooped again. Twice in one day. I bit my tongue, pretended it really *wasn't* a big deal and headed for Rhonda's office.

Rhonda didn't have anything else with my name on it on her white board, so I ducked out early. Apparently, the twins had managed to bail Cody out and that was a good thing, no matter who reported it. Besides, I had several thoughts in mind for the ever-growing outline that I'd left at home on the kitchen table. I hoped my aunt was right—which she usually is—and that the outline was a good way to put my thoughts in order, because right about then I truly needed some order to my seriously jumbled thoughts. *Broken shot glass. Is Lucy dating her professor? Rampant course switching. Vision blue paperback book. Real blue paperback book. Mean, swearing Sam. Beloved mentor Sam. Innocent Cody. Guilty Cody. New murder. Old murder. Is the merengue a Haitian-Creole dance?*

Maybe what I needed was a nap.

Aunt Ibby's Buick was in the garage when I got there and I knew she'd be busy making preparations for our six o'clock meeting with the twins, the Angels, and Pete. O'Ryan met me at the back steps, then hurried back inside through his cat door. He paused in the hall, looked back at me, then scampered through the next cat door into my aunt's kitchen.

I knocked. "It's me," I called.

"Hold on. I'm coming." There was a click as she unlocked the door.

"You always remember to lock it when you're expecting Pete," I said. It was true. He reminds her regularly to keep her doors locked. The front door—on the Winter Street side of the house—is always secure, but the kitchen door? Not so much.

"Nobody uses it except you, the cat, and the paper boy," she said. "You and Pete worry about me too much."

"You're incorrigible," I said. "Do you need help with anything before everybody gets here?"

"I think I'm all set. I have soft drinks and wine and cheese and crackers for nibbling. It's too early for anything heavy." She smiled that sly smile I know so well. "If we happen to work right up until dinnertime, I have a lovely coq au vin simmering in the slow cooker, homemade rolls ready to pop into the oven, and a fresh-baked apple pie in the pantry."

"Sounds delicious. And you look quite gorgeous." She definitely did, in a slim-fitting emerald green sheath. "I'm pretty sure Pete and I can be talked into staying for dinner," I said. "I'll run upstairs and change. I'll be back before six. I can hardly wait to see the twins." Roger and Ray had been more than simply students in one of my classes at the Tabby. They'd become my friends, and a couple of times actual lifesavers, and I'd been delighted with their success on Boston television. I dashed through the shower, clothes selection, makeup routine and—as

I'd promised—was on my way down the front stairs by five-forty-five.

I'd been watching the twins' show, *Street Beat*, fairly regularly, and I'd noticed that they'd both lost weight and that they still dressed identically. I'd always had trouble telling them apart and assumed that would still be the case. They'd never seemed to mind; in fact, they seemed to get quite a kick out of confusing people.

I'd just stepped into the foyer, when the doorbell chimed. O'Ryan was already positioned at the long vertical windowpanes beside the door, and I'd arrived there in time to welcome my old friends. I unlocked the door and pulled it open.

"Roger! Ray!" I held out my arms and hugged them one at a time. "It's so good to see you both." They accepted my enthusiastic greeting with somewhat embarrassed pats on my shoulders and stepped inside the house. By-the-book, just-the-facts-ma'am police officers, they'd never been much for affectionate gestures—but I knew they were every bit as fond of me as I was of them. "Come right on in here. Aunt Ibby is in the kitchen. She's dying to see you too."

I'd almost closed the door behind them, when I noticed that they weren't alone. "We brought our nephew, Cody, along," Roger/Ray said. "Hope that's okay."

"Of course. Please come in, Cody," I said, extending my hand, wondering how this had come about. "I'm so pleased to meet you. I'm Lee."

Cody McGinnis had a nice smile and a firm handshake. "I know this is unexpected. I'm as surprised to be here as you are to see me. I recognize you from television," he said. "And my uncles are probably your biggest fans." He bent and patted O'Ryan, who proceeded to give his hand a lick. "This must be O'Ryan, your very smart cat. My uncles talk about him sometimes too."

I faced the twins. "I'm more than surprised," I said. "How did you do it?"

One of them answered. I think it was Roger. "We called in a couple of favors." He gave a little shrug. "Cody has no past arrests. He's not a flight risk. We posted bail, and he's been remanded to our custody until a trial date is set. He had to turn in his passport and wear an ankle bracelet, but for a while at least he'll be able to help us prove his innocence."

"You say Ibby is in the kitchen?" said the twin I guessed (by the interest in his tone) was probably Ray.

"That's right, Ray," I said. "Right through the living room and the door to the right. You can follow O'Ryan."

"I remember," he said, and the three men walked single file behind the cat.

I dared a glance at the hall tree as we passed. Nothing there but a reflection of me. Relieved, I joined the parade to the kitchen. A rhythmic knock at the back door announced that the rest of the Angels had arrived, and soon the kitchen rocked with the happy sounds of old friends greeting one another, along with polite introductions between those who were still strangers. Since by then it was six o'clock and Pete hadn't arrived yet, Aunt Ibby suggested that we all adjourn to the dining room where Merlot, diet cola, cheese, crackers, pencils, and notebooks, along with a laptop, were arranged on the table. "Pete Mondello will be joining us, but we may as well get started."

Since none of us had expected that Cody would be with us for this meeting, things were a little awkward at first. After all, we were discussing murder, a quite violent one, and the man who might or might not be the killer was sitting there eating cheese and crackers and sipping wine with us. Awkward for sure.

Aunt Ibby had seated Roger at the head of the table, and all of us looked silently toward him. "Thank you all for being here," Roger began. "Ms. Russell, Mrs. Leavitt, and Mrs. Abney-Babcock, I especially appreciate your willingness to help us prove Cody's innocence." He tilted his head toward his nephew, who so far hadn't said anything except "How do you do?" each time he was introduced. Louisa reminded him that they'd met before, but by then he had a deer-in-the-headlights look in his eyes and it was hard to tell if he remembered her at all.

"Cody, want to say a few words?" Ray encouraged the man.

I knew that Cody was a teacher, and a popular one at that. It was unlikely that the near paralysis we were witnessing was his normal classroom demeanor. *This poor guy is terrified.* It must be horrifying for an innocent person to be suspected of murder—to realize what the penalties could be if he was convicted of such a crime.

"Cody, Professor McGinnis," I began, hoping I'd be able to find the words to put him more at ease. "It must be gratifying for you to know that you have so many friends eager to defend you—to be there for you during this difficult time . . ."

Holy crap! I sound like a Hallmark sympathy card. I tried again.

"Look, Cody. Roger and Ray are the best in the business. They dot every i and cross every t. They believe in you. We—all of us in this room—we believe in you too, and we want to help in every way we can. These women"—I gave a wave of my arm toward my aunt and her girlfriends—"they're not cops. They think outside the box. They color outside the lines. You might say we're all kind of nosy—and sometimes a few nosy women hear things—see things—professionals might miss."

"She's right, son," Ray said. "These ladies have agreed to do a little . . . well, unofficial 'snooping' on your behalf. I've seen Lee and Ibby in action before, and believe me, it's good to have them—and their friends—on your side."

"Good to have them on your side," Roger agreed.

The beginnings of a smile played around Cody's lips. "I get it. Thank you. All of you."

Betsy, looking remarkably Farrah-like with her new hairstyle, was the one to get the proverbial ball rolling. "Glad to help. We've already dug up quite a lot about old Sam. Ibby has it all on paper for you. But listen. I heard something new about Sam Bond at the beauty parlor today." She picked up her pencil, stabbing the air with it. "Shall I just blab it out or are we supposed to put everything in writing?"

"Just blab—I mean, tell us about it, please," Roger said.

"Tell us about it," Ray echoed.

"Okay." Betsy leaned forward, both elbows on the table. "Here it is. Sam Bond, in addition to being a name-dropping, social-climbing weasel, was also a lying cheat."

"How so?" Louisa asked.

"One of the women getting her nails done—gel coat of course, a yummy lavender shade—anyway, she said that Sam wormed his way into the men's Friday night poker game at the yacht club, and her husband told her that they had to ban him for cheating. A card cheat. Can you believe it?" She leaned back in her chair. "Then the shampoo girl told us when she was a waitress at IHOP they used to laugh at him because when he was eating with someone else, he'd leave like a fifty-cent tip and the other guy would leave two bucks, and when he thought no one was looking, he'd switch the tips around so it looked like he left the most. What a weasel. Then somebody said that he also used to cheat on his late wife too, but she didn't give details, so I don't know if that counts. Before I left, one of the older ladies—she was getting a weave—said that she'd gone to school with him and back in the seventh grade he used to sit behind her so he could copy her math answers."

"Kind of establishes a pattern, doesn't it?" Roger said. "Thanks, Betsy."

"Along the same lines," my aunt said, "perhaps it's a small thing—but rather than pay some fairly substantial library overdue fees, Samuel Bond was in the habit of having students check out books for him."

"Weasel," Betsy said.

"I've already told you that Sam has been dealing with some financial difficulties recently," Louisa said. "But he apparently expected some sort of windfall was forthcoming. According to some local bank scuttlebutt, it has to do with a publishing venture."

Cody frowned. "I know about that one," he said. "I'm kind of involved in it. But I'm sure it's not going to be a significant moneymaker."

"Yes," I said. "Alan Armstrong told me about it. It's a student handbook. A how-to book on taking exams, doing research, that sort of thing, right?"

"Right," he agreed. "Alan and Sam and I co-wrote it. Fortunately we finished it before Sam—um—passed."

"I spoke with Edwin Symonds this afternoon. He said the same thing."

He didn't smile. "How do you know Eddie?"

"Friend of Louisa's," I said.

Ray and Roger looked back and forth between Cody and me as though they were watching ping-pong—identical heads moving in unison.

"Edwin Symonds?" Roger asked.

"Eddie?" said Ray. "Where did you find him?"

Louisa handed Ray a slip of paper. "I brought along his phone number for you."

"We had a meeting with Pete Mondello today," Roger said. "He told us Eddie Symonds works right here in Salem. He's a dancing school teacher at the Tabby."

"Merengue," said Betsy.

"Of course. Merengue," Louisa agreed.

Cody did the ping-pong look between Louisa and Betsy.

Aunt Ibby snapped her fingers. "Now I remember. No wonder the man in Louisa's picture looked familiar. Rupert introduced me to Mr. Symonds at the Tabby some time ago. Later he helped out with a bookmobile promotion. Seemed like a nice fellow. You say Pete knows him too?"

"Where is Mondello anyway?" Ray glanced around the table. "Isn't he supposed to be here?"

As if on cue, the front doorbell chimed "The Impossible Dream." I hurried to let Pete in, hoping he'd be able to bring some order to the table tennis tournament going on in Aunt Ibby's dining room.

Chapter 24

"**S**orry I'm late," he said, pulling me close for a kiss. "Is everybody here?"

"Yep. Everybody. Aunt Ibby, the Angels, and the twins. Also, Cody McGinnis."

"No kidding? Angels and twins sounds like a baseball game. Cody's here too? Interesting."

"It's getting that way." I returned the kiss. Pete's back was toward the hall tree. I couldn't help looking over his shoulder. The lights and colors showed up right away, melding into Old Jim's picture of the blue book in Eddie's hand—only the man's hand had turned into a red handprint—a bloody red handprint. Then, blink. It was gone.

Pete held me at arm's length, looking into my eyes. "You okay, babe?"

"I'm okay," I told him. "Seeing things in the damned mirror for a second. I'll tell you about it later." ("Seeing things." That's what Pete calls my visions.) We started through the living room. "Pete's here," I called as we headed for the dining room. Everybody shook hands and greeted one another. More crackers and cheese and another bottle of Merlot appeared on the table. The three cops, the three snoopers, the prime suspect, and I got down to the nitty-gritty business of solving a murder.

Pete's presence at the table didn't seem to affect Cody one way or another. Pete announced that he'd refrain from commenting, but if no one objected, he'd sit in as an observer. No one objected. It turned out to be a good thing that Cody was present. He was able to answer some of the questions we—the Angels and I—had wondered about from the start. For instance, how did Cody's ladder get from his tool shed to Sam Bond's house? Cody's answer was a simple one. "That tool shed is a literal shed behind my mom's place," he said. "It was my playhouse when I was a kid. My grandfather built it. It has one window and a rickety unlocked door. There are some old lawn tools in there, a few garden rakes, extra hoses, two or three wooden ladders. Nothing valuable. No power tools or anything like that. I guess anybody who knows it's there can borrow anything they want to from it. I have no idea when that ladder went missing."

"Seems pretty darned circumstantial to me," Betsy said. "Isn't it, Pete? Darned near anybody in Salem had access to that shed, it seems like."

"It is circumstantial," Pete agreed.

"Cody's prints are on it, and it was found at the scene of the crime," my aunt said.

"Correct," Roger said.

"Right," said Ray.

"And what about his prints on a glass in Bond's house?"

Roger raised one hand. "So he drank there occasionally with Bond and a couple of other professors and the girl. Nothing strange about that at all."

"The shoe prints? What about that?" Louisa asked. "Has anyone determined that they were in fact his shoes?"

"I can answer that one," Ray said. "The prints are definitely from his Nikes."

I saw Pete nod in agreement.

"Oh my." My aunt's tone was one of surprise. "That wasn't in the papers."

I was surprised too. "That seems more than circumstantial, doesn't it, Roger?"

"It does." Roger looked at Pete. "And it justifies the charge. But since Cody is innocent, we need to find the explanation for it."

"Can you explain it, Cody?" Betsy's voice was firm.

He looked down at the table. "I can't. It's not as though I wear them every day. I don't work out nearly as often as I should. But I'm sure I would have noticed if they were ever missing from my gym locker when I was there."

"There were traces of soil on the sneakers. Forensics is analyzing the dirt," Ray said. "It's likely the killer wore them. We know it wasn't Cody, so who was it?"

Actually, we don't exactly know it wasn't Cody, do we? I could tell immediately that others at that table shared that thought. All of the Angels, including my aunt, sat up a little straighter in their chairs, seeming to physically distance themselves from Cody McGinnis.

O'Ryan, though, had a different reaction. He left his spot beneath my chair and circled the table, then leaped gracefully and gently into Cody's lap. I had no doubt the cat believed the man was innocent. Good enough for me.

"Doesn't Cody have any sort of alibi for the time Bond was killed?" I wondered aloud. "The paper said he spent part of the evening at the Tabby."

"I did," Cody said, stroking O'Ryan's fuzzy head. "Then I went home. Nobody saw me. Nobody called or texted or knocked on my apartment door. I have no alibi for most of that night."

"Then somebody saw somebody with a ball cap like yours near Bond's place," Aunt Ibby said.

"Doesn't mean a thing," Roger said. "The papers picked it up because of that old eighteen-thirty case—where one of Dick Crowninshield's accomplices was spotted outside Joseph White's house the night he was killed."

"They recognized that man because of his hat," Louisa said. "I looked it up. There truly are remarkable similarities between this case and the Joseph White murder."

"Too many similarities to be coincidental," Betsy said. "And they match up with the course on Salem history that Cody teaches at the Tabby."

I thought about the bloody handprint I'd seen so recently in the mirror, and about the bloody scene Joseph White's housekeeper had seen on that long-ago morning. Too many similarities to be coincidental? I wondered what River might have to say about it. Pete, Aunt Ibby, and River are the only people who know about my so-called gift. Pete doesn't like to talk about it. Aunt Ibby reluctantly accepts it. River, being kind of psychic, likes, accepts, and *loves* talking about it. I knew that visions in a mirror had no place in this conversation. I decided to call River. ASAP.

There was quite a bit of discussion about the tell-tale sneakers, which according to the police definitely belonged to Cody and definitely had made the prints beneath the window at Samuel Bond's house. Nobody came up with an explanation of how that could happen if Cody wasn't there.

The broken shot glass was the accepted explanation for those bloodstains in the old man's bedroom, although the reason for Lucy Mahoney's presence there in the first place raised questions. No answers.

Betsy, Louisa, and Aunt Ibby each contributed a few more snippets of gossip related to Sam Bond, and my aunt told once again about her poodle-sitting friend who'd overheard two men arguing, and about Bond's new passport picture. Roger asked for names. By eight o'clock we'd exhausted the cheese, crackers, wine, and most of the conversation.

Aunt Ibby invited everyone for a potluck dinner, but the twins and Cody were due back at Phyllis's house, and Louisa and Betsy had "other plans." Pete and I accepted as usual. We said good night to our friends, and accompanied the twins and Cody to the front door and the women to the back door. Then Pete and I settled ourselves comfortably at the kitchen table while Aunt Ibby popped the rolls into the oven.

Murders—both old and new—and phantom bloody handprints could wait. For now there were steaming bowls full of coq au vin, hot rolls, apple pie with vanilla ice cream, and coffee.

We'd all be dealing with reality soon enough.

Chapter 25

When Pete and I, full of good food and with a bag of leftover rolls for breakfast, eventually climbed the front stairs to my apartment, it was nearly time for the ten o'clock news. "Want to watch my interview with Edwin Symonds?" I asked as I turned on the kitchen TV.

"I guess I'm about to," he said, smiling.

"I haven't even seen the fully edited version myself," I said. "I think I did okay though. He was a pretty easy interview. Seems like a nice guy."

"He's for sure the mysterious editor, right?" Pete sat at the counter, facing the TV, and I sat beside him.

"He is. Mr. Pennington recognized him from Louisa's pictures. But, know something? I mentioned that I'd spoken with Symonds before you got here, and Cody didn't seem too pleased about it."

"What'd he say?"

"He didn't actually say anything, but he had kind of a stony face."

"Stony face doesn't mean a thing. The man is facing a murder charge," Pete said. "Can't expect him to look happy about much of anything."

He was right, of course. "Before we watch the interview," I said, "there's a part of it we left out." I told him
about the book in Eddie's hand—with his fingers covering most of the title or whatever the words on the cover
were. "It has something to do with the thing I saw in the
mirror tonight."

"Want to tell me about it?" Pete reached for my hand.

"Yes, I do." I faced him, glad for his gentle touch. He
knows I don't enjoy the visions. "In the mirror the man's
fingers were replaced with a print. A bloody handprint."

"You think it has something to do with the girl's
bloody prints on Bond's bedroom wall?"

"Maybe. Or maybe it has to do with Joseph White's
blood. I don't know what to think," I admitted. "You have
any ideas?"

"It's likely that the killer wore gloves of some kind,"
he said. "The gloves would be bloody. Does that make
any sense?"

"Maybe. I think I'll ask River what she thinks too.
She's good at symbols. She's probably at the station by
now."

"Couldn't hurt to ask," he said, and pointed to the
screen. "Here comes the news."

Phil Archer does the ten o'clock newscast—mostly
local events and high school sports. Buck Covington
comes on at eleven with national and regional headlines,
along with investigative reports. That leads into River's
midnight show—*Tarot Time with River North*.

Phil led with Scott Palmer talking with the mayor about
the possibility of reestablishing the start-of-summer picnic
for school kids at the Salem Willows, followed by some
film of the latest under-the-city tunnel entrance a home-
owner had discovered in his basement. There was a teaser
about my interview, then a Stromberg's Cove restaurant
commercial. Scott's piece about Cody being released on
bail followed and took only a few seconds. Marty was

right. I would have milked it for more. Finally, there I was in the Tabby's new Starbucks with Edwin Symonds. I looked okay. Eddie in spandex looked fabulous. I listened to myself asking questions and Eddie answering them. Was Old Jim right? Did I have reporter's instinct? Should I have pushed a little more on the broken shot glass episode? Was the fact that Eddie had been one of Professor Bond's students important—or another coincidence? Is anything about all this a coincidence? I watched Pete's face. "Well," I asked. "What do you think?"

"I think you're a damn good reporter," he said, "and getting better all the time."

"You do?"

"Of course I do." He ruffled my hair. "Do you think I'm trying to talk you into bed?"

"That'd be too easy," I said, leaning into his shoulder. "But seriously, whenever I watch an interview like that one—one that's important, not a pet store or a crystal shop—I always wonder if I should have been more aggressive. Pushed harder for answers. Like I wanted to ask Eddie who his and Cody's dates were, but I thought it would be rude."

"It might have been," he agreed. "Fortunately, I didn't have to be polite when I questioned him. I guess I can tell you Lucy Mahoney was Cody's date. Eddie had brought along one of his ballroom dance students—a lady of impeccable character and a ton of money."

"I'd guessed that Lucy was with Cody. I gather that Eddie's date isn't a person of interest?"

"Clean as a whistle," he said. "Symonds admitted very frankly that he likes older women with money. No law against that."

"True," I said. "I guess he was kind of hitting on Louisa when they were all in Alaska."

"No surprise there," he said. "I think I'll hit the shower while you call River about the hocus-pocus stuff."

I called River's number. She picked up right away.

"Hello, Lee. I saw you on the news. I'm almost ready to sign up for dancing lessons!"

"Mr. Pennington says the classes are popular. Maybe you and I should go together," I said. "Meanwhile, I need your advice about a vision."

"A bad one?"

"Kind of unpleasant," I said. "More confusing than bad, I guess."

"I have time. Shoot."

I told her about the book I'd seen in Eddie's hand and about the blood smears in Professor Bond's room. "I think both of those images got mixed up in my brain," I told her, "and what I saw in the mirror tonight was a bloody handprint where Eddie's fingers were on the blue book. What do you think it means?"

"What matters is what *you* think it means." Her tone was serious. "I think it's possible that *you* think your new friend Eddie may have blood on his hands."

"That never crossed my mind," I protested. "Honest, it didn't!"

"Maybe not your *conscious* mind," she said. "Any other visions lately?"

"There was a brief one in the car mirror—it showed the blue book with a red stain on it. And another one had the Knight of Pentacles riding on a giant Monopoly game piece."

"Knight of Pentacles," she repeated. "Dark hair, dark eyes, red gloves. I don't get the giant game piece though."

"It's a display piece at the Toy Trawler. I'd done a segment about it."

"Gotcha. It seems as if all of the recent visions point to one person, doesn't it?"

"Seems so." I agreed reluctantly. "But I like Eddie. I'd rather it was Alan or even the girl, Lucy."

"What about Cody McGinnis?" she asked. "Doesn't Pete think it was him?"

"I guess he has to. But the twins are so sure their nephew is innocent that I have to believe in him too. And Eddie Symonds seems so positive that Cody couldn't have done it. We met Cody in person tonight, and he seems like a nice guy who's in a tough position and is scared to death."

"Okay. So tell me about the girl, Lucy. Have you met her?"

"I spoke to her briefly once at a 'Save Cody' rally at the college," I said. "She's apparently dating him, and she was the one whose bloodstains were found in Sam Bond's bedroom. She was also on an Alaska cruise where Bond, Cody, Alan, and Eddie were all present."

"Wow. Toss that into the mix and we've got quite a mystery. How about I come over soon and do a reading for you?"

"Yes. Soon, for sure. Meanwhile, I have a couple of classes to teach at the Tabby. Filling in for Cody."

"You have a pretty full plate, girlfriend," she said. "Take care of yourself."

"I will," I promised. "Pete and I will be watching your show tonight. Bye."

I'd put down the phone when Pete returned, bare chested, hair wet from the shower, wearing blue sweatpants and smelling wonderful. He sat on the stool next to me again. Extremely distracting. "Did River have any bright ideas about your seeing things?"

"She thinks that I think Eddie has blood on his hands."

"I can understand that." He spoke quietly, calmly. "Yes. That's a logical interpretation of what you saw. Don't you think so?"

"I don't *want* to think that. But I don't want to think Cody did it either. I don't like Alan Armstrong much, but I don't think he's capable of the kind of emotion it would take to kill somebody." Big sigh. "I still don't know what to think."

"Maybe you should stop thinking about it so much. That's my job. Think about other things. I heard you say something to River about subbing for Cody at the Tabby. How're the plans for that coming along?"

"His lesson plan is pretty solid. I can work with that. Maybe I'll be able to weave in some thoughts of my own too."

"Why don't you do that? It will be more fun than worrying about blood-stained gloves."

"You know? You're right. I should do something special for that class." I liked the idea already. I'd been pretty good at lesson planning when I'd taught there before. "I'll work on a new Salem history game plan."

There was that cartoon lightbulb shining over my head again!

"Game plan!" I said. "The game! What a great idea!"

"Game? You've kind of lost me there, babe. What game?"

"Wait a minute." I grabbed my handbag from the back of a kitchen chair. "I'll show you." I fished out the directions for the Clue mystery party game. "Brilliant," I declared. "If I do say so myself."

Chapter 26

Once I'd decided to do the Clue mystery party for Cody's history class, I could hardly think of anything else. Pete and I went to bed and watched River's show and even stayed awake through most of the movie—Jessica Biel in *The Tall Man*—a creepy thriller. But the characters from the Clue game kept intruding on my thoughts. Professor Plum, Colonel Mustard, Mrs. White, Mr. Green, Miss Scarlet, and Mrs. Peacock danced around in my head. I'd have to make up some kind of a mystery story—with a murder for my characters to solve.

In the morning I was up before Pete was—a rare happening. I'd even made coffee and fed the cat.

"Pete, do you think I should ask the students in Cody's class to play the parts of the characters in the Clue game?" I asked, "or should I get some of the people from the acting classes?"

He spread some of Aunt Ibby's homemade strawberry jam onto a toasted dinner roll and took a bite. "How many are in the class?" he asked.

"Three men and two women are still signed up. Two

dropped out when Cody left. Lucy Mahoney and another woman."

"So the three men could play Colonel Mustard, Mr. Green, and Professor Plum. Then if you could get one of the dropout women to come back, you'd have a full cast."

"Right. The Toy Trawler even sells plastic replicas of all the weapons and even some costume props for each character." My enthusiasm for the project grew. I cut a roll in half and popped it into the toaster. "It would have to be staged at the time of the regular class. But if I use the entire class to stage the murder, won't we need an audience?"

"I shouldn't even suggest it," Pete looked thoughtful. "But if you stage it in the student theater, since the school seems to be behind Cody, maybe you could ask for donations and give the money to his defense fund."

"Great idea," I said. "But we only have the weekend to pull this all together. No one would have time to memorize lines or anything like that."

Pete picked up the party directions I'd left on the table the night before. "It says here that they don't have a regular script. It's more or less a general story, and they give the clues that are on the playing cards. Exactly like in the game. Why don't you call Pennington and see what he thinks about it?"

"I will. And I'll contact all the students again. If they agree to do it, and if one of the dropouts will come back, we could walk through it at class Monday night and do the game on Tuesday." I reached for my phone. "If they don't want to do it, I'll use Cody's lesson plan." I called Mr. Pennington's private number. I could ask him to narrate the whole thing. He'd probably love that idea.

So I did call him, and he did love the idea. I gave him a brief rundown of the Clue mystery party rules. "I'm very familiar with the game myself," he said. "Played hours of it when I was at university. The dorm students here play it a lot when we have board game night. I'd be pleased to narrate."

"If we use the student theater," I worried, "how will we do the stage settings? The game has several different rooms."

"Easy," he said. "Rear-screen projection. We get slides of a library, a parlor, a bedroom, and so on and project them onto a large screen from behind. Piece of cake. As soon as you give the go-ahead, I'll get the Art Department going on signage and brochures."

That was a relief. Now if six of my students would agree to participate, we were good to go. If all seven agreed, I'd use the seventh to understudy everybody else. Pete and I cleaned the kitchen together, he left for work, and I dressed for the day in jeans, a white Irish knit turtleneck, and navy flats. Getting rid of the heels felt better all the time.

Rhonda had several destinations on the white board for Francine and me, but it looked as though I'd have an hour-long break at noon. Plenty of time to call the seven prospective game players. Things were beginning to fall into place neatly, I thought. I was actually humming a little off-key version of "Jesus, Take the Wheel," Pete's country music influence no doubt, as we headed across the parking lot to the mobile van.

"You're in a good mood," Francine said. "Pete spend the night?"

"Yes, he did," I said, happily. "But it's not only that. Things in general seem to be moving along a little better than they have been lately."

She put a finger to her lips. "*Shhh.* Don't jinx it. But catch me up on what's going on in your life. Haven't had a chance to talk to you since we did the Christopher's Castle video. How'd it go with Old Jim and the VW?"

"It went well," I said. "Got a good interview with a handsome dance teacher. Did you see it?"

"Sorry. No. They've kept me pretty busy trucking Scott around. He sure talks about himself a lot, doesn't he?"

"He does that," I agreed. "But he's a good reporter."

"So are you," she said. "Here we are." We'd arrived at our first assignment for the day. It was one of my favorite Salem events. The Chestnut Street car show. The beautiful historic street was lined with a fabulous array of antique and vintage automobiles, along with pre–WW II era bicycles. I'm such a car buff—some friends call me a gearhead—that I didn't even need Rhonda's prepared notes. My late husband Johnny's career as a NASCAR driver solidified my lifelong interest in all things automotive. With Francine filming, I strolled the street and chatted with proud owners about amazing auto finds and professional restorations. We did more than twenty minutes, and I was sorry when it was over. "I could have spent the rest of the day there," I told Francine as we put away our gear and prepared for the next stop on our list. The Farmers' Market at Old Town Hall.

"No chance of that," she said. "Here's a text from Rhonda. She says to eighty-six the farmers and head for the courthouse. Something's going on." We made a U-turn and picked up speed. "Shoot," she said. "I wish we had a siren and lights on this thing!"

There were already quite a few cars lining Federal Street outside the courthouse, but it looked as though we were the only media there so far. We both grabbed our press credentials on their dark blue lanyards hanging from the rearview mirror and hastily put them around our necks.

"Looks like the police have made another arrest in the Bond murder. Court will be in session in about ten minutes. Get on it!" Rhonda reported as Francine and I—me with a stick mic and Francine with a shoulder-mounted

Sony camcorder—ran toward whatever was going on beyond the tall gray columns in front of the place. I stood on
the top step and did a quick standup. "Lee Barrett reporting from the Essex County Courthouse in Salem," I said.
"There has been another arrest in the Bond murder. We'll
be bringing you the news as it unfolds."

We raced inside the building. All those official press
credentials didn't make a bit of difference. We had to get
wanded, pass through the metal detector, empty our
pockets—pretty much the same procedure as at the air-
port. Cameras weren't allowed inside the courtroom, but
Francine began filming as soon as we reached the open
double doors. I knew right away who'd been arrested.
Lucy Mahoney—even with her back to me she was impossible to miss. The judge had already begun the pro-
ceedings. The charge was "accessory after the fact of
murder." A uniformed police officer stood beside her. A
man I presumed was an attorney flanked her other side.
Lucy didn't speak. The attorney answered a few questions about Lucy not being a flight risk and requested that
she be released on personal recognizance. That was denied. He requested that bail be set. That was denied too.
"The court will enter a plea of 'not guilty' for you," the
judge said. "A trial date will be set. Council may ap-
proach the bench." The lawyer and judge conferred in
low tones. Lucy was fingerprinted right there in front of
everyone. I thought of how embarrassed she must be.
Even worse, I saw that she was handcuffed too. Then, escorted by the policeman and the lawyer, she left the room
via a side door. The bailiff called for the next plaintiff to
come forward.

Francine had recorded the whole procedure, but what
exactly had happened here? We looked at each other, left
the way we'd come in, and went outside. "Is there a back
door to this place?" I asked.

"Sure. Follow me."

We raced around the side of the building and positioned ourselves beside an exit Francine selected as the most likely. I texted Pete. "At courthouse. Why Lucy?"

Message came back. "Print on knife. Positive ID."

Cody and Lucy? Both of them?

There was no time for more questions. I needed to tell the viewers of WICH-TV what had happened as well as I could. "We're outside the Essex County Courthouse," I said, "where Lucy Mahoney, a student at Essex County University, has been arraigned here this morning. As you know, Professor Cody McGinnis, a teacher of history at the same university, was recently arrested for the murder of his fellow professor, Samuel Bond. McGinnis is free on bond while awaiting arraignment. Ms. Mahoney has apparently been arrested as an accessory after the fact of murder in the second degree."

Where are the twins? I wondered. *Doesn't she have anyone who can help her too?*

That last question was answered right away. Roger and Ray, as well as the lawyer and Cody McGinnis, appeared behind the door. Next came the officer and poor handcuffed Lucy. The lawyer pushed it open and all five left the building. "Here come Ms. Mahoney and an arresting officer," I said. "Also, we recognize Professor McGinnis, as well as his attorney and McGinnis's uncles Ray and Roger Temple, retired twin Boston police officers who host the popular talk show *Street Beat*."

Spotting me with my mic, the lawyer, who I now recognized as one of the team who'd accompanied Cody earlier—held up his hand. "Neither Ms. Mahoney nor Professor McGinnis will be answering any questions." He turned and put the hand in front of Lucy's face. I expected her to duck her head down, but she didn't. Shoulders back, chin up, she looked straight into Francine's camera, blue eyes defiant. "We've done nothing wrong. Neither of us. You'll see." The officer led her quietly but firmly toward a waiting police cruiser.

Cody reached out to her, but she'd already turned her back. The twins wordlessly positioned themselves on either side of their nephew. I thought of a hundred questions I needed to ask. Instead, I put down my mic and signaled to Francine to stop filming. "That'll be enough," I said, knowing full well that I'd allowed friendship to overcome whatever reporter's instinct I might possess, and watched the three men hurry downhill to a waiting limo.

Chapter 27

I called Pete while we were on our way back to the station. I barely said hello before I began firing questions—maybe the ones I should have aimed at Lucy and the lawyer.

"Is Lucy going to jail? Why 'accessory after the fact'?" I demanded. "And I thought the knife was clean?"

"Whoa. Slow down. 'After the fact' is because Bond was already dead from the blow to the head before he was stabbed. That's why he didn't bleed much from the wounds. And Forensics found a clear partial of Lucy Mahoney's right forefinger on the handle of the murder knife."

"This is weird, Pete," I said. "Captain White was dead when *he* was stabbed too. There are too many coincidences. Someone duplicated that murder on purpose."

"Looks that way," was the calm reply. "Things aren't shaping up well for McGinnis and the girlfriend, that's for sure. Have you talked to the twins today?"

"No. They were in a hurry to leave after poor Lucy's arraignment."

"*Poor* Lucy?" I could almost see that raised eyebrow.

"That kind of slipped out," I admitted. "But, yeah. I feel sorry for her. And Cody too. It was awful to watch."

"The evidence is stacking up against them, Lee. Try not to let your friendship with the twins interfere with your objectivity on this."

"I'm sure you're right," I said. "That's exactly what's happening, though, and I don't know how to stop it."

"I understand," he said. "Sometimes I have to fight it too."

Francine pulled the mobile unit into the parking lot. "Gotta go," I said. "We're at the station. Talk to you later."

"Stay strong," he said.

I helped Francine secure our gear, anticipating that we'd be on the road again very shortly. She'd already sent ahead the footage from both the car show and the courthouse. I was sure Marty probably had it all ready to roll for the next newscast, and hoped against hope that nobody would question my decision to stop recording when I did.

No such luck. Even the ever-faithful Marty wanted to know why I hadn't pursued Lucy, the lawyer, and the others. "Scotty would have been yelling questions at them all the way to their car," she said. "Cat get your tongue?"

I had no answer for her question—at least not one I could articulate at that moment. I made a fast decision to brazen it out. "I thought the comment from Lucy Mahoney was dramatic enough for a strong close."

Surprisingly, it seemed to work, at least for Marty. She bobbed her head. "It is dramatic. Might have been a good call after all, Moon. We'll see what Doan thinks soon enough. It'll be the lead for the noon news. By the way, I've managed to figure out a couple of words in that photo of a book."

I checked my watch. Noon was only twenty minutes away. I had mixed emotions. I don't get the lead story all that often, so that pleased me. On the other hand, what if

I could have—should have—done a better job with it?
And I definitely wanted to know what Marty had learned
from that photo.

"Want to go upstairs and watch it with Rhonda?"
Francine suggested. "We could spend our lunch break here
and send out for pizza."

"Sure. Why not?" *Everything goes better with pizza.*
"You guys order it and I'll be up in a minute."

Marty pulled the photo from the envelope. She'd high-
lighted a couple of places. "See this up in the corner? It
says *versity Pr.* I'd say the publisher is one of the university presses. And see here? Between his fingers? It says
id-Cent. Could be 'Mid-Century.' There were lots of new
dances in the fifties. Maybe he was looking that up. Who
knows? Anyway, I'd guess it's one of those academic
journals that professors like to get published in. Probably
a history one. Why don't you ask him?"

"Thanks, Marty. I think I will." *Or not.*

I opened the green metal door and went back upstairs.
Rhonda and Francine had already lined up three of the
chrome-and-turquoise chairs facing the big screen behind
Rhonda's desk, and the Pizza Pirate had delivered a large
combination pizza and two liters of Pepsi. We moved a
purple artificial iris arrangement out of the way, parked
the feast in front of us on a glass-topped chrome end
table, sat back, and waited for Phil Archer to read the
intro to the news.

My story was indeed the lead. Phil gave a brief introduction, and there I was standing on the courthouse steps.

"You looked good," Rhonda said, pouring Pepsi into
paper cups. "The flat shoes are fine. I wouldn't worry
about wearing heels all the time if you don't want to."

"With the running around we did today, she would
have broken her neck in heels." Francine took a bite of
pizza. "Seriously."

"*Shhh.*" I shushed them both and leaned closer to the

TV. "I want to hear it all." I sipped my Pepsi, picked up a slice of pizza, and concentrated on the screen. Rhonda was right. The flats looked perfectly presentable. Francine's camerawork was spot on—maybe even better than usual. She'd let the camera linger for a few seconds on some of the details of the old building—the graceful ionic pillars and the massive iron lampposts. The boring security ritual had been omitted, but she'd grabbed the shot through the doorway of the bailiff with the traditional call to order and the judge approaching the bench. Lucy, hands cuffed behind her back, looked very small between a policeman and the tall lawyer while the charge was read.

I was so engrossed in watching every detail that several minutes passed before I realized that Bruce Doan had joined us. He stood behind my chair, not speaking until the segment ended and Wanda the Weather Girl appeared on screen. He reached for a slice of pizza.

"Mind if I have a slice?"

Rhonda handed him a paper plate. "What did you think?" she asked. "Good job, huh?"

He didn't answer immediately. I put my halfway-eaten slice on my plate, almost holding my breath.

"I'm surprised about the girl being arrested," he said, pulling up a chair. "The front of the courthouse intro looked good, Ms. Barrett. Of course, you didn't have to say much, did you? I mean the action—the judge—the cop with the handcuffs—that said it all. Damn good job, Francine. Considering you didn't have a sound man, you did fine capturing the conversation. All in all it was a good segment. One thing though, Ms. Barrett . . ."

Uh-oh. Here it comes.

I gritted my teeth and waited to be chastised for letting all of the principals simply walk away without pursuing them with questions. He picked up his empty paper plate and tossed it into Rhonda's wastebasket. "I don't appreci-

ate your giving a big on-air plug to a competitor." He
shook his head. "*Street Beat*. I can't believe you did that."

He turned and faced Francine. "Great camerawork,
Francine. Ending with the girl like you did, nice dramatic
touch. Liked it." He disappeared into his office.

Feeling as though I'd dodged a bullet on that one, I
high-fived Francine, finished my slice of pizza, and helped
myself to another.

Rhonda tossed her plate away and returned her chair to
its regular position beside the window. "Looks like it's
going to be a pretty afternoon for some outdoor work,"
she said. "You two ready to do the farmers' market?"

My mouth was full, so I nodded. Francine agreed that
the farmers' market would be fine, and that she'd be eating vegetables for a while to make up for the pizza.

"Me too," I mumbled, wiping crumbs from my lap and
standing. Francine returned the flower arrangement to its
original spot while I got rid of the remaining paper plates,
pizza box, and plastic cups. By one-fifteen we were on the
road again, heading to Old Town Hall. "After we finish the
shoot, let's take a quick detour past the Toy Trawler," I
said. "I want to get those costumes and weapon props he
showed us."

"You're going to do the Murder party?"

"For that Salem history class I've inherited," I told her.
"And I've got less than a week to pull it all together."

"I went to one of those parties once. I was Miss Scarlet. Wore a great red dress. I still have it."

"I might have to bring you in to play her again," I said.
"I don't know whether the students will be the characters
or not. Up to them. If they don't want to do it, maybe I'll
get some actors from the Theater Arts Department at the
Tabby."

"You should use your aunt and her girlfriends," Francine
suggested. "Then find three guys." Long pause. "Maybe the

hot professor and the dance teacher would do it. Then you only need one more."

I had to smile at the idea. "It would make for an interesting production," I agreed, "but one that's unlikely to happen."

We searched around for a parking space for a while. Landed a good one almost next door to the town hall. This market is always full of color, and this day was particularly pretty. Flowers, fruits, and vegetables—brilliant greens, yellows, reds, oranges, blues, and purples—were bright against the mellow red and pink bricks of the building and street paving, all below a cloudless blue sky. Rhonda's prep notes gave me a tiny bit of history on Old Town Hall. Most everybody in Salem knows about it, but maybe the kids don't, so we usually lead with that on market days, then do a walk-through and talk to the vendors. It's not all about fruit and vegetables. T-shirts, jewelry, books, assorted tchotchkes, and the usual witch-related items are there too.

Francine and I had strolled onto the busy brick concourse, when I heard a male voice. "Hi there, Ms. Barrett! Francine! Over here."

It was our new friend, Captain Billy, decked in his full captain's regalia, waving to us from behind a red plastic dory decorated with nautical flags and a prominent Toy Trawler sign. "Glad to see you ladies again so soon," Captain Billy said. "That TV spot you did on me and the store brought in plenty of business. I want to thank you. Hey, Ms. Barrett, have you given any thought to doing that Clue party we talked about? I have all the makin's of a good time right here!" He gestured toward a stack of Clue games and plastic bins filled with the make-believe weapons.

"What a happy coincidence," I said. "I've been talking about you." *And maybe I'm starting to believe in coincidences.*

"Nothing bad, I hope." He watched Francine as she panned across the colorful merchandise.

"All good," I assured him. "I'm planning to do a Clue party after all. I'll need a game and a set of those weapons and a few of the brochures about how to run a party." I studied the display. "Did you say you have some costume components?"

"Back at the store I do. Sometimes I come here to sell some of my overstock. I don't have a lot of the costume stuff left." He'd already begun to fill a handled shopping bag with game, weapons, and brochures. "Shall I call the store and put a complete set aside for you?"

"That'd be great." I handed him a credit card. "So glad we ran into you."

"Me too," he said. "Say, by the way, right after that TV spot ran a fellow came into the store asking questions about you."

"Questions? What kind of questions?"

"Like, you seemed to be especially interested in the murder—you know—the new one, not the old one. He'd like to discuss it with you. And did I happen to know where you live. That one bothered me."

"Bothers me too," I said. "What did you tell him? Did you get his name?"

"No name. He didn't buy anything. I told him you seemed most interested in the giant game pieces and that I never share information about my customers."

"Thanks. That's good. What did this guy look like?"

He frowned. "Youngish. Average height. Average weight. He wore sunglasses and a ball cap. Nothing special about him."

"What kind of ball cap?"

He closed his eyes for a few seconds. "Red Sox, I think."

Chapter 28

Francine tugged at my elbow. "The light's so pretty right now. Want to do a walk-through starting with the local honey display over there?"

"Okay." I put my credit card back into my wallet, told Captain Billy I'd pick up my purchases on our way out, and followed Francine. I talked with vendors, admired produce and pottery, sunflowers and sushi. I discovered Hawaiian sweet potatoes and New Hampshire clover honey. We spent half an hour or so and were both pleased with the result. I told Captain Billy I'd stop at the Toy Trawler soon to buy the costumes, then picked up my Clue collection and packed it into the van along with mic and camera.

"You're kind of quiet," Francine remarked as we neared the station. "You haven't said two words since we left the market. Anything wrong?"

I told her what Captain Billy had said about the guy who'd asked questions about me. "Probably it's another fan who thinks he's in love with you," she said. "Good thing he didn't get your address."

"That wasn't the question that bothered me most," I

admitted. "Why would anyone care about my interest—
or lack of it—in the Samuel Bond murder?"

"I don't know," she said, "it's probably nothing, but if
I were you, I'd tell Pete about it."

"Don't worry. I will. Today."

When we unloaded the van, I carried my Clue party
purchases over to the Vette, along with the two Hawaiian
sweet potatoes and the jar of New Hampshire white
clover honey I'd been unable to resist. I opened the trunk
and put the game and the toy weapons in, pausing for a moment to examine the plastic gun and the neatly tied noose. I
picked up the make-believe lead pipe—smooth and light in
my hand—and tried to imagine Cody McGinnis bringing
the real-life version down onto a sleeping man's head. I bal-
anced the plastic knife in one hand and thought of young
Lucy repeatedly plunging a real one into a dead man's
chest. Couldn't do it. I couldn't picture anyone else doing
it either, so maybe my objectivity was still intact. I closed
the trunk and walked slowly back to the WICH-TV building.

I spent a half hour in the dataport again, contacting the
Salem history students I'd be meeting soon. Since all of
them had day jobs, I knew I'd be leaving voice or text
messages but wanted to get their input on my Clue mystery party idea. Since Lucy's arrest, the student pool was
down to six members—Harrison, Conrad, Carl, Kate,
Penny, and the other student who'd dropped out when
Cody left, Shirley. I asked each one to contact me ASAP,
and promised I'd see them on Monday.

If even one didn't choose to participate, my all-classmate
cast idea would have to be scrapped. I could try asking the
theater arts classes to do it, but they were usually pretty busy
preparing for their own productions. Maybe Francine's
suggestion had some merit. The Angels in the three female roles were a distinct possibility, but we'd need to
recruit three men. Alan was practically a sure thing, I fig-

ured, with his fondness for being noticed. Eddie would be good, but if he had a dance class on Tuesday evening, he wouldn't be available. Another man from the dance class maybe?

I told myself to stop worrying. If we couldn't pull the Clue mystery party together, I'd go with Cody's original lesson plan. No problem. Besides, I knew the game and props I'd already bought wouldn't go to waste. Planning a party at Aunt Ibby's house would be a sure thing.

Next I called to check in with Rupert Pennington. I told him I'd bought basic supplies for the party. "I don't know whether the class members will want to be the players," I told him, "but I have a couple of alternative ideas. I'd like to hear your input."

"I'm excited about the idea of using the student theater for the production." I heard the enthusiasm in his voice. "I've asked one of our projectionists about the rear-screen idea, and he says it'll be no problem. I've taken the liberty of preparing a preliminary script for the narration. It basically sets up the premise, a dinner party at a stately mansion in a remote location. I'll introduce the invited guests with a little backstory on each one. We'll distribute some flyers around the school as soon as your plans are firm. I think many of the day students will come back for it, and the dorm students are always looking for something to do in the evening. This is going to be such fun no matter who plays the parts!"

I felt my fake smile coming back. "I'm sure it will be. Of course I hope it'll be the class members. If not, I'm thinking of asking Aunt Ibby and the Angels to play the female roles. For the men, I'd thought about Professor Armstrong and Eddie Symonds for two. Don't know about the third. If you weren't narrating, you'd be a fine Colonel Mustard."

"Thank you, my dear. Shall I ask the two gentlemen you mentioned if they'd consider such a venture? I know them both quite well. By the way, I believe you have an admirer in Professor Armstrong. He wants to send you flowers as an apology. He said he thinks he might have offended you recently and asked for your home address. I told him I'd have to ask your permission."

"He can send them to the station if he wants to," I said, "but there's no need for him to apologize."

That's two requests for my address. I'll definitely tell Pete about both. And soon!

I told Mr. Pennington I'd stay in touch, thanked him for his offer to speak to Alan and Eddie, closed the data-port door, and returned the key to Rhonda, feeling sort of confident that, one way or another, Tuesday evening's class would be all right. I was also absolutely confident that I'd be extremely happy when Tuesday evening's class was over.

I texted Pete. *Two men asked others for my address. Worry?*

It didn't take long to get a phone call. "Heck yes, I'm worried. Who? What men? Who'd they ask? Did they get it? I hope not. Hell, Lee, I wish you'd stop poking around in murder."

I kept my voice steady. "Neither one got it. Alan Armstrong asked Mr. Pennington and a stranger asked Captain Billy."

"It's easy enough to get anybody's address these days. Why did Armstrong want it?"

"Wants to send me flowers. It's an apology I guess for being such a jerk."

"Uh-huh. And the other guy?"

"That's the one I'm sort of concerned about. He'd seen the interview I did with Captain Billy and thought I seemed to be especially interested in the Bond murder. He wants to 'discuss it' with me and asked if Billy knew where I live. And Pete, he was wearing a Sox cap."

"I'll check with Captain Billy. It's the new toy store that looks like a ship?"

"A trawler," I corrected.

"Whatever. Anyway, he probably has cameras all over the place. Maybe we can get a look at the guy. Find out what he's all about. The ball cap is showing up too often."

I had to smile at that. "Pete, remember when we were at Greene's Tavern the other night? Darn near every person in the place wore a Sox cap. Except me."

"You're right. I'm overreacting. But where you're involved, it's hard for me to stay impartial. Please be careful." He sighed—loudly enough for it to carry on the phone and sounding surprisingly like my Aunt Ibby's own exasperated sigh.

"You worry about me too much," I said. "I promise I'll be extra careful. And I'll avoid all men wearing ball caps."

"Good. And for God's sake, Lee. Tell your aunt to keep that damned back door locked!"

"I will," I promised. "Now I need to get back to work on my Clue party."

"How's that coming along?"

"Well, I've bought a new game board, ordered costumes, and I have a set of creepy fake weapons. All I'm missing is a cast of characters. Say! How would you . . . ?"

"Don't even think about it! Talk to you later. Bye."

Back at the reception desk I checked Rhonda's white board. Nothing there in purple marker. Scott and Old Jim in the VW had been sent to cover a high school soccer match, and Francine was downstairs helping Marty with the farmers' market edits.

"Doan would like to see you in his office," Rhonda said. "You can go right on in."

A summons to the boss's office? Now what?

I approached the door marked "Station Manager" and gave a tentative knock.

"Come in, it's open." His voice sounded gruff.

That doesn't mean anything, I told myself. *He almost always sounds that way.*

"It's open," he repeated in the same tone of voice. I turned the knob and stepped inside.

"You wanted to see me, sir?"

"Yes, indeed, Ms. Barrett. Have a seat, please." He gestured to a purple suede upholstered club chair facing his desk. I sat.

"It's about your moonlighting job over at the Tabby."

Moonlighting?

"Hardly moonlighting, sir," I protested. "Not even a job. The director, Mr. Pennington, has asked me to fill in for a couple of evening classes."

"I know. You're filling in for the Bond murderer."

"Suspect, sir. Cody McGinnis is a suspect."

"Right. Suspect. How are you doing with my idea about getting a camera in there?"

Lightbulb moment!

"Even better, sir. Remember the segment about the Toy Trawler? Captain Billy is ready and willing to sponsor a live Clue party—and it happens that I'm planning one for my class at the Tabby next Tuesday evening. We can get a camera into the school and sell the time to Captain Billy."

"Now you're talkin'!" His tone had changed from gruff to jovial. "I'll make a good reporter out of you yet! I'll have Rhonda draw up a contract for the Toy Trawler. You firm up the details, and let's get moving on this. Pronto."

Pete and Old Jim and Francine think I'm pretty good now.

"Thanks," I said. "I'll get right on it."

Sure. All I need to do now is assemble a cast and get a production onstage by next Tuesday. Piece of cake.

By the time I'd closed the office door and reached Rhonda's desk, she was already typing up a contract. Even though getting all this pulled together in a hurry was intimidating—even a little scary—I was excited by the prospect, excited enough to call Aunt Ibby and ask her to put the Angels on alert for possible onstage appearances within a few days, to call Mr. Pennington to get the slides ready for rear-screen projection, and to leave a message for Captain Billy that a TV broadcast of the Clue party was a go.

Chapter 29

The first person to respond to my barrage of Clue party calls and messages was Aunt Ibby. "The Angels are in," she said. "We're all willing to do it. Louisa was a little reticent, but if she can be Mrs. White, she'll agree, and of course Betsy wants to be Miss Scarlet. I don't mind being Mrs. Peacock. We're working on our costumes already. Rupert is excited about it too. He's delighted that you want him for narrator."

The next call was from Conrad, who said he was "absolutely terrified" at the idea of appearing onstage ever, followed rapidly by Shirley, who said okay, she'd do it only if Penny would too. The next call revealed that Penny would but now Shirley couldn't. Carl and Kate were reluctant, but said they'd do it if I couldn't find anyone else. By then it was obvious that the all-class-as-actors idea was kaput, even though Harrison called and said he'd absolutely love to do it and had once thrown a Clue party himself.

So with the addition of Harrison I had my three females and one male lined up. If Mr. Pennington had convinced Professor Dreamy and Eddie to take the remaining two parts, we'd be good to go. Things were definitely looking up on the Clue party front.

I headed for home in a pretty good frame of mind. I decided I'd pick up some nice pork chops and a bag of chopped salad at Shaw's. Tonight I could grill the chops, bake my Hawaiian potatoes, and invite Pete for dinner. Maybe I'd get some english muffins too and we could try out the clover honey with breakfast.

I did my shopping and made the ten-items-or-less line, even with the addition of two packages of fancy sardine-flavored snacks for O'Ryan and a brand-new flavor of Ben & Jerry's for me. I also noted the fact that at least a dozen men in the store wore Red Sox caps.

O'Ryan met me at the garage door. Unusual. He usually waits for me on the back steps. Must be the kitty snacks in my grocery bag, I decided. I tapped on Aunt Ibby's door as I passed through the back hall, intending to drop off one of the fishy treats. O'Ryan enjoys them for happy hour. "It's me, Aunt Ibby," I called, fully expecting the "Come on in. It's open" reply.

"Wait a minute." I heard the click-click signaling that she'd remembered to lock the door. Amazing!

"You remembered to lock it!" I marveled, putting the bag on the table. "Pete will be proud of you. I invited him to dinner. Pork chops. I'll tell him you took his suggestion seriously."

"He called and reminded me." She struck a hands-on-the-hips pose I remembered from childhood. It usually meant I was in trouble. "What's this about strange men trying to get your address? Pete is upset about it and so am I. Weren't you going to tell me?"

"Pete called you?"

"He said it was a general reminder to keep my doors locked. You know. Because there *could* still be a murderer loose in Salem." She gave a dismissive flap on one hand. "I knew it was more than that. Had to pry it out of

him—about the men asking where you live. Have you
any idea who they are?"

"Well, one of them is Alan Armstrong. He wants to
send me flowers because he thinks he offended me."

"Did he offend you?"

"Yes. Kind of."

"Hmm. Might be a legitimate reason. Might not. And
the other one?"

"Haven't figured that one out. Francine thinks it's a
fan. He told Captain Billy he'd seen me on TV."

"Pete sounded worried."

"I am too, a little bit," I admitted. "The man was wearing a Red Sox hat."

"Everybody wears a Red Sox hat," she said. "Oh, I
see. You're thinking of the man outside Samuel Bond's
house the night he was murdered."

"Yes. He wanted to know if I seemed especially interested in Bond's murder."

"What did Captain Billy tell him?"

"The truth," I said. "That I was more interested in the
giant game pieces."

"I see. Let's hope Francine is right. He's only a fan."

"Aunt Ibby?"

"Yes."

"How did you pry the information out of Pete? I never
can do that."

"Dear child, I'm a reference librarian. I have a master's degree in prying." She clapped her hands. "Now
scoot upstairs and put your groceries away, then come
right back down. It's almost happy hour. O'Ryan gets impatient if I'm late with his treats."

I did as I was told, leaving through the front hall instead of the back staircase so that she wouldn't have to
unlock her kitchen door again. O'Ryan trotted along,
close beside me. Once on the third floor, balancing the
grocery bag with one arm, I pushed open *my* kitchen door

and started inside. The cat stopped short on the doorsill. "Come on, silly cat," I prompted. "It's almost happy hour." He didn't budge, but sat there, switching his tail, doing that cat-stare thing they all do.

"Move it!" I commanded. "My ice cream will melt."

Without breaking eye contact, he sprawled out full length, effectively blocking the entire doorway. I frowned. "You want me to leave it open?"

He did the equivalent of a cat eye-roll and voiced an exasperated sounding "Meh!"

"I don't get it," I said, "but stay there if you want to. I have to put these groceries away." I hummed a little of "I Hope You Dance," sneaking peeks at him from behind the freezer door. After a moment, he changed positions. With a soft *mmrrrow,* hind feet still firmly planted on the sill, he stretched upward against the frame until his right paw touched the latch.

"It wasn't locked!" I said. "My door to the front hall wasn't locked!"

O'Ryan immediately strolled into the room, hopped up onto the chair beside the window, muttering a cat-comment that sounded remarkably like "duh," and proceeded to groom his whiskers.

"O'Ryan, you are so darned smart!" I crossed the room, picked him up, and hugged him. If he was surprised, he didn't show it. He gave me a fast lick on the chin and squirmed to get down. He was right, of course. If Aunt Ibby left her downstairs door unlocked, and I left my upstairs door unlocked, what was there to stop some unknown someone from walking right into my apartment? As Councilor Mercer had pointed out, it was entirely possible that there was still a killer loose in Salem. Properly cat-chastised, I closed and locked the door and put the keys in my pocket.

With the ingredients of a good dinner refrigerating, I texted Pete, feeling sure he'd accept my invitation, and smarty cat and I headed down the front stairs to happy hour.

Aunt Ibby had been doing some extra research at the library on the long-ago Captain White murder and had checked out several books on the subject for me. She'd spread them out on the table next to the wineglasses and the snack tray. "Several of these had been checked out recently," she said. "There's even a waiting list for a couple of others. The recent murder has apparently sparked a good deal of interest in the eighteen-thirty one."

"I can see why," I said. "Even the Boston newspapers and TV stations are covering it. I heard that a team from the History channel is in town too."

She made the familiar "tsk-tsk" sound. "Not the nicest publicity in the world for our lovely city, is it? As if there wasn't already enough hype about the unfortunate witchcraft delusion."

O'Ryan left his treats long enough to investigate the library books. He walked around the display, tapping each one lightly with a paw, then returned to his red bowl. It gave me an idea. "Aunt Ibby, did all of these books get popular after the Bond murder? Or were some attracting attention before that?"

"Professor McGinnis's class members borrowed a good many of them. Professor Armstrong checked out a few too. Cody McGinnis has probably read them all, along with nearly every academic history publication in the stacks," she said. "Edwin Symonds reads academic papers too but not so much focused on Salem. I've brought a few of the academic ones, a random selection. We have plenty of them. Other than that, I hadn't noticed. But I can check the borrowing histories easily enough." She gathered the books together and pushed the pile into the center of the table.

"Good. I'm not sure what it might prove, if anything, but I'd like to know who's been reading what lately."

She raised her glass of Chablis. "To all readers everywhere, may their tribe increase."

"To readers," I said, and we touched glasses. O'Ryan looked up from his bowl and gave a gentle mew. "Especially readers of books about cats," I added.

"Is it my imagination, or is O'Ryan being particularly attentive to you recently?" she asked. "He was doing his nervous pacing thing this afternoon until he heard your car in the driveway, then he absolutely bolted through his cat door."

"He came all the way out to the garage to meet me," I recalled. "I thought it was because he smelled those fishy treats."

"He didn't try to race you upstairs either," she said. "He stayed right beside you. I think he's worried about you."

I told her how he'd reminded me to lock my kitchen door. "He was quite insistent about it. Wouldn't come all the way into the apartment at all until I got the message."

"I'm trying to be careful," she said. "It must be important if both Pete *and* O'Ryan are concerned about us. Here. Eat something. If Pete's coming over, your dinner will probably be late." She passed the vintage painted tole tray across the table, carefully avoiding the books. I selected a couple of wheat crackers with neat squares of extra-sharp cheddar and a stalk of cream-cheese-and-olive-stuffed celery.

"I love the way you make everything so pretty for happy hour," I said, "even though it's usually only you and me and O'Ryan here to appreciate it."

"Not always," she reminded me. "Everybody knows O'Ryan and I celebrate at about the same time every evening. Occasionally a friend or two drop in. I like to be prepared."

"All the more reason to lock the doors, I suppose," I said, "if you don't know exactly who might drop in."

"Never thought about it that way," she said. "Not a happy thought."

O'Ryan looked up from his dish and ran toward the kitchen door. My aunt and I each jumped a little at the sound of knocking. "Hello?" she called. "Who is it, please?"

"It's me, Ms. Russell" came a masculine voice. "Eddie Symonds. We met some time ago at a bookmobile fundraiser. You invited me to drop by some evening for your regular happy hour. Remember?"

Chapter 30

"**D**id you really?" I whispered.

"Maybe," she whispered back. "I mean, I guess so. He's quite attractive, you know. I didn't expect he'd actually take me up on it."

"Well, you'd better let him in," I said, remembering Pete's comment that Eddie enjoyed the company of wealthy older women. I folded my arms. "I'll stay right here to chaperone."

She stood, smoothed her dress, and patted her hair. "Coming," she cooed, unlocked the kitchen door, and welcomed the "quite attractive" dance teacher. "What a pleasant surprise, Mr. Symonds. I'm so pleased that you could join us." She waved in my direction. "I believe you know my niece, Maralee Barrett?"

He stepped into the room. "Please call me Eddie," he said, "and yes, Ms. Barrett and I have met. How do you do, Lee. I had no idea you two were related, although now I see a definite family resemblance." He grinned. "Two gorgeous redheads."

My aunt blushed. I stifled a rude snort. "Can I get you

a glass of wine, Eddie?" I asked. "That's what happy hour's all about."

"Thank you, yes," he said, choosing the chair next to Aunt Ibby, and helping himself to crackers and cheese. "Lee, I take it you're a regular at Ms. Russell's happy hour celebrations?"

"Pretty much," I said.

"Maralee lives right upstairs," she announced with pride. "She has her own apartment."

I heard a soft *mrroow,* from under the table as O'Ryan sat on my foot. He couldn't get much closer to me than that. Maybe he was truly worried about me. "Red or white?" I asked.

"Whatever you're having will be fine," Eddie declared. "It's good to be with family. My folks are still in Iowa, and I miss them a lot. My mom still teaches ballroom dancing. My dad's retired from the aerospace program out there. I sure miss them."

"I'm sure they miss you too," my aunt said, "and that they're very proud of your accomplishments both in your dancing and your writing."

"And possibly a bit of playacting," I added with fingers crossed, "if Mr. Pennington has convinced you to be part of our upcoming Clue game party. Will you do it?" I poured a hefty amount of Chablis into his glass.

"Will I! Would a ham like me turn down an onstage appearance? I guess I'm going to be Mr. Green."

"I'm so pleased," I told him. "We had such a short time to pull this together, I appreciate your help."

"Happy to do it. I'm trying to figure out how to work a few dance moves into the story. Rupert tells me it's possible, Ms. Russell, that you'll be part of the cast too?"

Is that the reason for this surprise visit?

"I will," Aunt Ibby said, "as will Mrs. Abney-Babcock and our friend Betsy Leavitt. It sounds like such fun!"

Sounds to me like a feast for a man who likes wealthy older women.

He beamed. "I'm sure it will be. It's my hope that Cody will be cleared in time to join us. I'm quite sure the police will figure out soon that he couldn't have killed Professor Bond."

"You seem quite confident about that," my aunt said.

"I am." He swirled the wine around in his glass, then took a swallow. "*Mmm.* This is good. Cody and Lucy both have perfect alibis. I don't understand why either of them is being held."

"Alibis?" By this time O'Ryan had stretched out so that he covered both of my feet.

"Sure. They were together at a play in Boston that night."

It was the first time I'd heard a word about that. "A play? Are you quite sure?"

"Positive," he said. "What kind of cheese did you put in the celery?"

"Cream cheese and olive," my aunt said. "What play?"

"Olives. Interesting. Hmmm. It's delicious. *Shear Madness* at the Charles Playhouse. They loved it. Ever seen it?"

"Of course. Everybody has seen it."

"They hadn't." He took another bite of celery.

This was puzzling. If while Sam Bond was being murdered Cody and Lucy had been in Boston at a theater where plenty of people could see them, where they would have undoubtedly been caught on multiple security cameras, why were they still the prime suspects? I could tell that Aunt Ibby was puzzled too. I wanted to ask more questions, but waited to see what the professional information-prying librarian would do with it.

Oddly enough, she changed the subject. "Mr. Symonds," she began.

"Eddie," he interrupted.

"Eddie." She favored him with a smile full of sweetness and light. "Tell us some more about the book the professors wrote."

"The book?" He frowned. "Oh, the *how-to*? Nothing much to say. It's kind of basic." He took what could only be called a gulp of his wine. "It might be helpful to students." Sly smile. "And to some teachers too." He glanced at the kitchen clock. "I understand that my friend Mrs. Abney-Babcock sometimes joins you at around this time."

"She does," my aunt said. "But she's busy with some of her grandchildren tonight. I understand you two met on an Alaska cruise. That must have been a wonderful adventure."

"That's the cruise Cody and Lucy were on," I said. "Louisa shared lots of pictures with us."

"And Professor Armstrong was there too." Aunt Ibby refilled his glass. "Here, Eddie, try one of the stuffed figs."

"No thanks, Ms. Russell," he said, looking at the clock again, this time pointedly. "I have a dinner date pretty soon." He refused the stuffed fig, but tossed back the wine in a hurry.

"I'm glad you stopped by, Eddie," my aunt said. "Don't hesitate to come again."

"Thank you, Ibby. May I call you Ibby?" He stood.

"Of course you may." She stood too, and unlocked the door.

"Nice to see you again, Lee."

I realized that with the cat on my feet, I *couldn't* stand (at least not without rudely dislodging O'Ryan and possibly hurting his feelings). "Nice to see you too, Eddie. My friend River and I are thinking of joining one of your classes."

"I'll look forward to that," he said as my aunt closed the door behind him and relocked it.

O'Ryan immediately abandoned his foot-warming position and left the room via the cat door. "He's watching to be sure that man leaves," my aunt said. "I wonder what Eddie is up to. Mostly I wonder why he suddenly decided to drop in here."

"I'm wondering the same thing, and I'm wondering on several levels."

"Of course, it's possible that he's telling the truth. I guess I *did* tell him about happy hour, and I probably *did* say he was welcome to drop in."

"Uh-huh. But what if *he* was one of the men who wanted my home address? Average height, average weight, sunglasses, and a ball cap. Could be almost anyone."

She put on her wise old owl look. "But your address would have taken him to the Winter Street side of the house. He came to the back door, on the Oliver Street side. How did he happen to know about that?"

"We always leave that door unlocked during the day, don't we?" I worried. "Maybe we should keep that one locked all the time too."

"This is becoming so inconvenient," she said. "What ever happened to the good old days when we used to leave *all* the doors unlocked *all* the time?"

"I'm afraid those days are gone forever," I said. "But, back to Eddie. Pete told me that he often dates older women. Women with money."

"I thought of that too. He was interested in Louisa, and she's sure it was because of her wealth." She refilled both of our glasses. "I'm certainly not in Louisa's league, moneywise."

"You're very attractive. And single. Eddie's not the only man showing an interest in you."

She looked thoughtful. "True," she said, not exactly modestly. "Now what about his story about Cody and Lucy being at a play in Boston while Samuel was being murdered. Has Pete said anything about it?"

"No, and as far as I know, neither have the twins."

"Eddie seems so sure about it. He said he was positive. Will you ask Pete about it?"

"Sure. If he comes for dinner, I'll tell him tonight," I promised. "I'll tell him about Eddie knowing his way to our back door too."

"Good idea," she said, "and when Ray calls, I'll see what he has to say about it."

"Ray is calling you now?"

"Yes, every night since they've been here." *She's blushing. So cute.* "But this time it's to confirm a nine o'clock brainstorming meeting tomorrow morning. The Angels are coming over too. Roger and Ray seem to find us helpful."

"Especially Ray," I teased.

She blushed again and wished me a firm good night.

Chapter 31

I was still smiling when I climbed the front stairs. I got a kick out of Aunt Ibby's casual mention of an expected phone call from Ray Temple, and I'd certainly be interested in what the twins might have to say about their nephew and Lucy attending a play on the night of the murder. Also, as attractive as my aunt apparently is to gentlemen, I'd like to know what the twins have to say about the reason for Eddie Symonds's happy hour back-door visit, and I still intended to check further into Eddie's reading habits. I'd surely try to drop in on the next morning's meeting. I might learn the answers to several questions.

With O'Ryan still close beside me, I unlocked the door to my kitchen. He didn't even attempt to use his cat door, but waited for me to go inside. Then he sat on one of the tall stools beside the counter, watching me while I double-checked the contents of the refrigerator. Satisfied that dinner prep could be achieved fairly easily, I reached over and patted his fuzzy head. "Are you worried about me, big boy?" I whispered. "That's okay. I'm a little bit worried about me too, and I don't even know exactly why."

He licked my chin, then escorted me down the hall to
the bathroom. Gentleman that he is, he didn't attempt to
follow me inside, but sat, upright and alert, in front of the
door. I emerged later, shampooed, showered, wearing
white satin pj's with embroidered red roses on the collar
and breast pocket. Pete is accustomed to the fact that I
can't wait to get out of work clothes and into pajamas
practically as soon as I get home. I save the prettiest ones
for the nights when I expect his company. O'Ryan was
still at his self-appointed post, ready to accompany me
back to the kitchen. I'd left my phone on the table and
missed a text from Pete.

"Be there in an hour. Bringing vanilla in case I don't
like the new B & J."

I put the sweet potatoes into the oven, hit the timer for
one hour, put the George Foreman Grill on the counter,
and sat in the Lucite chair closest to O'Ryan's favorite
window. He took his usual spot on the windowsill where
he watches for birds in the daytime and peers at whatever
might be going on out there at night. This time he alternated between looking outside and watching me. It was
disconcerting.

"Come on, O'Ryan," I said. "Let's play a quick game
of Clue. It's been years since I've even looked at it, and
I'm pretty sure you've never played it." I opened the box.
"Here's the deck of cards. See?" I spread them out, showing pictures of the six suspects, nine rooms of the house,
and six weapons. I picked up the miniature weapons.
"Look at these. They are instruments of death." I lay the
tiny rope, lead pipe, knife, wrench, candlestick, and gun
above the cards. "These little playing pieces represent the
suspects—the people whose pictures are on the cards.
See?" One at a time, I named the pieces according to their
color. "Colonel Mustard," I said, putting the yellow piece
next to the appropriate card. I followed with the red piece
for Miss Scarlet, the white one for Mrs. White, blue for

Mrs. Peacock, purple for Professor Plum, and green for Mr. Green. The cat nodded and tapped the purple piece with a dainty paw.

"So, you like Professor Plum," I said. "Now, here are the rooms. It's a big house, like ours. Lots of rooms." I pulled the appropriate cards from the deck and lay them in front of him one at a time. "Kitchen. Study. Hall, Dining room. Lounge. Library. Conservatory, Billiard room, Ballroom." He examined each one with seeming interest, but no paw tap, still turning nervously toward the window from time to time. I'd finished my Clue game explanation and decided to make it easier on his neck swiveling by turning my chair around. That way we could watch the backyard together, the cat would know exactly what I was doing, and we'd see Pete when he arrived.

There wasn't much happening out there. The occasional car and one bicycle passed on Oliver Street. Solar lamps illuminated the path between the garage and the back steps, giving a pretty glow to Aunt Ibby's garden, where sunflowers reached above the wrought-iron fence. A white-faced owl paused on a low branch of a maple tree, arousing O'Ryan's interest for a moment. I wondered again why Eddie had chosen the Oliver Street route, and wondered even more about Cody and Lucy and the Boston theater alibi.

O'Ryan abruptly left his chosen post and started for the hall leading to my living room. He stopped short at the edge of the kitchen, looking back at me. I knew what was going on. He knew that Pete was approaching, wanted to meet him downstairs, but didn't want to let me out of his sight.

"Don't worry, boy," I told him. "I'll come with you. I'm anxious to see him too." We hurried down the hall, across the living room, and through the locked door to the upstairs landing. The cat stood at the top of the twisty staircase, apparently expecting me to follow him down two flights. This is one reason I don't need a step class. Between this house and the station, I think I travel up and down a mile or two of stairs every day. I followed the cat, and a surprised Pete was greeted by both of us as soon as he stepped out of the Crown Vic.

He greeted me with a quick kiss and put one arm around my waist. "Here's a quart of vanilla," he said, offering me a very cold paper bag. He reached down and patted O'Ryan. "To what do I owe this special escort committee welcome?"

"We're both happy to see you," I said, "but the curbside reception was his idea." I pointed to the cat, who by then had moved slightly ahead of us on the path. "He's in one of his protective modes. Won't let me out of his sight."

Pete tightened his grip on my waist and frowned. "What do you think he's worried about this time?"

"Who knows? He's a cat." I tried to keep my tone light, but I knew why Pete was frowning. We'd both seen this behavior from O'Ryan before. I'd tried to ignore it, to make light of it before too. But every time that cat gets overprotective about me, it's at a time when I definitely need protection—whether I know it or want it or not.

"Hey, O'Ryan," Pete said. O'Ryan stopped in the middle of the path and turned to face us. "How about I take over watching Lee tonight? You can relax. Okay?"

"Mrrou," said the cat, resuming his position ahead of us.

"I don't think he's ready to relax yet," I said.

"Well, like you said, he's only a cat. How's that dinner coming along? I'm hungry."

"Potatoes are in the oven. Everything else is ready to go." We entered the back hall, locked the door behind us, and started up the twisty staircase, O'Ryan still in the lead. It was all right with me if he wasn't ready to relinquish his protective mode. With both wise cat *and* strong man watching over me, I felt doubly safe.

Pete's look was approving when I pulled keys from my pocket and unlocked the door to my apartment. This time O'Ryan used his own door and waited for us inside. "He *is* acting nervous, isn't he?" Pete said. "He usually gets right up on that zebra chair and pretends to be asleep."

"I know," I said. "He's been that way all afternoon."

"We'd better put that ice cream in the freezer." Pete took the bag from my hand and headed for the kitchen. "Did anything special happen this afternoon to upset him?"

"Nothing," I said. "He did remind me to lock my kitchen door though."

"Good cat." He opened the freezer, read the label on the B & J, shook his head, and tucked the vanilla carton in beside it. "Good thing I brought this. Can you think of anything else that would set him off like this?"

"Like sitting on my feet to keep me from standing up when Eddie Symonds came in?"

He closed the freezer door a little harder than necessary. "Symonds? What the hell was he doing here?"

"That's what Aunt Ibby and I have been trying to figure out." I told him how my aunt had admitted to giving Eddie a casual invitation to "drop by" for happy hour sometime, and how he'd arrived via Oliver Street and the back entrance. "Also, he's going to play one of the characters in the Clue party game I've been planning." I pulled the bagged salad mix from the refrigerator. "What kind of dressing do you want on the salad?"

"Ranch, please. So do you think he's hitting on your aunt? Or is he checking on you for some reason?"

"I don't know. Maybe he's one of the men who was looking for my address."

"Maybe he is." Pete used his cop voice.

"Maybe. Sunglasses. Ball cap. Maybe he could be."

"How are the twins and the Angels doing? Anything new there?" he asked.

I sprinkled some mesquite seasoning on the chops, along with a little meat tenderizer. "They're due for another brainstorming session here first thing tomorrow morning. I'm going to try to sit in on it. I'm sure you can too if you want to. Listen, what do you know about the idea that Cody and Lucy were watching a play in Boston when Sam Bond was being killed? Eddie seems quite positive about that."

"That was the first alibi they offered," he said. "Not true. Oh, they had tickets for the play. They even had bought train tickets for the trip into Boston. But they never went. Those tickets were never used."

"So they were here in Salem when the murder happened after all?"

"Looks that way."

"So they'd made up the alibi ahead of time? Doesn't that look like they'd preplanned everything?" I had a sinking feeling about Cody and Lucy's innocence.

"Looks that way." He said again, but not with a lot of conviction.

I decided to try prying. "If they weren't in Boston and they weren't murdering the professor, where were they then? Somebody must have seen them somewhere."

"Not necessarily." He plugged in the Foreman Grill. "How soon will the potatoes be done?"

"About ten minutes. Have they told you where they were?"

"Only that they were together."

"That's not helpful, is it? Do you think they've confided in Cody's uncles, and the twins maybe haven't told you and the chief everything?"

He arranged four chops neatly on the grill. "No. Roger and Ray are still cops, first and foremost. They're working with us on this. All the way. Even if the kids turn out to be guilty."

I tossed the salad and put plates on the table. "I don't

know, Pete. Even with all the evidence from the ladder to the fingerprints on the knife to the unused tickets, I still can't see those two as killers."

"I understand," Pete said. "I've been boning up on the Joseph White case. Everybody in Salem knew Dick Crowninshield and the Knapp brothers were lowlifes. This is different."

"Very different," I said, "and every bit as mixed up and confusing as a game of Clue."

Dinner turned out well, if I do say so myself. The chops were tender and flavorful and had those cute grill marks on top, the salad crisp and pretty, and who knew that Hawaiian sweet potatoes are purple on the inside? Anyway, Pete liked everything except the new flavor of ice cream. (Actually, he didn't even try it. Didn't like the name.)

We talked some more about the Bond murder—more than we usually do about police business. "I wonder why Eddie was so certain that they'd gone to Boston that night," I said. "He seemed to be convinced of it."

"Apparently they told everybody at the school they were going, then came back the next day with rave reviews of the play." He waved one hand. "Said what a great time they had."

"Not a good way to establish an alibi, is it? I mean, it was pretty easy to check, wasn't it?"

"Pretty easy," he agreed, not offering further comment on how the police had checked it.

I tried a little more gentle prying. "They don't have a lot of money between them, I guess. Were the tickets expensive?"

"They were good seats at a good theater," he said. "Not cheap."

"Aunt Ibby said everybody has seen *Shear Madness*. It wouldn't be hard to read enough reviews so they'd sound as if they'd been there."

"True," he said.

"So that's what they did."

"Seems so."

Clearly I'm not as good at prying as my aunt is. I turned on Mr. Coffee. "You sure you don't want to try the B & J? It's good."

"No thanks. Got any of those Girl Scout Cookies left?"

I pulled a sleeve of Samoas from the Little Red Riding Hood cookie jar. We enjoyed our coffee, Pete with cookies, me with delicious ice cream. I tried prying one more time.

"Does anyone know when Lucy might have had access to that kitchen knife? Besides on the night of the murder, I mean?"

"She says she was in Bond's kitchen almost every time the group met there. She was often the only woman and usually got stuck with putting the snacks in bowls, slicing cheese, and all that kind of duty."

"Yep. Some things never change," I said. "So that means *anybody* who visited or worked in the Bond household had access to the knife—which may already have had Lucy's prints on it. Am I right?"

"Yes, Nancy." He sighed. "You're right. Now can we stop talking shop and enjoy each other's company?"

"Okay," I agreed. We put the dishes in the dishwasher, wiped down the table and the counters, turned out the lights, went to bed, and enjoyed one another's company very much.

Chapter 32

The weekend passed uneventfully, considering that there might still be a murderer loose in Salem, and on Monday morning, Pete was the first one up as usual. But I wasn't far behind him. I wanted to get a call in to Rhonda early. I was pretty sure Mr. Doan would okay my clocking into work late in favor of sitting in on a meeting with the Temple twins. I made it clear that this time I wouldn't mention their popular show on a rival station.

Rhonda called back before I'd finished my first cup of coffee. "Okay, Lee," she said. "Doan says you can go to that meeting but as soon as it's over, he wants you in his office with your complete plan for that Clue party you're throwing at the Tabby. Seems your friend Captain Billy has already signed on the dotted line—big-time! Looks like it could be an hour-long prime time special. Doan's already got the sales team out selling spots around it. Christopher's Castle wants to do the costumes. Scott's on his way to the Toy Trawler to shoot some promos. Better get a move on, girl!"

My complete plan? I'd barely put together the cast, and I'd never even met Cody's students. Had Mr. Pennington prepared a script? Did the Angels all know how the game is played? What about Professor Dreamy and Eddie and Harrison? I hadn't talked specifics with any of them. Why hadn't I simply gone along with Cody's perfectly good lesson plan?

Pete knew something was wrong when I put the phone down. "You all right, babe? What's going on?"

"Holy crap," I whined. "How am I going to get out of this one?" I told him what she'd said. "So Mr. Doan wants my complete plans. I don't have any complete plans." I was close to tears. "I'm supposed to show up in his office, plans in hand, directly after this morning's meeting."

He looked at Kit-Cat. Seven-fifteen. "You've still got some time to pull it together." He sounded so calm, it made me feel better.

"You think so?" I sniffled.

"Sure. The meeting downstairs is at nine o'clock. The Angels will all be there. I'm sure they all have photos you can use. You can get pictures of Eddie and the other guy from the school files. The cast pictures will take up some room in the presentation."

I was beginning to believe. "I'll call Mr. Pennington now and see if he's got a script ready. I'm betting he has. He was so excited about doing it."

"Why not take a game of Clue with you?" Pete suggested. "The party rules are almost the same as the board game rules, aren't they?"

"They sure are. They use the same clue cards and everything. And Pete, I already have the toy weapons and I can call Captain Billy now and have him ask Scott to bring the costume stuff I ordered back to the station with him."

"See?" Pete refilled our coffee mugs, popped a couple of english muffins into the toaster, and opened the jar of New Hampshire clover honey. "You've got this."

"Maybe. At least enough to impress Mr. Doan." I laughed. "It feels a little like a third-grade show-and-tell presentation, but I think it'll work for now. Thanks, Pete. What would I do without you?"

"I'm thinking maybe you'll never have to." He leaned forward with the kind of kiss that could have delayed the hastily made plans for quite a while. "As soon as I leave here, I'm going to check in at the station, and I'll be back by nine for the meeting downstairs," he said. "See you there."

I finished my coffee and honey-drenched muffin and got to work on my show-and-tell project immediately. I called Mr. Pennington first. "Sorry to call so early," I said, "but if you have a script of your narration for the Clue party ready, could you send me a copy?" I held my breath and mentally crossed my fingers. *Please have a script!*

"Yes, certainly. I was going to send it along to see if you approve," he said. "I've taken the liberty of preparing a little backstory for each character, along with a bit of explanation of the supposed connection between the game and the Joseph White murder. I've described the rooms too. Would you like me to send photos of the scenery we've selected?"

Wow! Can things get much better? "Thanks, Mr. Pennington. That would be great. I'm putting together a presentation package for Mr. Doan, and your material makes a perfect addition."

"It is I who should thank you, Ms. Barrett," he said. "The idea has absolutely caught fire here at the Tabby. We should have a full house for our little production. The Theater Arts Department is already planning an adaptation of Scrabble for next year. Something with dancing alphabet letters."

"That sounds amazing, sir," I said truthfully. "One more thing. Could you please send me your staff photos of Professor Armstrong and Mr. Symonds? And one of yourself, too, of course."

"Certainly. Right away."

Things were going well. Kit-Cat said seven-forty-five. *I've got this.* I texted our third man, Harrison—not sure if he was an early riser—and asked if he had a photo he could send for the cast program, which didn't exist yet, but I assumed it would at some point.

He responded immediately with a professional model's comp card with four studio-quality headshots and a couple of beach poses. This man was serious about an acting career—and was a gray-haired, tanned, well-muscled senior citizen hottie. Naturally Betsy had plenty of photos on her webpage, Louisa had an excellent recent studio portrait on hers, and I already had Aunt Ibby's newest.

I called Captain Billy and asked if he'd send the costume components along with Scott. I knew that the Angels would come up with much more creative outfits, but the premade ones would do for the immediate future. I already had a Clue game and the toy weapons. So far, so good.

By eight-forty-five I'd printed out the script, headshots, and scenery backgrounds. I'd collect the costume stuff from Scott, and along with a Clue game and the fake weapons, I'd be ready to do a quickie live standup for Doan as soon as I got to the station. I could even do a PowerPoint presentation for the sales staff before the day was out. Pleased with myself—and a bit surprised at the speed with which it'd all been accomplished—dressed, combed, and made up, I started downstairs, accompanied by my faithful cat companion.

When O'Ryan and I entered the warm, good-smelling kitchen, the twins were already seated at the table, clearly enjoying cinnamon rolls, coffee, and the company of my very attractive aunt. The men stood to greet me with handshakes and even a hesitant hug from Ray.

"So good to see you again, Ms. Barrett—Lee," Roger said. "We've been following up on the helpful leads you all gave us earlier, and we're moving ahead. We're encouraged."

"Very encouraged," Ray echoed. "Big help."

"I hope we can help more," I said, sitting beside Roger at the round table. "I felt so sad for Lucy and Cody when I saw them at the courthouse."

"We'll talk about that when the others get here," Roger promised. "There've been some new developments, and yes, we can use your help."

"It turns out that private citizens like you and Ibby and Betsy and Louisa can sometimes learn things that professional investigators might miss," Ray said.

"Now that you both are private citizens too," Aunt Ibby offered, "I'll bet you're finding things you couldn't have found when you were policemen. Am I right about that?"

"Maybe," was the guarded answer, spoken in unison. I smiled, remembering how often they'd done that in my class, much to the delight and amusement of the other students. *They're still cops at heart.* O'Ryan suddenly left the kitchen—and my side—via the cat door.

"The girls must be here," Aunt Ibby said. I assumed the cat must have felt comfortable leaving me in the care of the twins for the moment as he went outside to greet the arriving Angels.

Aunt Ibby was right. She opened the unlocked door, and catching my disapproving look, whispered, "I knew they were on the way." Louisa and Betsy entered the kitchen in a pastel panorama of orchid silk (Betsy) and pink linen (Louisa) accompanied by a whiff of Flowerbomb (Betsy). The gentlemen stood, greetings were exchanged, coffee poured, and the meeting was—more or less—called to order.

"Pete will be along when he can get away," Aunt Ibby said, "but we may as well get started. I know Ray and Roger have progress to report, Betsy has some news, and I've made a new discovery myself. Lee, will you take notes?"

"Is it all right if I do?" I looked from one twin to the other. "I already understand that it's all off the record."

"Off the record," Ray said, and Roger bobbed his head in agreement.

I pulled my notebook from my purse and prepared to listen, learn, and take notes.

Chapter 33

Aunt Ibby tapped on a coffee cup with a spoon, halting all conversation. "Roger, why don't you get us started."

Roger pulled his chair a little closer to the table, leaning forward as he spoke. I recognized the motion. Announcers and newspeople, accustomed to camera and sound equipment, often assume that posture, even in informal settings.

"First, let me tell you all that we are more sure than ever that our nephew Cody is not guilty of killing Samuel Bond. His young lady, Lucy, is innocent too of course." His voice was cop-like, his stare, as he looked around the table at each of us, was intense. Roger, and Ray as well, I realized, had learned a lot about stage presence since they'd left my television production class a few years earlier. "Some of you may have heard that the two had originally claimed they'd been at a play in Boston on the evening in question," he continued. Heads around the table dipped in agreement. "That was not a true statement. They were, in fact, together. They were, in fact, each other's alibi. But unfortunately, they were not in a crowded theater where others would surely see them. No. Unfortunately, they were not."

Ray sighed. "So unfortunate."

"Tsk-tsk," Aunt Ibby said. "Too bad."

A gentle "Oh dear" came from Louisa.

"Then where the hell were they?" Betsy demanded. "In bed together?"

Roger held out both hands, palms up. "Unfortunately, that's exactly where they were."

"Tsk-tsk," Aunt Ibby said again.

A more forceful "Oh dear" from Louisa.

"Oh boy," Betsy said. "That could be a problem. Now what?"

"On so many levels," I agreed, putting down my pen.

O'Ryan chose that moment to dart through the cat exit, announcing Pete's imminent arrival. "I'll get it," I said, unlocking the door and following him outside. I stood on the back steps for a moment, waiting for Pete to park the Crown Vic, enjoying a cool morning breeze and trying to digest what Roger had shared with us. As Betsy had put it so succinctly, *"Now what?"*

Pete bounded up the flagstone path with O'Ryan a few steps ahead of him. "Sorry I'm late," he said. "Did I miss anything?"

"Apparently Cody and Lucy were definitely not in the orchestra seats at the Charles Playhouse," I said.

"Yeah. I know. They were alone at Lucy's parent's house all night." We hurried into the house, and Pete took a seat next to me. "Sorry I'm late," he said again. "Chief's getting anxious about this case. City Hall is after him."

"It's okay," Roger said. "Nothing's come up you didn't already know about."

I picked up my pen and waited for what might come up next.

It was Betsy's turn. "I did a little checking on your Professor Dreamy," she said, looking straight at me.

"He's not *my* Professor Dreamy," I insisted.

"Right," she went on. "Anyway, when you and he were having drinks at the Hawthorne lounge the other night, a few of my sorority sisters were there taking it all in."

"All what?" I said. "Besides, it was Diet Coke."

Betsy pointed to my aunt. "Ibby, make her stop interrupting my story."

Aunt Ibby put a finger to her lips. Properly chastised, I looked down at my notebook and listened to Betsy's story.

"Well, as I was saying, they got to talking about Alan Armstrong. They recognized you, Lee, and figured out that he was probably trying to get on TV somehow. They all know how conceited he is, even if he is gorgeous. One of them said that he'd invited her daughter to go with him to a party at Sam Bond's house and, wouldn't you know it, it was for the night old Sam got himself killed." Betsy looked around the table. "The daughter was glad she hadn't gone with him, naturally. But get this! She would have if he hadn't cancelled on her." Betsy dropped her voice. "Now this is a girl *nobody* cancels on! She was ticked. And know what his excuse was? He told her something was going down at Sam's that she wouldn't want to see. Something bad was going to happen there, and he didn't want her to be involved." Big smile. "Now what do you all think about that?"

"Interesting," Roger declared.

"Very interesting," Ray agreed.

"Could I have your friend's name, Betsy?" Pete asked. "I'd like to talk to her daughter."

"Sure." Betsy scribbled on the back of a card and handed it to him. "But I already talked to her. It was exactly what her mother said. Something bad was going to happen."

"That sounds pretty suspicious, doesn't it?" my aunt asked. "I guess you boys will be talking to Professor Armstrong too."

"We will," Ray said. "Thank you, Mrs. Leavitt—uh—Betsy. Ibby? You said you have some news."

"I do," she said. "Tyler Dickson, my assistant at the library, called last night to tell me that another person on my list had returned a book. It's one of the university press academic history journals from the stacks—a fall 2003 issue. Edwin Symonds returned it a few minutes before closing. She sent it over with the night watchman this morning." My aunt held up the blue-covered publication for all of us to see. I recognized it. "That's not all," she said. "This is one that Cody, Lucy, and Alan have all checked out, and some years back Sam Bond borrowed it too."

"May I see it?" I asked, reaching for the book. "I'm pretty sure it's the one Eddie was reading when I interviewed him in the coffee shop." She handed it to me. I was right. The part that had begun with "Mid-Century" turned out to be "Mid-Century Arts and Humanities." I opened the cover and looked at the index. One name popped out at me right away. Professor Samuel Bond. He'd written about mid-century New England architecture. I opened the book to Bond's article and passed it to Pete. "This must be what all four of them were looking at."

Pete studied the open pages for a moment. "Mid-century architecture? I wonder what the fascination with that is all about."

"Eddie has a degree in architecture." We all turned to look at Louisa. "He told me so when we were in Alaska. He was especially interested in photographing Alaskan postmodernist buildings. Our hotel was one of them, which was why he happened to mention it."

I took notes as fast as I could. This was getting more interesting by the minute. Alan thought something bad was going to happen at the Bond house, dance teacher Eddie has a degree in architecture we didn't know about in addition to his journalism degree, and lovebirds Cody and Lucy had made up an elaborate but easily disproven alibi for the night in question.

"Cody and Lucy are both interested in New England history," Aunt Ibby offered. "Cody as a teacher and Lucy as a student. I expect architecture is part of the Salem history course. That would explain their interest in Bond's article."

"It's possible that Lucy didn't want to go to Bond's house anymore, after that shot glass–throwing incident," I suggested. "Did she say anything about that, Roger?"

"She seemed to still be embarrassed about it," Roger said. "She told us that she'd had a little too much to drink and Bond began teasing her about her looks. You know, the blue hair and the little diamond thing on the side of her nose and the tattoo and all."

"She has a tattoo?" Betsy asked.

"It's a fairly discreet one as tattoos go," Ray said. "It's on her—um—her upper thigh."

"What is it?"

"It's a picture of that statue of Samantha Stevens over on Washington Street. *Bewitched,* you know? Some of the college kids have been getting them. The kids love the statue. Most of their parents hate it." He shrugged. "A little generational rebellion, I guess."

"She was angry with Professor Bond, then, because of the teasing?" Louisa asked.

"She was," Roger said. "But she didn't throw the shot glass at *him*. She smashed it in the fireplace." He smiled briefly. "She says she saw it done at a Jewish wedding and thought it was cool."

"It is," Betsy said. "Mr. Leavitt and I did it at ours. But was Sam Bond angry about it?"

"According to the others, he wasn't. He said he was

sorry if he'd hurt her feelings, and instructed her to clean it up. Which she did."

"Yes," I recalled. "Eddie told me she'd cleaned it up. That's how her bloodstains got in the professor's room, right, Pete?"

"It seems to be entirely possible," Pete admitted. "She'd cut herself on the broken glass. The housekeeper vouches for all that."

"Speaking of the housekeeper," Louisa said, "she occasionally does some sewing work for me. Pete, did you know that the professor had a safe in his closet?"

"Yes. We have it. Roger and Ray know all about it."

"Can you tell us what's in it?" my aunt asked.

"Nothing much of interest. Papers. Manuscripts. Some of those journals like that one." He pointed to the blue-covered book on the table. "It seems to be where he put his writings for safekeeping."

"I always thought he was kind of stuck on himself," Betsy said. "Probably believed every word he ever wrote should be preserved for posterity."

"Cody did a lot of polishing on the professor's writings," Ray said. "He told us he thought the main reason his own full professorship was held up was because Bond didn't want to lose his copyediting talent."

Roger agreed. "That's true. Cody says he often had to rewrite the first paragraphs and change the titles on practically everything Bond gave him to work on, in addition to making sure all of the footnotes were correct."

"I wonder why he didn't ask Eddie to do it," Aunt Ibby said, "since Eddie was working on the book they co-wrote."

"Cody had majored in history and Eddie hadn't—that we know of," Ray said. "Cody was more apt to find factual errors."

"But you believe Cody was resentful of the extra work Bond piled on him." Aunt Ibby spoke gently but firmly. "In fact, he thinks it cost him the professorship he'd earned—along with the considerable financial benefits."

"Cody didn't kill him," Roger stated.

"Cody wouldn't kill *anybody*," Ray agreed.

"To be fair, we have to look at all the facts," my aunt said. "Several people have said there was an argument between Cody and the professor."

"Most everybody called it 'a disagreement between colleagues,'" I said. "At least that's the way it was described to me."

"It was an argument." Roger's cop voice was back. "Cody admitted it."

Ray solemnly agreed with his brother. "A real argument. Yelling and everything. Cody admitted it."

"That's not good for his case, then, is it, Pete?" Betsy asked.

Pete sighed. I knew he wanted to stay out of this conversation as much as possible. "We try to collect facts, Betsy. Some of them are bound to reflect badly on the accused."

"Okay then," Betsy continued. "I'd like to know more about how Professor Armstrong fits into all this. How did he know there'd be something bad going down at Bond's house? Are we supposed to think he has some psychic ability?"

"We hadn't ever heard about that until this morning," Roger pointed out. "You can bet we'll be following up on it." He waved the card Betsy had given him. "Today."

The very possibility of Alan Armstrong having psychic ability had never occurred to me. I thought about my own strange "gift." Was it possible that Alan saw things in mirrors, or had a crystal ball? *This is Salem, after all. Maybe he's a witch.* I shook the silly thought away. What if I went around babbling about the things I'd seen in mirrors lately? How about the blue book with a bloodred stain—then the same book with a bloody handprint on it?

I'd seen both of those *before* the actual book showed up on the table right in front of me—stain-free.

Pete's hands were in his lap, and he'd begun peeking at his watch. "Do you have to leave?" I whispered. He nodded and shrugged his shoulders at the same time. Mixed signal. I decided to bail us both out.

"Excuse me, folks," I said, "but I have an appointment with Bruce Doan, so I'll have to say goodbye for now." I stood. Pete stood and added his apology to mine. O'Ryan had already headed for the cat door. Once in the back hall, I gave Pete a quick kiss and started up the twisty staircase while he headed for his car. I needed to gather my "show-and-tell" equipment for the morning's presentation. O'Ryan preceded me on the stairs, but only by one step at a time. He was still staying close by. *What's up with that?*

We entered my living room side by side. "Are you planning to go to work with me too?" I asked, with the strong feeling that if he could, he most certainly would.

Chapter 34

I parked the Vette in my regular space and grabbed the Clue game and my briefcase from the passenger seat. It's a nice one, smooth tan leather with my initials in gold. Aunt Ibby gave it to me a couple of Christmases ago. I don't use it very often—WICH-TV isn't a briefcase sort of place—but I figured it, along with my pinstriped business suit, added a bit of formality to my presentation for Mr. Doan.

I rode Old Clunky up to the second floor, where Rhonda waited for me. "Wow. Looking good. Doan's in his office. He says to send you right in." She raised perfectly arched brows. "Scotty just dropped this off for you. Toys?" The bright pink bag was marked "Toy Trawler."

"Suggestions for party costumes," I said, tucking the bag into the briefcase. "A feather boa, some different colored neckties, a fake mustache, stuff like that. Part of my presentation for the boss."

"Cool," she said. "He seems anxious to see you. He's all gung ho about your Clue party show, and he's super happy about the Captain Billy deal." She paused and glanced around the room. "Maybe you'll get a big bonus," she whispered. We both laughed at that one.

"Wish me luck," I said, and knocked on the station manager's door.

"Come right in, Ms. Barrett." The voice sounded almost jovial. *Is he too happy?*

What if he's disappointed in what I've done so far? I pushed the niggling negative thoughts away. *Nope,* I told myself, *like Pete said, I've got this!* I turned the knob and pushed the door open.

"Good morning, sir," I said. I stepped right up in front of his desk, slid the Clue game across the polished surface, and snapped open the brass lock on my briefcase. "Let me invite you to a Clue party." I heard the unmistakable sound of a throat being cleared, then turned and faced three members of the sales team standing in front of three purple chairs. (It was, in fact, the *entire* sales team.) Therese Della Monica gave me a pinkie wave and a wink.

"Good morning, Ms. Barrett." Bruce Doan motioned to the three. "You sales people can sit down. Ms. Barrett, I guess you know these folks. Proceed, please. We all need to know exactly what we're selling."

I took a deep, cleansing breath like they taught us in yoga class. "Well, then," I said. "Let's get started."

I began with Mr. Pennington's script with his descriptive sketches of each character. I'm no Buck Covington, but after so many years in front of the cameras, I read a script pretty darned well. I showed the pictures of the cast, one at a time. Then I opened the Clue box and gave a quick explanation of the game's rules. "The party is run by the same rules," I said. "For instance, Colonel Mustard did it with a candlestick in the library." I could tell by their expressions that everyone was familiar with the game, so I moved on to the costume artifacts and the toy weapons.

"The game will be played against authentic backgrounds," I said as I passed the prints around, along with a promise that a PowerPoint presentation they could share with prospective time buyers would be available to everyone by afternoon. "The director of the Tabitha Trumbull Academy of the Arts has assured me that the student theater will be filled near capacity by showtime, and we know from experience that any production Captain Billy is involved in is strictly first-class. Our own Marty McCarthy will handle postproduction. The entire broadcast will be shown in prime time. Your clients will be proud to be part of it."

I hadn't expected applause, but I got it anyway. I even got a "Good job, Ms. Barrett. We appreciate the time you must have put into this. Thank you," from the boss himself.

If only you knew how little actual time I've put into this! I mentally gave myself a pat on the back, thanked them all for their kind attention, and scooted out of the office. I needed to get busy on the promised presentation package for the sales department. I wished Aunt Ibby was there to help. She'd have this thing put together in twenty minutes, while it would probably take me half a day. I told Rhonda I'd need a dataport for a while.

"No problem. Doan said to clear the decks for you." She handed me the key, giving me a smiling up-and-down look. "Dressed for success and no place to go, huh? The suit is great. Scott and Francine have already left. If you finish whatever it is you're doing, Old Jim is on standby for you."

I picked up the dataport key. "Thanks, Rhonda. I'll probably be done by noon." I headed downstairs, determined to keep up the head of steam I'd had going since early morning. I hadn't put one of these together for a while—not since my television production classes. Thankfully, I hadn't forgotten how to do it. I had a credible product ready to share with the sales department by eleven. I ducked outside, replaced the Clue game and the fake weapons in the trunk of the Vette, then clattered back up those metal stairs, wishing I could ditch the heels in favor of sneakers, but that would seriously mess up my dressed-for-success image big-time. I opened the door to the reception area and darned near bumped smack into Alan Armstrong.

He was carrying flowers. Roses. In a glass vase.

"Lee," he said. "I hope you can forgive me." His expression was perfect "naughty little boy who wants to be forgiven." *It must have taken hours in front of a mirror to perfect that lost puppy-dog look.* He thrust the vase into my hands.

"Hello, Alan. Thank you." I sniffed the roses. "These are beautiful. You shouldn't have."

"I wanted to send them to your house, but I don't have your address," he said. "I was such a snot the other day. I'm so sorry."

"No harm done, Alan," I said.

"No, really. I took the heat when you asked about the editor. Sam swore us all to secrecy about that. We'd all promised we wouldn't tell that there was a ghostwriter involved." He reached over and touched my arm. "Then when Eddie admitted it on TV, it didn't matter anymore. I want to make it up to you," he said, lowering those long eyelashes. "Let's go over to the Hawthorne. I'll buy you that glass of wine I promised." He glanced around, then whispered, "I have something I need to tell you. About who killed Sam."

"Can we talk about it here?" I asked, putting the vase on the Formica counter. "I'm sure I can commandeer an office."

He frowned. "Please come with me. One glass of wine." He gave me that look again. "You look so beautiful today. It's a shame to waste it in a borrowed office."

"Dressed for success and no place to go," Rhonda had said. She was right. He wanted to talk about who'd killed Sam. One glass of wine. What harm could it do? "Okay, Alan," I said. "You're on. Your car or mine?"

"I have a Lexus," he said.

"I have a Corvette Stingray."

"You win."

"I know. Rhonda, will you take care of my roses? I'll be back within the hour."

So pinstriped and high-heeled me and gorgeous Professor Dreamy made our grand entrance into the Hawthorne lounge. We drew the expected stares, which actually felt pretty good. I wondered how soon the news would get to Betsy. Alan ordered for us.

"One glass," I warned, keeping my voice low. I didn't want the early lunch crowd to overhear. "It's early in the day for drinking, and I don't have a lot of time. Let's get to the point. What's this about who killed Sam? Do you think you know who it is?"

Our wine arrived before the question was answered. His words were halting. "It's not so much that I have a definitive answer. I mean, like, can I tell you for sure who climbed in the window? Who beat the old man over the head? Who stabbed him? I can't say that exactly. It's more like I have some facts. Some things I know." A short laugh. "The only thing I'm positive about is that it wasn't me."

I looked at my watch, not even trying to hide the fact that I was already getting impatient. "What *do* you have, Alan?"

He leaned forward, expression earnest. *Real emotion or practiced? Hard to tell.* "Listen, Lee. All of us—Cody and Eddie and Lucy and me—we *all* have good reasons to—um—to dislike Sam Bond. And we *all* were frequent visitors to his house. I'm sure that every one of us has left fingerprints—even DNA—somewhere in the place."

"So it wasn't unusual for Lucy's prints, even her blood, to be there."

"That's right."

"You believe Lucy is innocent, even though she has no alibi?"

"Lucy!" He gave a dismissive wave with his wine-glass, not spilling a drop. "Lucy is a vegan. She's a member of PETA. She won't step on an ant. She thinks a cockroach has a soul. Lucy Mahoney would not, could not, stab anybody. Ever. She was angry with Sam. No doubt. He gave her an undeserved D and he made fun of her appearance. But stab him? No."

He makes a good case. "Okay. What about Cody? Do you believe he's innocent too?"

"I don't know. It looks bad for him, doesn't it?" Alan didn't wait for an answer. "He says that ladder was stolen. I don't know how to explain the shoes. I told you, we all must have left fingerprints in the house. But Cody was the only one of us who kind of liked the old guy. At least he respected him in a way, you know? Even though he was pissed about the associate professor thing. God only knows he deserved the title more than I ever did." He shook his head. "I think he was actually sorry to hear Sam was dead—even though everything pointed to him being the killer."

I sipped my excellent Chablis and recalled that Cody had already admitted to a yelling-at-each-other argument with Bond. "What about Eddie?" I asked. "What was his problem with Bond?"

"I told you, we all had reason to dislike him, but Eddie didn't try to hide it. He liked to needle Sam, about money, politics, women. Sam hardly ever responded, just humored him. It made everybody uncomfortable."

I thought then about Aunt Ibby's friend who'd heard Sam Bond arguing with a man in Bond's backyard. *You've stolen from me for the last time. . . .* Was that the argument Cody admitted to? Or was the other man Eddie?

"Did you ever hear them get into a serious argument about Sam stealing something from Eddie?" I asked him.

"No. I never did."

The waitress had refilled our glasses while I wasn't looking. Remembering that I was the designated driver, I pushed it gently, regretfully away. "That leaves you, Alan. Why did you dislike Sam Bond?"

"It doesn't matter. I told you I didn't do it."

"That's not playing fair," I told him. "You started this conversation by saying all of you had reason to dislike him."

"All right, but this part is off the record. Agreed?"

"Agreed."

"Did I ever tell you I started out as a history major?"

"Yes. And Professor Bond convinced you to change majors."

"Yeah. He flunked me out in history. Political science was a better choice for me anyway. I got my teaching degree and my master's in poli-sci from County U and a BFA in acting from BU. I'd always figured between those two and this face I'd go into politics."

"Seems like a logical plan," I admitted.

"I know. I still plan to do it when I'm a little older. Maybe add another degree or two. Law, probably. Learning comes easy to me. Always has. But flunking Sam Bond's history course still bugs me."

"Even after all these years?"

"Still off the record?"

"Of course" was my reluctant response.

"The old bastard stole my term paper."

"Stole it? What do you mean?"

"It was years later when I found it." I was pretty sure the faraway look wasn't faked.

"Found what?"

"My paper. He'd changed the title, rewritten the first paragraph, and added a few more footnotes, but I recognized my own work."

"He'd published your term paper as his own work? His own research? How did you find out?"

"Just by chance. I was looking up material on how courthouse environment possibly affects trial outcomes. Some of the suggested resources included professional journals. In one dated 2001, I saw Samuel Bond's byline on an article about the various locales involved in the Salem witch trials. Naturally, I read it." He paused, drained his glass, gazed toward the doorway, and stopped talking.

"It was your work?" I prompted.

"Yes. It was mine. Thinly disguised, some sentences reworked, but undoubtedly mine."

"Did you confront him about it?"

"Confront him? No. I was planning to sue him for a bundle. Now, who cares?"

"There's no statute of limitation on plagiarism," I said.

"I know. But filing suit costs money, and it turns out old Sam was in debt up to his ears. His estate is a big zero. You going to drink that wine?"

I pushed the glass toward him. "Nope. You enjoy it. I'm driving."

"Thanks." He took a sip. "*Mmm.* Good stuff." He leaned forward and dropped his voice to a whisper. He crooked a finger, beckoning me to lean in too. "We were planning a class action suit."

"We? Who?"

"All of us. We knew I couldn't be the only one. It wasn't hard, once we knew what we were looking for. He'd even grabbed one of Eddie's—something about architecture—

and Cody found his on the aboriginal peoples of Australia in an earth science journal."

"So you think Professor Bond took work from outstanding students, discouraged them with low marks, and suggested they find another major?"

"Exactly. He waited a year or more, changed the title, moved words around, and boom! He was published. Most of us don't have time to read the professional publications outside of our fields—or the cash to subscribe to them—so the odds of being found out were in his favor." A bitter laugh. "Heck, he even had Cody proofreading articles he claimed were his, adding footnotes. There are probably lots more of us out there who'll never know they've been ripped off." He tossed back the rest of the wine. "I've said too much. Let's both go back to work." He signaled for a check.

Now I had an ethical dilemma. I know what "off the record" means. I had no intention of reporting on WICH-TV anything Alan Armstrong had told me in confidence. I didn't plan to share it with Pete either. But I knew that the twins needed to know, even though it added to Cody's possible motive for the murder.

Chapter 35

I dropped Alan off next to his Lexus, parked the Vette, and hurried inside the station. Rhonda pointed to the starburst clock when I appeared beside her desk. "You said you'd be back within the hour, and you made it with minutes to spare," she said. "So how'd the second date with Professor Dreamy go?"

"It wasn't a date," I insisted, "and the other time wasn't either."

She pointed to the roses. "Oh, I don't know about that. Long-stemmed American Beauties in a vase? Drinks at the Hawthorne? Looks like dates to me."

"Stop it," I said. "It was strictly business."

"I'm just teasing." Sly grin. "Does he really know who killed the old professor?"

"You heard that, huh?"

"Rhonda hears all. Knows all," she deadpanned.

I almost believed her. "He had some interesting information," I said, "but unfortunately the good parts are off the record."

"Oh-oh. Doan's not going to like that."

"I don't intend to share that with him—or anybody.

'Off the record' means 'off the record.' Nothing I can do about it." I looked at the white board. There were still a couple of assignments posted. "Old Jim still here?" I asked. "We could do that plaque unveiling." Salem's good about putting plaques around town, keeping tourists and residents informed about different historic sites. Rhonda handed me a printout from the mayor's office. The plaque noted on the white board commemorated the site of the home of Margery Bedinger, a Salem-born suffragette who back in 1915 walked, biked, trolleyed, and drove all over Massachusetts promoting voting rights for women. "It seems like a worthy cause. Would you page Jim?" I recognized the address. Long-gone Margery had lived in the same neighborhood as recently-gone Samuel Bond. It would give me a chance to do a little snooping on what might be going on at the Bond house, which, according to Pete, was still festooned with yellow crime scene tape.

Jim was available and more than happy to film me at the site. He was also amenable to doing a little off-the-record snooping. I did the standup, using Rhonda's notes, thinking maybe Margery would have approved of the businesslike pinstripes and heels, then headed around the block to the Bond house. The yellow tape was still there, a little the worse for wear, fluttering where it had come loose and mud spotted in places. There was a state crime scene vehicle and a Salem police department cruiser parked in front and a long mobile unit in the driveway marked "Massachusetts Bureau of Forensic Evidence." "Jim," I said, "see over there where the tape is muddy? And the Forensic Evidence truck is parked? That's the side of the house where the ladder was. And the shoe prints. Let's wander over and see what's going on. Maybe we can find somebody who'll talk to us."

Jim, with a shoulder-mounted Sony camcorder, and me with my trusty stick mic got as close to the forensic truck as we could without crossing any tape. I knew this might produce useless footage, but you never know until you try, right? I ad-libbed a little background information about the case and pointed out the state vehicles, reading the lettering on each.

"It's clear that the investigation into the mysterious death of Professor Samuel Bond has not slowed down in recent days. It appears that there may be some new activity in the area of the window leading to Samuel Bond's bedroom. Someone put a ladder up to that window, stole inside, and killed him in his own bed."

With his free hand, Jim motioned toward a side door of the house where a uniformed man had just emerged. With a small shovel in one hand and a handful of what I recognized as evidence bags in the other, he walked toward the truck—and me.

"Good morning, sir," I said, edging as close to the tape as I could without stepping onto the forbidden area. "Lee Barrett. WICH-TV. Looks as if you're collecting more dirt samples from the yard. Is that right?"

His expression was not a happy one. He didn't answer. Mr. Doan doesn't like dead air, so I spoke again quickly. "I noticed the evidence bags and the shovel," I said. My peripheral vision told me that Jim had zoomed in on the items in question. Even if this guy was going to stonewall me, even if he didn't utter a word, the pictures would tell the story. I tried a smile. "It's obvious that the department is being meticulous in investigating the professor's murder. Our viewers appreciate your efforts."

"Uh, thanks." He dropped his hands to his sides, shovel in one hand, bags in the other.

"Excuse me, I need to get back to work." He climbed into the front seat of the truck, but made no move to leave the yard. Clearly, he wasn't about to talk to me, and certainly wasn't about to dig in the dirt while the camera was there. Too bad. I moved so that I stood beside the truck, trying not to block the lettering. Jim's camera followed me. "The state's Bureau of Forensic Evidence is responsible for collecting and analyzing physical evidence. It appears that in this case an investigator is interested in the soil outside Professor Bond's bedroom window. Soil samples can reveal a lot of information. If the police have already found the shoes that may have made the prints allegedly found at this site immediately after the professor's death, a match of soil from the site and traces of the same soil on the shoes would be significant."

For over two years I've been taking an online course in criminology, which fortunately includes a significant amount of extra-credit reading—including *An Introduction to Forensic Science.* Pete is a year ahead of me in the same course, so I need all the extra-credit I can get.

I wound up the shoot with a fast rundown of the basic facts of the case so far, then signed off. No point in hanging around. I knew the state cop in the mobile unit could outwait us. I decided to call the twins right away, though. I wondered if this meant they'd officially matched up the dirt from Bond's yard with Cody's shoes. "Let's head back, Jim," I said. "Maybe we can use what we have for a newsbreak and later on the five o'clock." As we pulled away, I tilted the rearview mirror so that I could see the truck. The driver's side door opened as soon as we approached the corner of the street.

I called Roger the minute we were out of sight, taking the phone off speaker. "Roger? Lee here. Did you know they're gathering soil samples again from under Bond's bedroom window?"

"We know," he said. "The tests are positive. Cody's gym shoes not only match the print in the damp soil they found the morning after the murder, but traces of the dirt collected earlier itself is on the shoes. No doubt about it."

"Oh, Roger. How's Cody holding up?"

"He's more worried about the girl than about himself, and his mother is making a novena to Saint Jude."

"I'm going to get together with Cody's class this evening. Eddie Symonds and Alan Armstrong will be there too. And look, Roger, Alan Armstrong has told me something that I promised to keep off the record. But it's something I guess you and Ray need to know. Alan and Cody had good reason to be angry with Sam Bond. There was more than tenure involved."

"Is it about Bond stealing their work? Getting it published under his own name?"

"You knew?"

"Cody told us. He and Alan were planning to sue Bond for plagiarism. He laughed at them. Told them to go ahead. He was already so far in debt they'd never collect a penny."

"Do the police know about it?"

"Not that we know of. It sure would look to them like a motive, though." I heard him sigh. "We know our boy is innocent, but somebody has gone to a lot of trouble to set him up. He's scared and embarrassed about the whole thing."

"I understand," I said, although I really didn't. How could I? What does it feel like to be suspected of a terrible crime when you didn't do it? "You and Ray will be there tonight, won't you? Aunt Ibby and the . . . uh, Betsy and Louisa are coming."

"Yep. Ray's been in touch with your aunt. He's had it noted in red ink on our schedule."

How cute is that?

"Good," I said. "I've tried to get in touch with Lucy, but her voice mail is full."

"Actually, Lucy's at Phyllis's. Staying in the guest room. Her mom threw her out."

"How sad. Because she's a suspect?"

"Nope. Because she's been dating Cody. The age difference, you know? He's almost fifteen years older than she is."

Since the age difference between my own parents had been almost the same, it didn't seem strange to me. "That's too bad. I'm sorry to hear it. See you guys tonight. You'll be among Cody's friends."

"I hope so. See you then. Goodbye."

"That's odd," I said, more to myself than to Jim as I slid the phone into my purse. "What does that mean?"

"What does what mean?" Jim asked.

"When I said the twins would be among Cody's friends, Roger said, 'I hope so.' Why would he say that?"

Jim didn't answer right away. "I'd say," he announced, after a moment, "the twins aren't sure all those folks you said would be there tonight *are* Cody and the Mahoney girl's friends."

"That's what I thought too," I admitted. "And it's not a pleasant thing to think about."

Jim parked the van next to Ariel's bench. "I'll lock up the van and run the video down to Marty," he said, "while you check and see if Rhonda has anything else for us."

"Okay." I let myself in the studio door and climbed the metal stairs once again.

Chapter 36

There was nothing else for us on the white board. "It's just as well," I told Rhonda. "I'm meeting with Cody McGinnis's class over at the Tabby in a few hours, and I could sure use some more prep time."

"Getting ready for that Clue party, huh?"

"That'll be most of it. Alan and Eddie, along with my aunt and her pals, are all going to be there, plus the twin cops."

"How about I send Old Jim along? Maybe we could use some rehearsal shots for teasers for the Captain Billy program."

"I'll have to check with Mr. Pennington, of course," I said. "It's just a rehearsal. Just a teaser for a client's show."

"Sure," said Rhonda. "Want to go in and see what Doan thinks about it?"

"You kidding? He's been dying to get a camera into the Tabby since the day after the murder. He'll say yes. I'm not sure how Pete's going to feel about it, though."

"It's not as if you're going to be doing a news show.

It's just a rehearsal." She repeated my words. "Just a teaser for a client's show."

"Sure. That's all it is. Is Mr. Doan busy? I'll ask him now." I'd already *almost* convinced myself that filming the meeting would be no problem for anybody concerned, and it definitely would be a good promo for Captain Billy's program. It didn't take much to convince the station manager. I had my okay in seconds. I called Mr. Pennington and had the same response. Rhonda confirmed with Jim, so we were good to go.

I decided, though, in spite of all the positive aspects of the idea, that I'd better check it out with the twins. I called Ray.

"Roger and I are used to being on camera, so we'd have no objection. Might even grab a clip or two from it for our own show," he said.

"I'm thinking it might be a good experience all around," I said.

"Good instincts," Ray pronounced. "You've got 'em. Follow them. You'll be fine. We'll see you tonight."

"See you," I said, feeling pretty darned good about my instincts and just about everything else in my world at that particular moment. Too bad feelings like that never last very long. I took the elevator down to the lobby, slipping one shoe off at a time, rubbing sore feet. For once, I was glad for the slow ride.

The Buick wasn't in the garage when I reached home. I knew the Angels all had hair appointments at Betsy's favorite beauty shop in anticipation of the rehearsal. They'd be doubly excited if they knew Old Jim would be filming the whole thing. I decided to surprise them with that news later.

As soon as I'd locked the garage door and started up the flagstone path, O'Ryan approached me at a near gallop. "Whoa, boy." It was a very special welcome, even from him. I picked him up and gave him a hug. He showered me with enthusiastic cat-kisses. "You must have worried about me all day," I whispered. "I'm sorry I can't take you with me, so you'd know that I'm all right. Really I am."

Big Cat and I let ourselves in the back door. I put him down, and he led the way up the twisty staircase, looking back every few steps as though checking to be sure I was there. He didn't even stop in my living room, just stayed close as I headed down the hall to the kitchen.

"Back off a little, O'Ryan," I said. "You're getting tangled up with my feet." I opened a fresh box of sardine-flavored crackers and put a few into his bowl. "There now. Relax. I'm going to take off my executive clothes—and especially these shoes. I promise I'll be right here."

The crackers, and maybe my promise, seemed to calm him, and I got to shower in solitary peace. I donned jeans, a white cotton shirt, and soft, well-worn sneakers. The look needed a little something extra. I tied my favorite silk scarf—the long, floaty one with pictures of cats all over it—loosely around my shoulders. That worked. Rehearsals have never been dress-up occasions for me. I'd just be doing some general helping, leaving most of it up to Mr. Pennington. When I returned to the kitchen, O'Ryan was perched on his favorite windowsill, washing his face, apparently enjoying the cool evening breeze that gently ruffled his fur.

"That's my good boy," I told him. "I'm going to have to leave you for a couple of hours tonight. Your favorite show—*Wicked Tuna*—is on tonight, and you can watch it on the bedroom TV. I've already set the timer. Okay?"

He said "Meh," which lately seems to mean anything he wants it to, and continued washing his face and watching the backyard. I took that as "Okay." After a few minutes, he moved from the windowsill to a chair to the floor and padded down the hall toward the living room. A glance at Kit-Cat told me it was a little past O'Ryan's expected happy hour. "You've already had your crackers," I told him. I leaned across the vacated chair and saw the Buick turning into the garage, along with Betsy's Mercedes pulling into the driveway. I followed the cat downstairs to greet the newly coiffed Angels. I heard the three of them giggling like teenagers before they even opened the door.

Newly Farrah-styled and blonde-streaked Betsy wore a bright red feather boa draped over her shoulders. Louisa's stylish french twist was topped with a vintage white satin pillbox hat with a white puffy polka-dotted half veil, and Aunt Ibby's dangling earrings made from real peacock feathers accented soft red curls. "We're saving our real costumes for tomorrow," my aunt explained, "but we thought we'd set the mood this way."

"Works for me!" I laughed. "I hope the men get into the spirit the way you three have!"

"We hope so too," Louisa said. "We're all going to ride over to the school together in Ibby's car, but first we're going to celebrate happy hour with cheesecake instead of wine. Like the Golden Girls." She held out a string-tied cake box for my inspection. "Will you join us? It's strawberry."

I couldn't resist. "Absolutely. And you all look totally adorable."

"If we're going to be Golden Girls"—Betsy struck a pose—"can I be Blanche?"

"Naturally," my aunt agreed, cutting the string and placing the cheesecake on a Spode platter.

"Certainly," Louisa said, making the first cut in the pink-and-white confection. "Who else could be Blanche? Big slices or dainty ones?"

Everyone agreed on medium, but not *quite* large, portions. I explained that O'Ryan had already had his treats, but Aunt Ibby poured a few Friskies into his bowl. "So he won't feel left out." The happy hush that often accompanies the consuming of forbidden foods descended on

Aunt Ibby's kitchen as we four enjoyed our Golden Girls moment.

The small amount of leftover cheesecake was reverently bagged and refrigerated, and as the Angels collected wraps and purses and headed for the garage, I took a final look around—checking locks on both front and back doors, making sure alarms were properly activated—then left the house myself. I looked around for O'Ryan, realizing that *Wicked Tuna* was due to begin within minutes. He'd undoubtedly already scooted up the back stairs and was by then curled up on my pillow. That cat rarely misses happy hour or any of his favorite TV shows—including *Wicked Tuna*, *Deadliest Catch*, and *River Monsters*.

The Angels piled into the Buick and drove off in a giggling flurry of feathers and polka dots. I backed the Vette onto Oliver Street and followed. The Tabby parking lot was more crowded than usual for early evening. It appeared that my aunt had grabbed the last available spot. I circled around a bit, then scooted around the corner of the building to a downhill, dimly lighted lot that years ago had been used by Trumbull's department store employees. These days it's used mostly by dorm students and faculty, and sometimes as an overflow parking area. I recognized Mr. Pennington's Lincoln and Alan Armstrong's Lexus there, as well as the WICH-TV Volkswagen. Old Jim had arrived early too.

Mr. Pennington was just inside the big glass double doors, greeting everyone. There'd been some internal debate as to whether to hold the evening's event in the large street-level student theater where the actual Clue party would happen the following night, or upstairs on the rehearsal stage in the Theater Arts Department. (Aunt Ibby had told me that area was once Trumbull's furniture department.) The decision had apparently been made. Susan, the student receptionist I'd met earlier, directed guests to the elevators for the ascent to the third floor. I joined two women and two men who, I learned on the slow ride up, were my Salem history students, Conrad, Carl, Kate, and Penny. "I'm so happy to finally meet you all in person," I said. It was true. The four had seemed to me like missing puzzle pieces or—perhaps more appropriately—missing game pieces. "Where's Harrison?" I wondered.

"He's already gone up there. Backstage. Mr. Pennington told him to."

It turned out that all were WICH-TV fans, and they asked the usual questions about the station's on-air personnel. "Is River as nice as she seems? Is Buck Covington single? How old is Phil Archer?" Naturally, the four were mostly concerned about their teacher, Cody, and their classmate, Lucy.

"None of us believe that either of them could have done what they're saying," Conrad stated. "We know them. They're good, honest people." The others voiced agreement.

"Lucy even babysits my kids sometimes," Kate offered. "They love her. Little kids have good instincts about people."

Penny agreed. "That's right. Kids and dogs. They can tell if a person is okay or not."

Some cats can too.

Chapter 37

We stepped out of the elevator. There'd been improvements on the third floor since I'd last visited Theater Arts. The stage, which had once been fairly rudimentary—bare wood and no curtains—now had a polished, professional look. I was happy to see that Costume still used complete families of 1950s-era mannequins for various periods of dress, and that Scenery, with its rows of painted backdrops, assorted doors and windows, and what looked like a forest of artificial trees and plants, still had the old S&H GREEN STAMP REDEMPTION CENTER banner above the entrance.

"Have you been up here before?" I asked.

"Cody brought us up here once," Penny said. "He showed us the kind of clothes people wore back when—you know—that other murder happened."

"Right," Conrad said. "Cody is a really good teacher. He wanted us to be able to visualize what happened to Joseph White. We saw an old-fashioned nightshirt like Captain White might have worn."

I'll bet I know that nightshirt! They use it for Scrooge

every year when Mr. Pennington directs A Christmas Carol.

"He showed us a dress like the housekeeper might have been wearing when she found the body," Kate said. "It was a small size, so Lucy modeled it for us. We never did find a 'glazed cap' like Frank Knapp wore though. We think it was something like a newsboy hat or maybe a baseball cap."

Yes, a baseball cap.

"I wonder what Clue character Harrison is going to play," Carl said. "He's really excited about getting a part. I'd be so scared to do it. I mean, I've played the game at somebody's house, but get up in front of an audience? Not me."

"I'm sure he'll do well," I said. "Come on. I'd like you to meet my aunt and her friends."

Aunt Ibby, Betsy, and Louisa were just outside a door marked "stage." I introduced my newfound students to the Angels, and as they left for whatever lay beyond that door, we four found seats in the second row. There's not a great deal of seating in the rehearsal area, but we didn't expect a large audience. There were about a dozen people there so far, mostly, I guessed, dorm students. Old Jim had appeared at the back of the room, with his camera steadied on a tripod. Ray and Roger Temple, one on each side of Jim, stood with their backs against the wall. I've seen Pete take that exact position many times, watching, listening, observing.

There was a flurry of activity near the elevators as Harrison, Alan Armstrong, and Eddie Symonds arrived. "Oh, look," Kate whispered—loud enough for anyone in the first three rows to hear—"there's Harrison and Cody's teacher friends. Aren't they handsome?"

Heads turned, and there was a buzz of conversation as the men walked toward the same door where Angels had recently dared to tread. The guys had apparently consulted on outfits and had gone for a casual look. They each wore khaki slacks, white sneakers, and identical T-shirts—Harrison in mustard yellow as Colonel Mustard, Eddie in green as Mr. Green, and Alan in purple as Professor Plum. Simple, but effective. Aunt Ibby's peacock earrings would identify her as Mrs. Peacock, Louisa's satin pillbox confection marked Mrs. White, and Betsy, of course, was Miss Scarlet. So far so good. Everyone would know who was who in the game.

The chatter in the room hushed when Mr. Pennington appeared onstage and took a position behind an ordinary card table. He welcomed the audience, then introduced the players, beginning with Betsy as Miss Scarlet, naming each with his or her real name and character name. They stood in a row beside him. "My position this evening is as 'game master,'" he announced. "As most of you know, the game is played with cards representing three entities. Suspects"—he waved an arm toward the six onstage, who mugged appropriately to applause and laughter from the audience. "Rooms," he said with a gesture toward the back of the stage, where a slide show of the nine rooms flashed past, each one worthy of a mansion. More applause and some *ooh*s, and *ah*s. "Weapons," he pronounced, pulling the life-sized toy weapons one at a time from a canvas bag and placing each one on the table with a dramatic flourish.

"I've divided the cards into three decks," he said, placing three stacks of cards onto the lectern. "May I have a volunteer from the audience to select a card from each deck?" Kate, with encouragement from her classmates, blushingly volunteered, and hesitantly pulled one card, facedown, from each pile. Mr. Pennington, without peeking, put the three into an envelope, sealed it, and held it up. "The solution to the mystery is here!" he announced, tucking the envelope into his inside jacket pocket. "I have a surprise for you. I've invited a special guest here this evening to shuffle the remaining cards. Here from WICH-TV, Mr. Buck Covington!"

Applause, a few whistles, many *ooh*s and *ah*s. I was as surprised as anyone. Including someone from the station was a brilliant touch. Doan would be delighted and so would Captain Billy. Buck obliged with one of his fanciest Vegas-style shuffles, swiftly dealt six hands, one for each of the wide-eyed players, then bowed, smiling, and exited the stage to more applause.

Mr. Pennington gave a quick explanation of the Clue party rules. "Mr. Boddy is dead," he said. "The deceased was murdered somewhere in this great house." He looked from side to side, and his tone was hushed. "It's our job to discover which of the partygoers was the murderer, and what weapon was used in the dastardly deed. All of the players are free to ad-lib and alibi as they see fit." He pointed to Betsy. "Miss Scarlet, please come forward, and after consulting your own cards, pick a room. You will be followed in order by Colonel Mustard, Mrs. White, Mr. Green, Mrs. Peacock, and Professor Plum."

He moved the card table to stage left, then gave a quick rundown of the rules, explaining the use of the cards held by the suspects, how to use the cards to contradict another player's guess as to who had killed Mr. Boddy, where and how. "When somebody's accusation can't be contradicted and the room, the weapon, and the killer are identified"—he patted his pocket—"the game is ended. The murder is solved."

Betsy got into the spirit of the game right away. She selected the ballroom, and the slide depicting a formal ballroom zoomed into place. She commented on the beautiful gold mirrors, then sidled up to Eddie Symonds. "Good evening, Mr. Green." Hand on one hip, batting eyelashes, she pointed to his feet. "Are those your dancing shoes?"

Eddie looked blank for an instant, then quickly recovered and smiled, glancing down at his own white Nike-sneakered feet. "Absolutely, Miss Scarlet," he said, holding out both arms. "Shall we?" The two, sans music, performed a credible Viennese waltz. He bowed. She curtsied. The remaining players and the audience applauded. Betsy moved to center stage and pulled her cards from a pocket. "Here's my solution to this heinous crime." She pointed to Aunt Ibby. "Mrs. Peacock did it—in the library, of course, with a candlestick."

"I did not," said Aunt Ibby, holding up a card. "Here's the library to prove it." Properly contradicted, Betsy, holding Eddie's hand, pretended to pout, and the two stepped to the back of the stage. *Looks to me as if Eddie has his next "wealthy older woman" lined up.*

It was Colonel Mustard's turn to choose a room and take a guess as to who had killed Mr. Boddy. Harrison moved to center stage. Clearly intending to make the most of his debut Tabby stage performance, he began an obviously well-rehearsed description of his chosen murder site, the billiard room. He must have written mini-scripts for each room in the game. Good for him. It took a while for the rest to check their cards and contradict Harrison's guess that Mrs. White had bludgeoned poor Mr. Boddy with a lead pipe in the kitchen. The pipe and the kitchen setting gave him an irresistible opportunity to display a little stand-up comedy talent with some silly plumbing jokes. ("The plumber broke up with his girlfriend. He said, 'It's over, Flo.'") The audience groaned, and next it was Louisa as Mrs. White's turn.

So it went. As the evening progressed, and Mr. Pennington's running dialogue provided an increasingly exciting backstory for the fictitious murder of Mr. Boddy, the players became increasingly comfortable in their parts. The audience applauded often and with enthusiasm. By the time Mr. Pennington opened the envelope, revealing the solution to the crime, it was apparent that by the next evening, the Clue party would be ready for prime time.

When the cast lined up in a row for a well-deserved curtain call, they were suddenly upstaged by a large yellow cat walking along slowly, carefully, right in front of them.

Chapter 38

My first thought was *How did he get here?* and the next thought was *It must be important if he purposely missed* Wicked Tuna. Aunt Ibby used a ladylike version of a cop voice.

"O'Ryan! You naughty, naughty boy! Come here immediately." She pointed to the floor directly in front of her. The cat, unhurriedly, but obediently, strolled toward her and sat on the exact spot she'd indicated—and proceeded to wash his bottom. The audience loved it. Laughter erupted, accompanied by applause. The cast took another bow. Aunt Ibby picked up the cat, lifted one of his paws, and made him wave.

He hates that.

Mr. Pennington took center stage again, wished the showgoers a good night, reminding them to come back the following evening to see the finished production. The players chatted among themselves for a few minutes. I excused myself to Kate, Penny, Carl, and Conrad and hurried onstage. I reached for the cat, who favored me with a chin lick and purr.

What the heck was all this about? Had he stowed away

in one of the cars? Or had he walked all the way from Winter Street to downtown Salem? And once at the Tabby, how had he managed to get inside? I knew part of the answer. He didn't want to be away from me. He thought I needed protection. But protection from what? From whom?

The "how did he get in" question was soon answered by Susan, who'd seen him stroll in behind a few of the day-hop students who'd entered through the door from the attached cafeteria. "I tried to catch him," she said, "but he didn't look dangerous or anything so I figured he'd find his way out."

By this time the twins had made their way to the stage area. "What's up with the cat?" Roger asked.

"I'll ask him," I said, "but it was his idea. He wasn't invited."

"Fool cat always did have a mind of his own," Roger said. "Ray and I are going backstage to talk with the actors—or players—or whatever they are. Want to come with us?"

"I do," I said. I thanked Kate, Penny, Carl, and Conrad for coming. "See you tomorrow night."

"Sure thing," Penny said. "We're going to hang around here for a while and pretend we want Harrison's autograph."

With O'Ryan in my arms, his big front paws extending over my right shoulder, I followed the twins to the large onetime furniture stockroom, directly behind the stage, with entrances to either side of it. All of the players, along with Mr. Pennington, talked excitedly among themselves. A smiling Aunt Ibby left the group and walked toward me. Or O'Ryan. Or maybe she walked toward Ray. Hard to tell.

"It went well, didn't it?" she asked. "Rupert is so pleased. Tomorrow will be even better. You'll see." She reached for the cat and patted his head. "I wish you could tell us why you're here, dear cat," she said, "but I'm sure you have your reasons."

That's what bothers me. Why is he here?

I knew O'Ryan was protecting me—but from what? *It has to be somebody who is here tonight,* I thought. I looked around the long, almost bare, room. Eddie and Mr. Pennington now seemed to be deep in conversation. Harrison had rejoined his classmates with smiles and high fives all around. Alan Armstrong had cracked a bottle of champagne and was filling a plastic flute for Betsy—who seemed to be enjoying the attention. Aunt Ibby, Louisa, and Ray and Roger Temple had formed a circle of sorts and all seemed engrossed in whatever they were talking about, while Buck Covington and Old Jim inspected the viewer on his camera.

If there was something wrong with this picture, I couldn't see it. "Dear cat," I whispered, to the purring, totally relaxed feline, "help me out here. Who is it? Why are you afraid for me?"

"*Mmrrup,*" he said. "*Mmrrup mrrup.*" He squirmed in my arms, signaling that he wanted to get down. I loosened my hold, and he slid easily to the floor. Then, looking back at me every few steps, he walked toward Costume, where the 1950s family of mannequins, in the half darkness, had taken on a frightening aspect. I felt their dead glass eyes on me as I followed the cat past the entrance.

I knew immediately why he'd brought me there. A full-length mirror was straight ahead of us, lights already flashing, colors already whirling. I couldn't look away. It was a scene from *A Christmas Carol.* On a theater stage—not the simple one we'd just left, but a real theater stage with curtains and footlights—an old man in a long nightshirt sat on the edge of a four-poster bed. *Scrooge?* His face was indistinct. There was a huge safe next to the bed—the kind you see in cartoons. He opened the safe and pulled out a stack of magazines, spreading them on the bed. Then he did the strangest thing. He stood on the bed and began to dance on the magazines, the long night-shirt flapping around skinny legs as he turned in graceful circles. Blink! The vision was gone.

"What does that mean?" I turned, and asked the cat. But he'd already left Costume in favor of backstage, where the champagne celebration was in full swing. A second cork had been popped, and I was glad to see that River had joined the party. I wasn't surprised, since Buck was there. She hurried to greet me, with O'Ryan following close behind her. "Sorry I missed the performance," she said. "Overslept. I'll try to see the real thing tomorrow night." I understood completely. I'd worked that late-night show shift long enough to understand how sleep patterns get turned upside down. "It's okay," I said, "but I need to talk to you soon."

She took my hands. "You having visions?"

"Just had one. About two minutes ago. O'Ryan led me straight to it."

"I could tell he was nervous about something." She reached down and patted his head. "He's a good boy. So, what's going on?"

"I'm not sure," I admitted. "There's this murder, of course, and Aunt Ibby and I and Betsy and Louisa are try-ing to help the twins prove somehow that Cody didn't do it. Then there are the visions—which as usual, don't make any sense."

"Don't make any sense _yet_," River pointed out. "They will, you know. They always do." She looked around the room. "Where's Pete?"

"He's working late," I said. "Probably on Cody's case. And River, I don't mean to sound disloyal to the twins. You know I love them both, but it doesn't look good for Cody and Lucy. The truth is, everything seems to point to them."

"I know it," she said. "Talk around the station is maybe they did it after all."

"Really? I haven't heard that."

"That's because everybody knows you're friendly with the family. Want me to do a reading for you?"

"Yes, please."

"Can you come by the station before my show? I'll be there around eleven—to watch Buck do the news. I could do it then."

"You know? I think I'd like that. Maybe you—and the cards—can make some sense out of this mess."

"We'll try." She gave me a quick hug, patted O'Ryan, and with that glowy look she gets when Buck is nearby, hurried to where he waited for her with two flutes of champagne. Ray and Roger seemed to be working the room, moving from group to group, Ray grinning, shaking hands all around, Roger stone-faced, giving an occasional nod or headshake. *Good cop, bad cop?* I watched as they interrupted whatever was going on between Betsy and Alan Armstrong, and smiled as Betsy shook Ray's hand, waved a careless goodbye to Professor Dreamy, and darted across the room to join Louisa. O'Ryan got there before she did, and I wasn't far behind.

"Okay, girls," I said. "What are you two up to?"

"We're gathering information," Louisa said, lifting the polka-dotted veil away from her eyes. "The Temple twins need every bit of help they can get. It's not looking good for their nephew. Not good at all. I've been trying to get a chance to talk to Eddie, but Rupert seems to be monopolizing him. What did you find out from Alan Armstrong, Betsy? Anything new?"

"I think so." Betsy sounded breathless. "I mean, besides the fact that he's crazy about me. Listen to this. He's the one who gave Cody McGinnis those theater tickets!"

"He did? Are you sure?" That was a surprise.

"Oh, he didn't mean to tell me. It kind of slipped out.

Maybe it was the champagne." She giggled. "Anyway, we were talking about *real* plays we'd seen lately—not amateur plays like the Tabby puts on. He said he was supposed to tell Cody that he'd won those tickets on a radio show and that he knew Lucy really wanted to see *Shear Madness*."

Does Pete know that? Do the twins?

I looked around for Roger or Ray. One or both of them should hear this. If Betsy was correct, and Alan had given the tickets to Cody, had he been trying to set up an alibi for the couple? An alibi for the time of the murder *before it had actually happened*?

Another thought intruded on that one—as if the first one wasn't bad enough. Was this the reason Alan had broken his date for the gathering at Sam Bond's house on that fateful night? When he'd told the girl "something bad might happen"? I started across the room to where I'd last seen the twins, O'Ryan keeping pace close beside me.

"Hey, Lee! Wait up." I turned to face Eddie Symonds. He had a champagne flute in each hand and handed me one of them. "I've been wanting to talk to you all evening. Rupert Pennington had me kind of cornered there for a while. He's got some odd-ball idea about the Tabby's acting, music, and dance classes all getting together to produce some musicals based on board games." He put a casual arm around my shoulders, steering me back toward the seating area of Theater Arts. "Can you picture it?" He waved his glass toward the now-empty stage. "Kings and Queens and Knights dancing and singing on a giant chess board? Performing letters of the alphabet playing Scrabble?"

"He's already run the Scrabble idea past me," I admitted. "Can't quite visualize that one, but Candy Land might work."

He nodded. "You're right. I can see that. Giant slides with kids on them."

"They already have those at the Toy Trawler," I answered, scanning the room, still looking for one or both of the twins. "Captain Billy would probably lend them to the school for the performance."

"You think so?" Eddie's words were slightly slurred. *Too much bubbly?* "You looking for somebody?"

"Yes. I was wondering where the twins are. I have a—um—a message for them."

He stumbled slightly, surprising for the always-graceful dancer, tightening his arm around my shoulders. "Shall I help you look?"

"Sure. If you want to." I stepped sideways, extricating myself from the increasingly possessive arm, aware that O'Ryan had positioned himself between us. "Last time I saw them they were sort of table-hopping, chatting with everybody backstage."

"They chatted with me." He was no longer smiling. "It felt more like an inquisition than a chat though." I spotted Ray. Or was it Roger? His back toward me, he stood facing Aunt Ibby beside a forest of plastic stage-set trees.

"There's one of them now." I moved away from my unsteady escort. "Thanks for your help anyway, Eddie."

"No problem," he said. "I think I'll go down to my dance studio and just hang around for a while. Got a little last-minute research to do on a piece I'm working on about a jailbird I thought I knew. See you around." He smiled, giving me a brief wave. Then, hands in his pockets, he strolled back toward the elevators. He paused, picked up a full bottle of champagne from the improvised bar, tucked it under one arm, and pushed the DOWN button.

A jailbird I thought I knew? He's writing about Cody McGinnis.

Something in Eddie's conversation with the twins must have convinced him of Cody's guilt. No wonder he was drinking too much. He'd been Cody's biggest defender all this time. *Poor guy,* I thought. I hoped with all my heart he was wrong—for his sake and for the twins and Phyllis and the Angels and all those sign-carrying college kids who'd believed so completely in their teacher's innocence.

With O'Ryan a couple of steps ahead of me, I approached Aunt Ibby and whatever twin it was, anxious to deliver the information about theater tickets—information Alan had given—or let slip—to Betsy.

"Sorry to interrupt," I told them, "but I've just heard something that might be important." I repeated what Betsy had told me as exactly as I could. "He said he was supposed to tell Cody he'd won the tickets on a radio show."

Ray frowned. "He was *supposed* to tell Cody that?"

"Did he?" Aunt Ibby asked. "Did Cody say he got those tickets from Alan? That Alan had won them on a radio show?"

"Sure," Ray said. "As soon as we knew the two were lying about actually going to the theater, Cody admitted that Alan had won the tickets on some radio show and had already seen the play so he wasn't going to use them." Ray's cop voice was back. He faced me. "You're sure she said he was *supposed* to tell Cody that?" he asked again.

"For goodness' sake, let's just go and ask Betsy," my aunt said. "She's still here. I'm her ride. Come on." She started for the backstage entrance, Ray, O'Ryan, and I tagging along behind her.

The backstage crowd had thinned considerably. Both Alan and Eddie were missing, and River and Buck had left earlier. Louisa, Betsy, Harrison, and Mr. Pennington sat in folding chairs arranged around the stage-prop card table while Roger and Old Jim looked on. An impromptu champagne-fueled game of Clue was in progress.

Ray approached his twin, and after a brief, muted exchange, Roger tapped Betsy on a red feather boa–wrapped shoulder, whispered to her, and motioned for Aunt Ibby to take her place at the table.

Betsy handed her cards to my aunt, pointed out the orange token, and with a puzzled but pleased expression followed the twins to the stage left exit. O'Ryan, without hesitation, followed. So did I. No one objected to my presence—or to that of the cat—so we stood by quietly in a narrow off-stage corridor while the twins questioned the very willing and talkative Betsy. Roger and Ray used a tag team method—not good cop/bad cop this time. Roger said something like "Now Betsy, think very carefully about what Alan told you." While Betsy was presumably thinking, Ray said, "Take your time. Be as accurate as you can." Betsy closed her eyes. Everyone was quiet. Then, eyes wide, she repeated almost the same thing she'd said earlier.

"Alan said that he was supposed to tell Cody he'd won the tickets on a radio show and that he knew Lucy wanted to see *Shear Madness*."

"Think carefully," Roger said. "Did he tell you who told him to say it?"

Betsy shook her carefully coiffed head. "Nope. He didn't say anything more about the tickets at all."

"Do you remember what you and Alan talked about next?" Ray asked.

"After Alan told you what he was supposed to tell Cody, what did he say after that?" Roger wanted to know. "Can you remember?"

Betsy closed her eyes again, but only for a couple of seconds. "It was odd," she said. "It was an odd change of subject. We'd been talking about plays we'd seen. You know, the ones we'd liked and the ones we hated. Then all of a sudden, he asked me if I'd ever broken a date with someone then wondered later if doing it had changed the future somehow."

"What did you say?" The twins spoke in unison. I hid a smile. It always strikes me funny when they do it.

Betsy shrugged. "What could I say? It was a dumb question. I blew it off. Told him I had to go to the little girl's room and left him standing there."

"Thanks, Betsy," Roger said. "You've been a great help. We'll let you get back to your game now."

"Thank you," Ray said, motioning toward backstage. "Ladies first." Betsy and I, preceded by O'Ryan, followed by the twins, rejoined the others.

Chapter 39

Now what? Instead of clearing things up, Betsy's revelations about her conversation with Alan Armstrong had only complicated everything. Why had Alan provided an easy alibi for Cody and Lucy covering the time involved in the murder? At the same time, why had he broken a date for the gathering at Bond's house, claiming that something bad was going to happen there? If he'd kept the date, would the "bad thing" have been avoided? It began to look to me more and more as though charming Professor Dreamy might be the killer we were all looking for.

Did the twins see it that way too? Hard to tell. I wished Pete was with me.

The Clue game was still in progress when we returned. Betsy and Aunt Ibby changed places once again. Coffee had been delivered from the Starbucks downstairs, and the scene looked almost like an ordinary board game night in an ordinary home—not at all as though it was taking place in the middle of a real-life murder investigation.

Old Jim moved closer to me. "I'm about to head back

to the station," he said. "Need to turn this over to Marty—unless you want I should stick around."

"I'm okay, Jim," I said. "You go along. I'll see you in the morning."

"You sure?"

I knew Old Jim was worried about me. O'Ryan was worried about me. I'd started to worry about me too, and I didn't even know why. "I'm sure," I told him. "I'll be heading out soon myself." I pointed to the cat. "It's past this old boy's bedtime." O'Ryan promptly opened his mouth in a wide, pink-mouthed yawn. *Tell me this cat doesn't understand English.*

I did exactly what I'd told Old Jim I was going to do. Pleading a crowded schedule, I made a quick round of the remaining guests, bade all a good night, picked up the cat, and left the Tabby via the new automatic front doors.

I was actually glad for the company of my furry companion when I walked around the corner of the building onto the dimly lighted and slightly downhill path to the overflow parking lot. I clicked my key fob and watched for the welcome answering blink of taillights from my Vette. The WICH-TV van was gone, but Mr. Pennington's Lincoln was still there. So was Alan Armstrong's silver Lexus.

So was Alan Armstrong. He'd stepped from beside his car into the pale pool of light spilling from a bare bulb on the old department store's shipping and receiving dock. "Hey, Lee. Is that you?" He shaded his eyes with one hand.

O'Ryan uttered a low growl, and I felt his body tense in my arms. "It's me," I answered, straining to keep the very real fear out of my voice. "What's the matter? Car trouble?"

"No. I'm about to go home. I stopped in the diner to get a couple of tacos to go." He held up a brown paper bag, and his taillights flashed, signaling that he'd unlocked the Lexus. "Why don't you follow me to my place? I'll share my tacos." Even in the dim light I could see that brilliant smile.

"No thanks," I said, walking really fast toward the Vette. "I have this wayward cat with me." I pulled the passenger door open and dumped O'Ryan onto the seat. "See you tomorrow night, Alan." I literally ran around my car, climbed in, locked the doors, and gunned the big engine.

Overreacting? Maybe. But my heart was still pounding when I turned onto Washington Street and didn't resume normal rhythm until I'd nearly reached home. "What do you think, O'Ryan? Could the handsome professor be a killer? Could he climb in a window and beat a helpless old man to death?" O'Ryan said *"Mrrup,"* and pressed his nose against the side window, making little heart-shaped spots. No help there.

"Never mind," I said. "I'm going to see River at eleven. Maybe she can sort this out." It wasn't yet ten o'clock when I unlocked my living room door. I fed O'Ryan and closed the kitchen window, which undoubtedly had enabled his escape earlier in the evening. "I have to go see River for a reading tonight, O'Ryan, and you have to stay here. I wish you could come with me, but I promise I'll come straight home as soon as she's finished."

The cat looked up from his red dish briefly, but made no cat-comment one way or the other. I took this as a positive sign. I thought about changing my shirt and opened my closet to check out the possibilities. It wasn't until then that I realized my cat scarf was missing. "Darn," I muttered. "That's my favorite one. I'll call the Tabby in the morning and ask them to check the lost-and-found box." I chose a navy-and-white-striped long-sleeved blouse—same jeans and sneakers. Aunt Ibby wasn't home yet, so I decided to leave a note on her door telling her where I was. I texted Pete to tell him I'd be at the station for a while but that I expected to be back before midnight.

I used the twisty back staircase, pinned a note onto Aunt Ibby's kitchen door, and stepped out into the cool spring night. That white-faced owl was perched on a low limb of the maple tree again. It hooted softly, and I found myself walking a little faster toward the garage. It's no wonder an owl hooting in the night is a standard sound effect in creepy movies.

Once inside my car, with windows up and doors locked, I felt more comfortable. Salem's streets were quiet, with minimal traffic and not many pedestrians. I wheeled into the parking lot, not bothering to use my designated space in the far corner, but instead grabbing the well-lighted spot behind Ariel's bench, handy to the studio back door. Old Jim's VW mobile unit was in its usual spot, and I wondered if he was still inside working with Marty on the rehearsal footage. I'd just unlocked the car door, when my phone buzzed. Pete. Just seeing his name on caller ID made me feel good.

"Hi," I said. "What's going on?"

"Are you okay, babe?" he asked. "Your message only said you'd be home by midnight. What's happening at the station this late?"

"Oh. Pete, I should have been more specific. I'm fine, just a little confused about some visions and this murder and all. River's fitting me in for a quick tarot reading."

"River's hocus-pocus," he huffed. "I can't help much with your seeing things, but we've made real progress here with the murder. Forensics has come up with some convincing material. Chief's nearly ready to indict Cody McGinnis. First degree. Sorry about the twins though. They're both here right now, asking for a little more time to clear their nephew."

I climbed out of the car, locked it, and tapped my code into the security panel on the studio door. "He's going to indict Cody? What about Alan Armstrong?" The door swung open, and I stepped into the cool darkness.

"Armstrong? The good-looking guy who was hitting on you? What about him?"

"He was not . . . oh never mind. Did the twins tell you what Alan told Betsy Leavitt? About telling Cody he'd won those theater tickets on some radio show?"

"Yes. They did. But we already know they were purchased at the box office in Boston. The buyer used a pre-paid Visa. Said he was Cody McGinnis." He cleared his throat. "There was no radio station involved."

"That's silly. Why would Cody buy his own tickets, lie about where they came from, and then not even use them?"

"That'll get cleared up in time. Meanwhile, we're going strictly on evidence," he said. "What we've got is pretty darned strong."

I started down the center aisle toward the *Tarot Time* set. "What about Lucy?"

"Probably accessory after the fact."

"She thinks cockroaches have souls."

"Huh?"

"Never mind. River's waiting for me. Will you call me later? Or come over?"

"Yep. After midnight, right?"

"Right. Love you." I ended the call, slipping the phone back into my bag.

Chapter 40

River, gorgeous in a blue-velvet halter-topped side-slit gown, left the *Tarot Time* set to meet me halfway down the center aisle. "I'm glad you came, Lee." She pulled me close for a patchouli-scented hug. "Let's see if the cards can make some sense out of those visions and questions. Come on." She led the way back to the brightly lighted space where a pair of fan-backed wicker chairs had been pulled up to the round wicker table and a red candle burned. The familiar tarot deck lay facedown in the center of the table.

We sat, facing one another. River bowed her head. "I consecrate this deck to bring light wherever there is darkness, asking guidance and wisdom for myself and others for the higher good for all concerned." She handed me the deck. "Cut the cards please, Lee. Buck already shuffled it once to save time." As always, she'd selected the Queen of Wands to represent me. The queen holds a staff in her right hand and a sunflower in her left. The arms of her throne are lions' heads. There's a black cat sitting on the floor in front of her. River says she picked this card for me because of my red hair and hazel eyes, not because

of the sunflower—which I like—or because of the cat—
which I wish was yellow instead of black.

River shuffled the cards and began the familiar layout.
The first card she placed across the Queen of Wands was
the Seven of Swords. I'd seen this one before. It shows a
man carrying five swords he's stolen from a military
camp. Two more swords are stuck in the ground.

"Okay, Lee." River tapped the card gently. "The card
obviously is about somebody getting away with something—a deception or a betrayal. Does that make sense?"

"It does," I said. "Is he going to get away with it?"

"He has a lot of confidence that he will, but look. See
the small group of soldiers on the left? They may be coming after him. Let's see what the next card tells us."

Next came the Four of Pentacles showing a person
with both arms tightly wrapped around something. "He's
clinging to his gold, his material belongings. He doesn't
want anyone to take what he believes is rightfully his.
Does it fit?"

You've stolen from me for the last time! "Sure does," I
said, remembering the voice from Samuel Bond's backyard.

"Good." She nodded, the silver moons and stars in her
hair glittering under the lights. "Here's the next one. Well,
well. Here comes Pete!" It was the Knight of Swords, and
as always, I was overjoyed to see him in my reading. "You
know what he's all about," River said. "Moving on." She
flipped the next card over. "Another knight. The Knight of
Pentacles. We've talked about him before."

"The red gloves," I said. "Bloody red gloves. What is
he trying to tell me anyway?"

"He's usually a good guy," she said. "Sometimes he
has to deal with money—either coming in or going out.
In all the time I've been doing this, you're the only person who's associated the red gloves with blood though."

"I don't like him," I said. "He's scary looking."

"I understand. Let's see what's next." She turned up the next card, placing it crosswise on the Knight of Pentacles. "Interesting," she said. "The Five of Swords. Whoever you perceive this knight to be—bloody gloves and all—his troubles are escalating. Something he's hidden has been uncovered."

She lay the rest of the cards she held facedown on the table. "Before I go on, Lee, there's something here I rarely tell a client. But you're a friend. I don't like this. There's nothing good about this Five of Swords card. You see how he's captured the swords of his enemies? He's ruthless. Have you uncovered something about this man? And more importantly. Does he know you have?"

"I don't think so," I said. "I might as well tell you though, I think the Knight is Eddie Symonds. He's a dancing teacher. And a writer. But I haven't actually uncovered anything especially suspicious about him. Most everybody seems to like him."

"Maybe you have and you just haven't made a connection yet. Think hard. It might be important."

We both looked up at the sound of Marty's camera being wheeled onto the set. "Time to set up the bumper shot," she announced. "And we've got a last-minute new sponsor, so River, you'll need to do a fast live read on this. It's for a new yoga studio down on North Street. Here." She thrust a printed sheet across the table to River. "Sorry to interrupt you kids, but time's a-flyin'."

River gathered up the cards. "I'm so sorry, Lee," she said. "We'll have to finish this later. Try to remember whatever it is you know about the knight. And Lee, be careful."

"I will," I promised as I gathered up my hobo bag. "See you later. Good night, Marty."

The camera woman had already stuck her head under the camera's black hood but she waved an arm above her head. "Good night, Moon."

I made my way carefully down the darkened aisle to the door marked with a lighted red exit sign and, key fob in my hand, went outside. Even though I was only a few feet away from my car, I felt relieved when the taillights flashed on. *Silly me.* I was in familiar territory here in the WICH-TV parking lot, yet I found myself looking over my shoulder toward the door I'd just closed behind me.

I backed out of the space and headed the Vette toward home, checking the rearview mirror every few yards for . . . what? I drove slowly, trying hard to make sense out of all that had happened during that fine spring day in Salem.

Stop checking the mirror.

The rehearsal had gone well—better than I'd expected. Bruce Doan would be pleased with Old Jim's videography and so would Captain Billy. That part of my life was swinging along like it should. My relationship with Pete was a true blessing. But my attempts—all of our attempts—to help Ray and Roger in their efforts to save their nephew were not proving to be helpful. In fact, the more I learned about "The Case of the Murdered Professor," the more it looked as if Cody McGinnis might be guilty after all.

Stop checking the damned mirror.

There wasn't a car following me. There was no shadowy figure in the Vette with me and no hitchhiking cat in the seat beside me. Nothing. Was my worried cat the reason for this feeling of . . . of what? Dread? Fear? I gripped the steering wheel tightly. My palms were moist. "Maybe I'm coming down with something," I thought. "Maybe I've caught Scott's cold."

Don't look in the mirror.

I looked in the mirror. I recognized the man right away.

Pull over, dummy, before you hurt somebody.

I was almost home, but I pulled over across the street from the Witch Museum, the larger-than-life statue of

Roger Conant looming black against the lights of the Common. I dared to look at the mirror again. I looked into Dick Crowninshield's eyes.

I knew who he was. This was the face in the black-and-white photo I'd so recently stuffed into my briefcase. But now the face was in color, and around his neck was a scarf. Dick Crowninshield had hanged himself with a silk scarf—but not one with cats on it.

Eddie. His arm around my shoulders . . . untying my scarf . . .

Dick Crowninshield was the jailbird Eddie thought he knew—Dick Crowninshield, who'd hanged himself in his jail cell rather than face justice.

In almost one motion I reached for my phone, made an illegal U-turn, hit Pete's number, and sped back toward the Tabby. "Pete!" I yelled. "Edwin Symonds is the killer. He's at the Tabby. I'm on my way there to stop him from hanging himself. Hurry!"

Chapter 41

It wasn't yet midnight when I slammed on the brakes in the no-parking zone in front of the Tabby. I knew the doors would be open until twelve—curfew for the dorm students. The nighttime security guard looked up from the reception desk where so recently student receptionist Susan had greeted me. "Call 911," I shouted, running for the stairway. "Dance studio!"

"Hey, stop!" he called, but I didn't. I raced past the mezzanine. The dance studio was on the second floor, over my old classroom. I remembered the tap-tap of those dancing feet we'd often heard above us while I was teaching there.

Eddie's studio was one of the few enclosed classrooms. Most are laid out in the open plan of the old Trumbull's department store. Light spilled from under the door. Loud music played. A waltz. *The Blue Danube*? I turned the knob. Locked. "Eddie," I yelled. "Eddie, it's Lee. Let me in. I can help." No reply.

The security guard had caught up with me. I banged on the door with both fists. "Can you open it?" I pleaded. "Hurry." Distant sirens sounded. The man detached a ring of keys from his belt. He seemed to move in slow motion. "Hurry," I said again.

"I hope you know what you're doin', lady," he said, turning a key in the lock. "I called the cops. Sounds like they're on the way. I'll go tell 'em where you are."

I stepped inside the studio with its long expanse of polished hardwood floor—and its three walls of mirrors. Mirrors, of course. Dancers need to watch themselves. "Eddie?" I called again, my voice barely a croak. "Eddie, are you here? Are you okay?"

Dumb question. He's not okay. He's a killer.

I closed my eyes for a second, afraid because of all those mirrors. Then, forcing myself, I walked to the center of the room and, turning slowly, looked for Eddie. There was a desk in one corner. I moved closer. A desktop computer, a printer, and a green-shaded gooseneck lamp shared space with a pile of papers, some books, a pair of dark glasses. Peeking out from under the papers was a small letter opener—shaped like a dagger.

A long ballet barre ran along one side of the room, and one wall featured a row of uncurtained windows where city lights twinkled in the night sky. I almost smiled when I saw the single silvery stripper pole, imagining certain staid and proper Salem ladies pole dancing.

Running footsteps sounded from below. Good. Soon I wouldn't be alone here with the mirrors. And the killer. But where was he? Had I arrived too late?

I heard his voice. "Having a good look around, aren't you? What makes you think you can help me, Lee?"

I whirled. Looked behind me. No one there.

"I'm up here." Still wearing the green T-shirt, he stood upright on a wooden platform just above the stripper pole, where backup stock of ladies ready-to-wear, foundations, and millinery had once been stored. One end of my favorite scarf was tied to a sturdy ceiling beam—with the other end knotted around his neck.

"This is never the right way out, Eddie," I spoke louder, so he'd hear me above the music. "You know that. Let me help you."

"I thought I'd figured it out, Lee. The unsolvable perfect crime. Make sure all the evidence points to the wrong person, then make sure that person has a perfect alibi for the time of the murder. I was even writing a mystery with that plot."

"They didn't go to the play." I stated the obvious flaw in his plan. In the mirror directly opposite me I saw the welcome reflection of Pete in the studio doorway, backed up by several uniforms. I guessed that Eddie hadn't heard the sirens because of the music. He didn't know the cavalry had arrived.

"They didn't go to the play," Eddie echoed. "They didn't use the damn theater tickets." The platform faced the window wall. He wasn't seeing the same reflections in the mirrors I saw. He laughed. A bitter, unfunny laugh. "They went to bed instead. Now if I don't fix it, they'll both do time."

The music ended. The silence felt thick, suffocating, in that long, shiny mirrored room. Pete made a "stand down" motion to the uniforms. Was he actually going to let *me* try to talk this man, this killer, out of jumping—out of dying?

I looked up at Edwin Symonds then, standing there all righteous sounding, with my favorite scarf around his neck. My fear turned to anger. Cold, mean, pissed-off anger.

I raised my voice. "You think if you die, that'll fix it? What are you doing? Looking for sympathy?"

"What do you mean, sympathy?" His voice was almost a whimper. "I deserve to die for what I've done." He took a small step back from the edge.

"Oh great. You've pretty much fouled up Cody's and Lucy's lives, made them look like murderers. Now you want to blame your untimely death on them too?"

"No. I—I mean—I didn't want it to work out this way. I just wanted to pull off the perfect crime. I didn't want to hurt anybody."

"You hurt poor old Sam Bond. What was that all about anyway?"

"You really want to know?" The voice now was strong, confident.

"I'm listening." Pete and the cops had moved out of sight.

Is there a stairway up to that platform? There must be.

"He stole from all of us. Did you know that? Sold our work as his own."

"Yes. Cody and Alan were going to sue him for plagiarism."

"He laughed at them. Told them there was no money. But there was about to be. The thieving bastard had found a major publishing house with contacts to colleges all over the world. They wanted to buy world rights to *You Can Do This*. He'd copyrighted it in his own name. He bragged about it. Laughed at me. Said it was perfectly legal. A six-figure advance would be his. He planned to leave the country. Nothing we could do about it. He was right. We argued. That same night I put on some Latex gloves and went over and stole Cody's ladder."

"You bought the theater tickets and told Alan to give them to Cody."

"Right. I told Alan that Cody would never accept them as a gift from me. Too proud to accept 'charity.' Darn fool wouldn't ever even let me pay for his lunch. I knew he'd believe the radio show story." Again, the unfunny laugh. "It was the perfect crime. I even wore Cody's gym sneakers." He stuck out one of his own sneakered feet. "See? They're exactly like mine. Easy switch. I wore a Red Sox hat too because Cody's a Sox fan. Me, I love the Yankees."

"What about the knife?"

"I saw it in the bar after I slugged Sam with the pipe. I was going to use the letter opener, but the knife was better. I still had the gloves on."

Bloody gloves?

"I wanted to do it the way Dick Crowninshield had. Anyway, I wasn't sure Sam was dead." He shrugged, moving the scarf slightly, smiling when he said the words.

"You took the knife with you."

"Yeah. Carried it right down the ladder. I didn't know what to do with it. I dumped it in his office the next day. Sort of a little inside joke, you know? Listen, Lee, it's all in the manuscript on my computer. It's fiction of course. You ought to read it. It's about how Dick Crowninshield could have got away with it if he was smarter." He stepped closer to the edge.

"Smart like you?"

"Don't be a wiseass, Lee. You said you could help me."

"I can if I want to. First tell me how you knew to use the back entrance to my house."

"Easy. Nobody would give me your address, so I followed you home one day. That fancy car is hard to miss. Anything else?"

"Yeah. Untie my scarf. And don't tear it."

"I don't think so. I'll go out the same way Dick Crowninshield did. Silk scarf and all. Poetic justice, don't you think?" Another step forward.

"Oh, sure," I shouted. "Two losers. Centuries apart." By then I was so angry, so disgusted, that I almost didn't care anymore. If Pete Mondello, gun in hand, hadn't appeared behind him at exactly that moment, I think I actually might have told him to go ahead and jump.

Epilogue

Eddie Symonds didn't put up any struggle when Pete took him into custody. One of the officers took a knife and chopped the scarf down from the beam, while another one read the prisoner his rights. Eddie was charged with the death of Samuel Bond, but the various degrees of murder, the many aspects of perjury and deceit involved will have to wend their ways through the courts. He's safely locked up now though, so the good citizens of Salem don't need to worry about a killer wandering around in their midst. The police took custody of that manuscript Eddie talked about. I haven't read it, and I don't think I'll ever want to.

Cody and Lucy were cleared immediately, and Roger and Ray treated everybody—including Pete and me, Mr. Pennington, Alan Armstrong, and all three of the Angels—to a celebratory family dinner at Rockafellas. Lucy's mother was invited, and accepted, so things may be smoothing out there. Cody still doesn't have a full professorship and has resumed all of his teaching duties, including the Salem history class, but his lawyers are working on getting that fat publishing contract amended so that Cody and Alan can profit from their contributions to *You Can Do This*.

O'Ryan has stopped worrying about me, has returned to taking me for granted, racing me downstairs and making rude cat-comments whenever he wants to. He still reminds me now and then about locking my doors. I got the expected scolding from Pete for going by myself to the Tabby to save Eddie. I wasn't even one tiny bit sorry. I'm sure I did the right thing. Eddie is alive to pay for his crimes. I got an exclusive story, and I only wish Old Jim had been there to record every bit of it. The Clue party had to be cancelled under the circumstances, but Captain Billy has signed on to the Candy Land show and Mr. Pennington is still trying to figure out how to stage a Scrabble musical. Ray Temple and Aunt Ibby have stayed "in touch," and have dinner together occasionally. By the way, the Angels had such a good time snooping that they're thinking of opening their own detective agency.

I can hardly wait.

RECIPES

Joe Greene's Pizza-Dough Cinnamon Rolls

For the rolls:
Store-bought or homemade pizza dough
⅓ cup of sugar
2 teaspoons cinnamon
4 tablespoons unsalted butter

For the glaze:
4 tablespoons unsalted butter
2 cups of powdered sugar
1 teaspoon of good-quality vanilla extract
6 tablespoons of hot water

Joe Greene makes his own pizza dough, but you can use the store-bought kind. This recipe takes one pound of the dough, and it's easier to roll out if it's at room temperature.

Preheat the oven to 375°F. Grease an 8 x 11 inch baking dish. In a small bowl stir together sugar and cinnamon.

Lightly flour your work surface and roll out the dough into a 16 x 10 inch rectangle. Brush the entire surface of the dough with melted unsalted butter. Sprinkle it with the cinnamon/sugar mixture.

Start with the long end closest to you and gently roll the dough into a log. Cut the log into 12 rolls, about 1½ inches each. Now arrange each roll in the prepared baking dish about an inch apart.

Bake the rolls for 20 to 25 minutes until the rolls are fully cooked. Remove the rolls from the oven and cool

them while you prepare the glaze. Lee says check them after 20 minutes so they don't get too crispy on the edges.

Making the glaze: In a medium bowl stir together soft unsalted butter with powdered sugar and vanilla extract. Put hot water in a cup and whisk it, a tablespoon at a time, into the sugar mixture until it reaches a consistency you like. Drizzle the glaze over the slightly warm cinnamon rolls.

Aunt Ibby's Slow Cooker Coq au Vin

½ cup all-purpose flour
½ teaspoon salt
¼ teaspoon pepper
8 boneless, skinless chicken thighs
6 slices bacon roughly chopped
1 medium onion chopped
½ pound fresh mushrooms
4 carrots, halved
3 cloves garlic, crushed
1 cup of red Burgundy wine
1 cup of chicken broth
1 teaspoon thyme

Mix flour, salt, and pepper; coat chicken with mixture.

In large skillet or dutch oven, fry bacon until crisp, remove, and drain on paper towels.

Brown chicken well in bacon drippings, transfer to a large plate, and set aside.

Add onions, mushrooms, carrots, garlic to skillet. Cook and stir until onions are tender.

Transfer vegetables and broth to slow cooker.

Arrange chicken on top. Sprinkle bacon over chicken. Add Burgundy wine and thyme.

Cover and cook on low for 6 to 7 hours. Salt and pepper to taste.

Aunt Ibby likes to serve this with french bread and tossed salad.